GUNS TO THE FAR EAST

Historical Fiction by V. A. Stuart
Published by McBooks Press

THE ALEXANDER SHERIDAN ADVENTURES

Victors and Lords
The Sepoy Mutiny
Massacre at Cawnpore
The Cannons of Lucknow
The Heroic Garrison

THE PHILLIP HAZARD NOVELS

The Valiant Sailors
The Brave Captains
Hazard's Command
Hazard of Huntress
Hazard in Circassia
Victory at Sebastopol
Guns to the Far East

For a complete list of nautical and military fiction
published by McBooks Press, please see pages 237–239.

THE PHILLIP HAZARD NOVELS, NO.7

GUNS
TO THE
FAR EAST

by

V. A. STUART

MCBOOKS PRESS, INC.
ITHACA, NEW YORK

Published by McBooks Press 2005
Copyright © 1975 by V. A. Stuart
First Published in Great Britain by Robert Hale & Co.Ltd.,
Also published under the title *Shannon's Brigade*

Cover: *British Naval Boat,* from a drawing by J. W. Carmichael,
engraved by E. Brandard. Courtesy of Mary Evans Picture Library

Library of Congress Cataloging-in-Publication Data

Stuart, V. A.
  [Shannon's Brigade]
  Guns to the Far East / by V.A. Stuart.
    p. cm. — (The Phillip Hazard novels ; 7)
  Originally published: Shannon's Brigade. London : Hale, 1975.
  Includes bibliographical references.
  ISBN 1-59013-063-4 (trade pbk. : alk. paper)
  1. Hazard, Phillip Horatio (Fictitious character)—Fiction. 2.
India—History—British occupation, 1765-1947—Fiction. 3. Great
Britain—History, Naval—19th century—Fiction. 4. Great Britain.
Royal Navy—Officers—Fiction. 5. British—India—Fiction. I. Title.
  PR6063.A38S53 2005
  823'.92—dc22
                                                        2004019299

Distributed to the trade by National Book Network, Inc.
15200 NBN Way, Blue Ridge Summit, PA 17214
800-462-6420

Printed in the United States of America

9   8   7   6   5   4   3   2   1

FOR MY GOOD FRIEND

Colonel Harry H. Bendorf, U.S.A.F.

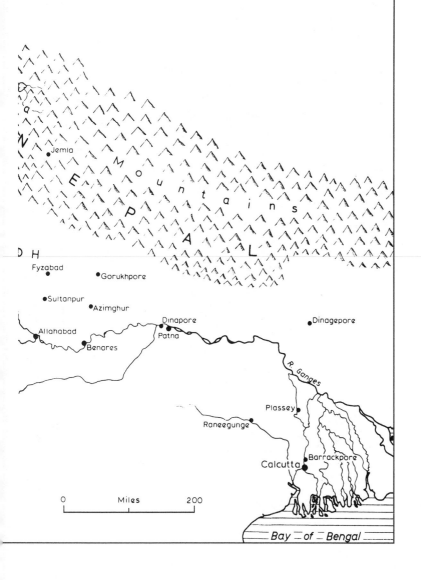

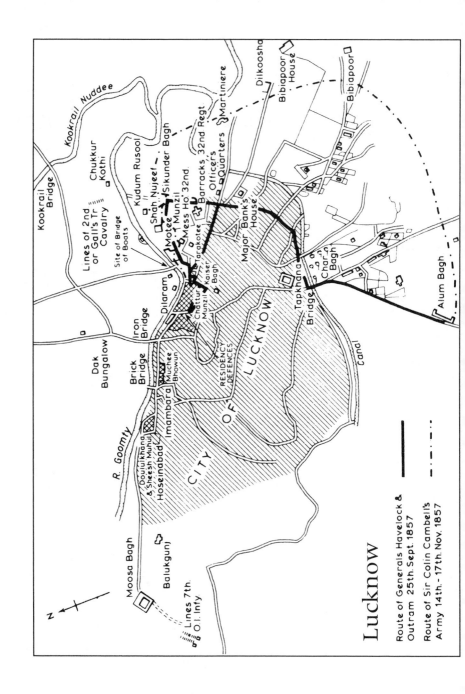

Lucknow

Route of Generals Havelock & Outram 25th Sept. 1857

Route of Sir Colin Cambell's Army 14th.–17th. Nov. 1857

PROLOGUE

At *seven-thirty* on the morning of Friday, 26th June, 1857, heralded by the stirring martial music of their bands, the troops chosen to represent those which had served in the Crimea began to converge on London's Hyde Park. It was a bright, sunny morning, with a promise of heat to come, and a light breeze stirred the leaves of the trees and rippled the surface of the Serpentine as thousands of spectators made their way to the Park. They came on foot and in carriages or hansom cabs, the women in crinolines, the men in tall hats or wearing uniform, all eager to witness the first presentation of the Victoria Cross by Her Majesty the Queen to sixty-two Crimean heroes.

Under the command of Lieutenant-General Sir Colin Campbell, G.C.B., the General whose "thin red line" of 93rd Highlanders had saved Balaclava Harbour from capture by the Russians, the columns of cavalry, artillery, and infantry wheeled into their allotted positions facing Park Lane. The cavalry, led by two regiments of the Household Cavalry—which had not taken part in the campaign—were followed by two regiments which had greatly distinguished themselves at the Battle of Balaclava—the 11th Hussars and the 6th Inniskilling Dragoons.

Resplendent in the striking uniform of the 11th Hussars

and mounted on the chestnut horse that had carried him in the now famous Charge of the Light Brigade, Major-General the Earl of Cardigan, K.C.B., rode at their head. The crowd cheered him excitedly although a few isolated catcalls greeted his appearance. Accustomed to the mixed emotions his name and reputation aroused, the Earl ignored both cheers and catcalls, but he bowed gallantly as he caught the eye of a smiling young lady in the gallery to the rear of the saluting base, which had been erected for the accommodation of peers, members of the Court, and the foreign military attachés.

The Commander of the Royal Horse Artillery troop and the two field batteries, Major-General Sir William Williams—no less distinguished, as the saviour of Kars—was less well known than Lord Cardigan and the crowd's applause was merely polite. It was enthusiastic, however, when Major-General Lord Rokeby rode into the Park at the head of three scarlet-coated battalions of Foot Guards. The 1st Battalion Grenadier Guards, the 1st Coldstream, and the Scots Fusilier Guards were heroes of the Alma and Inkerman and of the siege of Sebastopol—honours freshly embroidered on the Colours they bore proudly on to the parade ground—and the cheers were prolonged as they formed up smartly in the required quarter-distance columns and were stood at ease. They were followed by the 2nd Battalion of the Rifle Brigade, immaculate in their dark green uniforms, marching at their regulation 140 paces to the minute, and preceding them, brave in scarlet and swinging tartan, the 79th Highlanders.

From the opposite end of the Park, a detachment of two hundred seamen of the Fleet and a battalion of Royal Marines took their places to the right of a company of Engineers, Sappers, and Miners and detachments of ambulance, Army Works, and the Land Transport Corps. Last to fall in were boys from the Royal Naval and the Duke of York's Military Schools and the be-medalled veterans from Chelsea Hospital, who formed up in two lines to the right of the Royal pavilion and immediately in front of the public stand.

The officers who were to be decorated assembled opposite Grosvenor Gate at nine o'clock, to be joined by the other ranks, who had marched from Portman Barracks. The majority were in military or naval uniform, but a few of the officers were in mufti; one corporal wore the tricorne hat and scarlet coat of an enrolled pensioner, a tall, bearded fellow was dressed in the green livery of a Royal Park keeper, and a burly ex-sergeant of the 49th marched up in the tall hat and blue uniform of a Peeler, to earn friendly but faintly derisive applause from the crowd by the gate. Each man had a loop of cord—blue for the Navy, red for the Army—attached to the left breast of his coat, to facilitate the pinning on of his medal.

Just before ten o'clock, a 21-gun salute boomed out across the Park and a squadron of the Blues, with waving plumes and brightly burnished steel cuirasses, could be seen approaching Hyde Park Corner. Behind them, all mounted, came the Royal party. Her Majesty the Queen rode between her consort Prince Albert, and Prince Frederick William of Prussia and, in honour of the occasion, she had adopted a military style of dress. Above a dark blue riding skirt, she wore a scarlet tunic with a gold embroidered sash draped over the left shoulder, and a round hat with a gold band, a red and white plume attached to the right side. The Queen's appearance, thus attired, was greeted with loud and prolonged cheering and when it was observed that the Prince of Wales and Prince Alfred, mounted on ponies, were with their parents, the cheers were redoubled.

A cavalcade of brilliantly uniformed staff officers and equerries, headed by the Commander-in-Chief, HRH the Duke

of Cambridge—himself a veteran of the Alma and Inkerman—
passed in front of the reserved stands, followed by the Royal
party on horseback and the carriage procession. Reaching the
pavilion which had been prepared for her reception, the Queen
drew rein but did not—as had been expected—dismount.
Instead, sitting her magnificent roan charger, she faced the
line of officers and men awaiting decoration, who were drawn
up opposite the pavilion, the Prince Consort on her left and
the Duke of Cambridge—a burly, bearded figure in his General
Officer's uniform and plumed hat—and the Secretary of State
for War, Lord Panmure, in close attendance. Between them
stood a table, covered with a scarlet cloth, on which lay the
Crosses, fashioned, at the Queen's own command, by a Bruton
Street jeweller from captured cannon supplied for the purpose
by the Arsenal at Woolwich.

When all was in readiness for the presentation, a whispered order was given and the waiting line moved forward, to
approach Her Majesty one by one. Lord Panmure read out the
names and, as each man saluted and came to attention, the
Secretary of State handed a Cross to the Queen who, stooping
from her saddle, fixed the small bronze symbol of valour to
the cord suspended from his tunic.

As representatives of the Senior Service, the twelve naval
heroes were the first to receive their medals, pride of place
going to Commander Henry Raby of the Naval Brigade, whose
award had been won during the terrible carnage which had
followed the first full-scale British attack on the Russian Redan
on 18th June, 1855. Her Majesty addressed a few gracious
words to him, Prince Albert raised a scarlet-clad arm to the
brim of his plumed General Officer's cocked hat in grave
salute, Raby replaced his own and then a second youthful
Commander, John Bythesed, took his place. The Queen, it was

observed by those fortunate few who were in a position to see, paid marked attention to an even younger Lieutenant, William Hewett—fifth in line—who when acting-mate of HMS *Beagle,* had halted a threatened Russian breakthrough with his single Lancaster gun on the Heights of Inkerman, a few days before the battle.

As each man received his medal and returned to the line, he was enthusiastically clapped but—due to the Queen's failure to mount the raised dais—she was hidden from the occupants of the various stands and galleries by the mounted officers who surrounded her and by the ranks of Chelsea Pensioners drawn up to her right, in front of the main stand. There were audible murmurs of chagrin, particularly from this stand, in which—crowded to the point of acute discomfort and without seats—relatives of the sixty-two Victoria Cross winners, off-duty and retired officers of distinction and their families, and certain privileged members of the gentry were accommodated.

Leaning heavily on the arm of his handsome wife, the septuagenarian Admiral Sir George Hazard—Vice-Admiral on the retired list—peered with short-sighted blue eyes from his cramped vantage point at the back of the stand and said wrathfully, "That damned fellow Benjamin Hall and his department of works—I can't see a thing, damme, except the stern-ends of those infernal horses! Just as well Phillip isn't here to receive his Cross . . . we shouldn't have seen any more of the presentation than we'll see when it's made by Michael Seymour in China. Are those bluejackets who are being decorated now, Augusta?"

"Yes, dear, I believe so," his wife answered. "The officers have returned to their places." No better positioned to view the proceedings than he and considerably shorter in height,

Lady Hazard had glimpsed a naval cocked hat between the rows of tricornes and she spoke reassuringly, anxious to prevent any more expression of indignation on the part of her husband. His temper, never equable, had become more easily provoked with advancing years and, disgusted with the arrangement of the stands, he had several times given vent to his displeasure in terms better suited to the quarterdeck than to his present surroundings. Like herself, of course, she thought sadly, he was bitterly disappointed that their son Phillip, who had greatly distinguished himself in the late war, could not be present today to receive the Cross he had been awarded from the Queen's hands. But Phillip, ever eager to be at sea, had sailed from Spithead on 26th November with his old Commander, Henry Keppel—newly promoted Commodore of the China Squadron—in the fine sailing frigate *Raleigh* and . . . She felt the Admiral's bony fingers tightening about her arm. The Duke of Cambridge had moved from the Queen's side to quieten his restive mount and, for a moment, their view was unrestricted.

"That's young Alexander Dunn of the Eleventh Hussars," the Admiral told her, gesturing towards a tall young officer in the famous "Cherry Pickers'" uniform, fur-trimmed pelisse swinging from his left shoulder, who was now facing the Queen. "Won his Cross for riding back, after the Light Brigade charge at Balaclava, to save the lives of a sergeant and one of his private soldiers, who were cut off and under attack by the Cossacks. They say he accounted for at least three Russians singlehanded."

"He's a handsome young man," Lady Hazard observed.

Her husband chuckled. "Indeed he is—and quite a lively one, from what I've heard. Father was Receiver-General of Upper Canada and the boy was brought up there. Considers himself a Canadian and sold out, a couple of years ago—so what he's doing in uniform I don't know. Special permission, probably." He lowered his voice. "It's said he took his Commanding Officer's wife back to Canada with him but I don't know if that's true . . . certainly Douglas hasn't divorced her, has he?"

"I don't know, dear. But if—"

"Wonder what Cardigan thinks of it," the Admiral mused, his temper restored. "Dunn's a man after his own heart, I'd imagine—and now a V.C. Her Majesty didn't say much to him, did she? Must have been told, I suppose, and . . . damme, here's HRH back again on that infernal great horse! Now we shan't see any more of 'em."

"There aren't very many more to come now, George," his wife pointed out. "It's taking much less time than I had expected it would."

The ceremony had, in fact, taken only ten minutes. As the last man to be decorated—an officer of the Rifle Brigade—took his place in line with the other 61, the Guards' band struck up "See the Conquering Hero Comes" and, led by the cavalry and the Horse Artillery, the troops on parade passed in review between the Royal party and the newly decorated officers and men. Finally the whole force drew up in line, presented arms, and gave three rousing cheers for Her Majesty, which the Queen acknowledged graciously. To the skirling of the Highlanders' pipes, playing "Auld Lang Syne," the Royal cortège reformed and left the Park, and the main stand swiftly emptied as the families and friends of the new Victoria Cross holders hastened across the intervening space to offer their congratulations.

"Pity in a way, that young Phillip couldn't be here," the Admiral said regretfully. "It would have been a proud moment for both of us actually to be present when he received his Cross. But there it is . . . he's off to China, to what looks deuced like another war and, if it does come to that, I don't doubt he'll acquit himself well." His wife shivered involuntarily and he looked down at her anxiously. "Haven't caught a chill, have you, Augusta?"

She shook her head. "No. It's just that the thought of another war, so soon after the last one, and Phillip likely to be involved in it, is . . . well, I'm worried, I suppose."

"Wars offer a splendid chance of advancement to an ambitious young officer, m'dear," Admiral Hazard reminded her. "The only chance, really. And Phillip's ambitious . . . couldn't wait to go, could he? A couple of months' shore leave, after the *Huntress* paid off, and then Keppel had only to crook a finger and Phillip was on his way to Portsmouth to join him. It's what I'd have done myself at his age, of course but, for all that, I wish he'd waited a little longer. If he had, Their Lordships would have given him another command of his own—with his record and a Victoria Cross, they couldn't decently have refused. But with the *Raleigh* going down like that, it'll be in the lap of the gods, I suppose—both for Phillip and Keppel. I wish the boy would write, though, and tell us what's happening."

Lady Hazard, her attention concentrated on leading him through the surging crowd, scarcely took in what he was saying. Pausing at last so that her husband might regain his breath, she said quietly but with conviction, "I fancy Phillip had other reasons for wanting to go back to sea, George—other reasons than ambition and the desire for advancement, I mean."

"*Other* reasons? Nonsense, m'dear—what other reasons could he possibly have had?"

"Personal ones. I think it was a shock to him when Graham married Catriona."

"But good Gad!" The Admiral's heavy white brows rose in an astonished curve. "You're not suggesting that *Phillip* wanted to marry her, are you?"

His wife inclined her head. "I believe he did, yes. You see—"

"She's a charming girl," the Admiral conceded. "But for all that,—you're wrong, Augusta. Phillip knows perfectly well that any officer in Her Majesty's Navy who marries before he's reached post-rank is a fool. Why—"

"That was probably why he hesitated," Lady Hazard put in. She added, with a hint of reproach in her gentle voice, "You drummed it into him often enough, George."

"Of course I did—damme, it's the truth, isn't it? And if I did drum it into him, it was for his own good."

"Perhaps. Look, I think the crowd is thinning a little now— shall we go on?"

The old Admiral nodded. But, as they continued on their way to the Park gates, he returned to the subject of his elder son's marriage. "I thought it was a good match for both of them—and they seemed happy, 'pon my soul they did! It was high time Graham married . . . you said that yourself, Augusta. He needs the settling influence of a wife and he's fortunate in his choice of one."

"Yes, indeed, dear," Lady Hazard agreed.

"Well, then?" the Admiral challenged. "You are surely not suggesting that it was Phillip whom Catriona wanted, are you?"

His wife denied it. "Oh, no, nothing of the kind. But, if you remember, it was Phillip who brought her to the house initially, not Graham. I thought then that it was his intention to ask for her hand."

"But he didn't, did he?" the Admiral countered unanswerably. "In any case, it's worked out for the best for both boys, m'dear. Graham knew he couldn't make a career in the Service—Their Lordships may have restored his commission but they have long memories, they'd never have given him a command in peacetime. And what sort of future is it for a Lieutenant on half-pay these days, especially one with a black mark against his name?" He sighed. "I'm glad he did what he did, deuced glad . . . and proud of him! Because—if you'll pardon the expression, m'dear—it took guts. For an ex-officer to volunteer to serve on the lower deck when his country's at war is . . . damme, it's more than admirable."

"I am sure that it was for your sake that he did so," Lady Hazard said. "He wanted so desperately to win back your regard, you know. After his court martial, he—"

"Yes, yes," the Admiral agreed testily. "I was hard on the boy, I admit. But as I said, it's all worked out for the best, has it not?"

Perhaps it had, his wife thought. For a moment, tears filled her eyes as she remembered how, for years after their elder son's dismissal from the Navy, his father had refused sternly to see or communicate with or even to acknowledge him. She—and Phillip—had kept in touch, of course, but they had been compelled to do so secretly, like conspirators, keeping Graham's infrequent letters from the Admiral's knowledge, never so much as mentioning his name in the old man's hearing. And for Graham himself they had been cruel and bitter years, lost years, during which he had wandered the world, sometimes as mate but more often as a seaman in the merchant service, earning a precarious livelihood on long voyages to India and Australia, with no family to welcome him when he returned to a British port. But . . . Lady Hazard touched her handkerchief to her eyes, surreptitiously wiping away her tears.

The war with Russia had offered Graham his chance of redemption and he had seized upon it tenaciously and with courage. His commission had been restored to him—on merit, Phillip had told her proudly, and thanks to the personal intervention of the British Commander-in-Chief in the Black Sea, Admiral Sir Edmund Lyons, now the first Baron Lyons. So far as his father was concerned, all was now forgiven and forgotten. On his return from the Crimea, Graham had been welcomed back to the family circle and now, possessed of a charming and attractive wife, he had gone back to the merchant service, this time as the Commander of a fine Indiaman, owned by Mr Mark Pendleton, the wealthy and kindly East India Company Director, whose young daughters Catriona had companioned during a visit to the theatre of war.

As her husband had said, Lady Hazard reflected, it had all worked out for the best, for all three of them. Catriona was obviously happy, Graham ecstatically so and Phillip . . . She bit back a sigh, wishing for perhaps the thousandth time that a letter might come from him soon. They had heard nothing since the terse Admiralty message stating that the *Raleigh* had been sunk off Macao, without loss of life. But now, with war clouds looming in China and rumours of trouble in India, she was anxious—they both were—for news. Letters took weeks, even by the overland route, and the newspaper reports, based on brief accounts transmitted by telegraph, told very little. What they did tell—with two married daughters in India and two sons and a daughter-in-law on their way to the Far East— was frankly alarming but . . . Augusta Hazard came of a naval family and had married into one and, if she had learnt nothing else over the years, she had learnt to hide her feelings behind the appearance of optimism.

"Let's pause for a minute to get our breath, George dear," she suggested, sensing, from the weight he was putting on her arm, that her husband was again tiring. The Admiral halted gratefully, letting the crowd surge past them, as he mopped his heated brow.

"Never get a cab in all this rush, anyway," he said, gesturing with a gnarled hand in the direction of Kensington Road where, it was evident, from the number of people waving vainly from the pavements, hansom cabs were at a premium. "Have to walk, I suppose."

"Yes, I expect we shall," his wife agreed, without rancour. "But it's a lovely day. If we walk slowly and stay in the Park, dear, it won't be too bad. How are you feeling?"

"Me? Never felt better in me life," the Admiral assured her. He drew himself up to his full, impressive height, as if to prove his words, but Lady Hazard—whilst careful not to dispute them—led the way to a park bench which had just been vacated and seated herself firmly on its hard wooden boards. Since the attack of pneumonia that had brought him to death's door two years ago, the Admiral's health was another cause for anxiety. But, as a devoted wife, this concern was the one which, above all others, she went to great pains to conceal from him . . . although it was not always easy. Three hours' standing in the packed and airless spectators' gallery this morning had, she was uneasily aware, taken its toll of him. But at least they were in no hurry; they could linger here for a while, until the crowds thinned and then make their way, at a leisurely pace, to their house in Kensington Gore.

Quite a number of private carriages were passing them,

leaving the Park nose to tail and, as she watched the slow-moving procession, Augusta Hazard found herself wishing that their limited means, coupled with the expense of bringing up a family and marrying off their two elder daughters, had not compelled them to give up the unpretentious equipage they had once owned. She had derived much pleasure from ownership of the carriage, had enjoyed the afternoon drives, the visits to her friends in the country when her husband was at sea and, in their palmier days, it had not seemed so great an extravagance as it did now.

Not that they had ever been rich, of course. Contrary to the advice he had so assiduously drummed into his son, the Admiral himself had not waited to attain post-rank before taking a wife. He had married *her* when still a lieutenant—in command of his own sloop-of-war, it was true—and, promoted to a post-captaincy during the latter part of the Napoleonic war, had spent almost ten years on half pay when it ended, before being given another command. That had been the fate of all too many of the promising young sea officers of the Nelson era, alas . . . even Phillip's much-lauded Chief, Admiral Lyons, had been driven to abandon the Navy for the Diplomatic Service for this reason, and his exile had lasted over twenty years before Their Lordships had again found need for him. Augusta Hazard stifled a sigh. As her husband had said, a little while ago, wars offered the only real chance of advancement for ambitious young officers; when no enemy threatened the British coast or the sea-lanes of Empire, ships were laid up and the crews who manned them paid off and left to eke out a living as best they might on shore, whilst a parsimonious government conveniently forgot their existence. Yet no one wanted war, least of all the Queen and her ministers: the campaign in the Crimea had been a disaster which had cost nearly twenty thousand British lives, while those in Burma and Persia had also been costly and had achieved little. If there was now to be war with China and if the threat of a sepoy mutiny in India were not averted, then . . .

"Look, Augusta—" the Admiral's voice broke into Lady Hazard's troubled thoughts. "There's a carriage stopping and . . . damme, if it's not Lord George Melgund of the Foreign Office! Haven't seen him for over a year—ran into him at the St James's the night Phillip's award of the Victoria Cross was gazetted and we had a glass of champagne together, to celebrate."

"Lord George Melgund?" Lady Hazard echoed uncertainly. A footman had jumped down from the box to lower the steps of the carriage which had halted just in front of them and she studied the tall, good looking, grey-haired man who descended from it, top hat in hand. "I don't think I—"

"Nonsense, m'dear, of course you remember him," her husband reproached her. "Gave him passage to Rio in the *Hogue,* when he was Third Secretary at our Embassy there. Told you all about him, I'm quite sure. He went back in '48, as Chargé d'Affaires under Howden. Phillip met him then, when the *Maeander* called at Rio, on passage to the East Indies." He rose, smiling, to his feet, his own hat doffed, all trace of his earlier weariness gone. "Good day to you, Lord George!"

The newcomer extended his hand. "Admiral . . . I thought I recognised you! And Lady Hazard." He bowed, and added, gesturing to the waiting carriage, "Permit me to offer you a lift."

He ushered them into the luxuriously appointed vehicle, brushing aside the Admiral's protestations. "My dear sir, it is on my way, I assure you. And a coincidence I can't ignore, meeting you like this, on what must be a very proud day for you both. Your son was decorated by Her Majesty, was he not?"

"Unhappily, no," the Admiral admitted with regret. The coachman whipped up his horses and, as they rejoined the procession, Lady Hazard gave a brief explanation of Phillip's absence.

Lord George Melgund listened sympathetically. "Back with Henry Keppel is he . . . and seemingly on his way to another war? I can understand how you must feel, dear lady—my heart goes out to you. I recall most vividly the occasion when *I* saw young Phillip off to the Crimea."

"*You* saw him off?" the Admiral queried.

"Yes, indeed, Admiral. From Paddington Station, in March of '54. I handed over to his escort a member of the Russian Royal family, a charming young Archduchess, a niece of the Tsar, whose presence in this country had somehow been overlooked." Lord George smiled reminiscently. "We had to send her back as fast as we could, before hostilities broke out, so she and her governess were given passage in the *Trojan*. She was finally delivered—by another ship, I believe—to Odessa, under a flag of truce, just before the declaration of war reached the Fleet."

"Good Gad!" Admiral Hazard exclaimed. "The mysterious female passengers Phillip was waiting for when I dropped him off at Paddington! His 'Mademoiselle Sophie,' Augusta . . . at first, he mentioned her often in his letters and then"—he shrugged—"not a word about her. Even when he came home on leave, he never spoke of her, did he?"

"No," Augusta Hazard confirmed, her interest quickening. She had always wondered about Mademoiselle Sophie. Phillip was not, as a rule, secretive where his friends and acquaintances were concerned and his sudden silence had puzzled her. Socially, of course, a Russian Archduchess could scarcely be described as a friend but . . . She leaned forward in her seat. "Do you, by any chance, know what happened to the Archduchess, Lord George?"

Lord George Melgund smiled. "Oddly enough, I do, Lady Hazard. She married, soon after reaching Odessa. She had been betrothed in childhood to the Prince Andrei Narishkin but he was killed at Balaclava, I understand, and died in the British camp leaving Sophia Mihailovna tragically widowed. As possibly you are aware, I returned to St Petersburg with the Peace Mission last year and I saw her there. Only once and that almost by chance. The Princess told me that she had a son, born after her husband's death and she asked me, quite seriously, if—as a favour to her—I could arrange for the boy to enter the Royal Navy when he was old enough for a cadetship. Her voyage out in the *Trojan* must have impressed her very favourably, I can only suppose."

"Best training in the world for any boy," the Admiral said, with conviction. "Whoever he is . . . I trust you acceded to the lady's request, Melgund?"

"I told her I was sure that it could be arranged. There's time yet—the boy's only about two years old."

"It was a strange request," Lady Hazard said thoughtfully. "Strange for a niece of the Tsar to make. Russia has her own Navy and, after so bitter a war, one would hardly imagine . . ." Catching her husband's eye, she broke off and Lord George put in smoothly, "We are at peace with Russia under her new Tsar now, Lady Hazard, and pray God it will be a lasting peace. Not that *we'll* be allowed to enjoy it for very long, alas! Undeterred by Admiral Seymour's attack on Canton last November, Commissioner Yeh grows in insolence and appears to be spoiling for a fight with us."

"Pah!" The Admiral snorted his contempt. "Junks and

gingalls will be no match for our gunboats. They weren't in '42, as I know from firsthand experience. Once Lord Elgin gets to Hong Kong and starts things moving, Yeh will be kowtowing for all he's worth, mark my words."

"True, Admiral . . . but the news from India is becoming increasingly grave, you know. The Governor-General, Lord Canning, is recalling troops from Burma and Persia and now he's requested that those on their way to China should be diverted to his aid in India."

"Will he get them, d'you suppose?" the Admiral asked.

Melgund shrugged. "He will if Disraeli gets his way, certainly . . . and the House listens to him. *He* takes a graver view of the Indian crisis than the Government does and his last speech stirred up a good deal of feeling. John Russell really couldn't answer him. My own view is that Canning is yielding to panic. He's only just gone to India and . . ." He embarked on a lengthy dissertation on the possible consequences if troops were diverted from China, to which the Admiral offered well-informed comment and the assurance that, with or without additional troops, the Royal Navy could deal with Commissioner Yeh.

Their conversation involved strategic technicalities which had little meaning for Lady Hazard so, as the carriage turned into Kensington High Street and gathered speed, she leaned back against the well-padded upholstery, still giving the appearance of an attentive listener, but in fact, busy with her own thoughts. Her anxiety had been in no way allayed by Lord George Melgund's earlier observations. The situation in India must be very bad indeed, she reflected unhappily, for Lord Canning to request the diversion of troops intended for China. He, after all, was the man on the spot and as Governor-General, the one on whom the responsibility rested, and if the astute and far-seeing Benjamin Disraeli supported his request —even from the Opposition benches—the Prime Minister and his Colonial Secretary, Lord John Russell, would have to give it serious consideration.

The news that Delhi had been seized by mutinous sepoy regiments from Meerut, early in May, had only recently been received in detail and reported in the London newspapers. All England had been stunned and shocked when it was revealed that British civil and military officers of the East India Company—in many cases with their wives and children—had been savagely murdered in both cities and that, in Delhi, a wholesale massacre of native Christians had taken place as a ghastly prelude to the restoration of the King of Delhi to the throne of his Mogul ancestors.

Public opinion had been outraged as never before, even dignitaries of the Church joining in the demands for retribution and the severe punishment of the miscreants when letters, sent by overland mail, told of Christian places of worship desecrated and put to the torch in what, it seemed, the mutineers claimed was a holy war in defence of their own heathen beliefs. Moslem and Hindu, the enemies of centuries, had united together in the Bengal Presidency's Army with the avowed intent of ridding all India of her Christian rulers, and their initial success in taking Delhi—achieved by treachery— had dealt a very serious blow to British authority and prestige.

But that, the leader-writers insisted, was all the outbreak had done. Whilst not attempting to minimise the crime of mutiny, few of the influential journals had suggested that India was in serious danger of anarchy—many indeed, had criticised Disraeli for taking such a view, stating that he had no shadow of justification for so doing and even hinting that his motives were political. Delhi, the newspapers asserted, must at all costs be retaken and the self-styled Emperor deposed without delay. He was in his eighties, senile and almost certainly a puppet, who posed no real threat to the Company's rule. The Commander-in-Chief, General Anson, was reported by telegraph to be marching at the head of a European force for the purpose of driving the mutineers from Delhi. News of his death from cholera on 27th May had been followed by that of the appointment of General Barnard in his place and there was jubilation when it was learned that the new Commander-in-Chief had continued to march and, after defeating the rebels at the Hindan River, was now preparing to lay siege to Delhi.

Barnard was an experienced Crimean General; he would make short work of the siege, most of the newspapers agreed and, when Delhi was once again in British hands, the attempted mutiny would come to a swift and final end. It was the rebellion of a few disgruntled regiments, whose soldiers—drawn mainly from Oudh and resentful of the recent annexation of their corrupt and ill-governed kingdom—had stirred up trouble. An example would have to be made of them; innocent blood had been shed and mutiny was a crime punishable by death. It was even possible, one Whig newspaper declared, that the whole of the Bengal native army might have to be disbanded and . . . Augusta Hazard stifled a sigh. Until now she had believed all she had read on the leader-pages and in the news reports but now her faith was shaken, although . . . She glanced uneasily at Lord George Melgund and this time made no attempt to stifle her sigh. The most recent letters from her daughters had been calm and reassuring but they had been written almost six weeks ago and much could have happened in the interim.

The elder, Harriet, was in Sitapur—one of the Oudh out-stations some sixty miles north of Lucknow—where her husband was a regimental Commander and which, Lady Hazard knew, had an entirely native garrison. According to Harriet, all the native regiments were behaving perfectly and, although news of the Meerut outbreak and the loss of Delhi had reached the station, all the officers continued to repose complete confidence in the loyalty of their men. *"If the worst should happen, Sir Henry Lawrence has given instructions that we are to repair to Lucknow,"* Harriet had written. *"Of course, we are all horrified by what has happened in Delhi but here, I feel sure, all will be well . . ."* Please God she was right, her mother prayed silently. Please God that she and dear Jemmy and their three little ones would be safe . . .

She was no less anxious about her daughter Lavinia, who was married to an officer of the Queen's 32nd. The regiment had moved from Cawnpore to Lucknow and, although Lavinia's last letter had been written from Cawnpore, she wrote that she and her husband were expecting to follow the rest within a week or so. Tom had gone down with an attack of fever—not serious, she hastened to add, but somewhat debilitating—so they had remained with the regiment's invalids until he should recover sufficiently to return to duty. *"In any case, dearest Mamma"* the letter had ended, *"you need not worry about us. General Wheeler is making preparations for the defence of this station and two large buildings—one of them a hospital— are in readiness, with an entrenchment being constructed round them. They are close to the Allahabad road, and, should it become necessary, all the Europeans are to gather within the entrenchment, with our men and the gunners and reinforcements we are expecting from Allahabad to guard against a surprise attack. The Maharajah of Bithur, whose people call him the Nana Sahib (it means 'grandfather')—a most civilised man and a close friend of*

General and Lady Wheeler—has promised the aid of his troops should the sepoys here become disaffected.

"So we are in no danger, even if we have to stay here—and Tom doesn't think we shall. Sir Henry Lawrence wants the whole regiment in Lucknow and I, of course, would like to be there in time for the happy event we are expecting at the end of July, especially if Harriet should decide to join us, as Jemmy is urging her to . . ."

Tom and Lavinia had, as yet, no children but Lavinia had mentioned—almost casually in an earlier letter—the "happy event" they were expecting and Augusta Hazard added a prayer for them on this account. Giving birth to a baby in India could be fraught with difficulties but both Cawnpore and Lucknow were large stations, with European hospitals staffed by experienced civil and military surgeons. It was foolish to worry. Lavinia had urged her not to; she was a strong and healthy girl and Tom, of course, was the most devoted of husbands and could be relied upon to look after her.

There had been telegraphic reports, received via Lucknow and Agra, that Cawnpore was under attack by mutineers but, as yet, no official confirmation and all the newspapers had stressed the speed with which reinforcements were being rushed up country by road, river, and the partially completed railway from Calcutta. One entire regiment of the Company's European Fusiliers had been sent to augment the Cawnpore garrison and—after what was described as "restoring order" in Benares—had already entered Allahabad. If what Lavinia had written about General Wheeler's preparations for the defence of the station were true, then surely they would have little difficulty in holding out until the Fusiliers reached them? In any case, both Lavinia and Harriet were probably in Lucknow by this time, Lady Hazard told herself—in Lucknow, with a British regiment and under the care of that wise and widely respected

man, Sir Henry Lawrence. They . . . the Admiral gave vent to
a smothered exclamation.

"Good Gad! Held up in Allahabad, you say? Held up by
what, for heaven's sake?"

Startled out of her reverie, his wife turned to look at him
in mute question, the colour draining from her cheeks as
Lord George Melgund answered, in a flat, expressionless voice,
"By cholera and another threatened mutiny, I understand. But
Colonel Neill and his Fusiliers will deal with it and press
on to Cawnpore, have no fear. Indeed I—" He broke off in
mid-sentence, recalled to Augusta Hazard's presence by the little gasp of dismay which escaped her. "My dear Lady Hazard,
you must not let anything I've said upset you," he offered
apologetically. "This affair in India will fizzle out as soon as
General Barnard recaptures Delhi—and that, I'm assured on
the best authority, could be any day now."

"Yes," Augusta Hazard agreed faintly, "so the papers tell us
repeatedly and I . . . I try to believe it but . . ." She bit her
lower lip feeling it tremble.

The Admiral was unexpectedly silent, his hand closing
about hers, and Lord George went on, "There have been a great
many panic telegraph messages but none from Cawnpore
itself. The wires are down, so communication is cut off for the
time being. We don't even know for certain that the garrison
is under attack. Half the panic reports have proved to be false—
this one probably will be, too. The natives are said to cut the
telegraph wires wherever they can in order to make bracelets
for their womenfolk." He talked on, deliberately making light
of it, Lady Hazard sensed and added, as the carriage bowled
into Cornwall Gardens, "As to the sinking of the *Raleigh*, dear
Lady Hazard, Commodore Keppel must—as you will know better than I—stand trial by court martial for the loss of his ship.

But it will be the merest formality. Keppel's a fine seaman, with a reputation second to none, and he not only saved all his people, he saved his guns and most of his stores as well. He's bound to be exonerated and his officers with him, including your son Phillip. The talk about Keppel's being recalled is just talk . . . and political talk, most of it, I'm sorry to say. Certain people are jealous of his influence. But all that will change when a full report of the recent action at Fatshan Creek reaches the Admiralty. Keppel covered himself with glory on that occasion, I'm led to believe—they won't dare to recall him."

"No. No, of course not," Augusta Hazard echoed politely but somewhat at a loss. She had not heard the earlier part of Lord George's conversation with her husband and had no idea why he should imagine that there was any likelihood of Commodore Keppel's recall . . . and, until now, she had known nothing about his part in the actions in the Canton River. His part and—she drew in her breath sharply. Perhaps also Phillip's. The Admiral, however, had evidently followed every word, for he said gruffly, "The First Lord doesn't like Henry Keppel. Some difference of opinion over his C.B. award, if I remember rightly—Sir Charles Wood refused to put his name forward for a K.C.B.. which, in my view, he'd thoroughly earned as Commander of the Naval Brigade at Sebastopol. Keppel's a proud fellow and he wanted to refuse the lesser honour. They had words over it, strong words, and Wood isn't the man to forget a slight."

Lord George chuckled with what appeared to be great delight. "Well, he'll have to now, I fancy. May even have to eat his words!" The carriage drew up outside the door of the Hazards' modest residence but he refused Lady Hazard's invitation to join them for a glass of Madeira. "I must press on, to my regret, dear Lady Hazard . . . I've an engagement for luncheon." Top hat in hand, he bowed them farewell, brushing aside the Admiral's thanks. "I'm glad to have been of service and it has been a very great pleasure to see and talk to you both. I see too little of old friends these days, far too little. Good day to you, Admiral . . . your servant, Lady Hazard. I trust you will soon receive good news of all your absent children."

The luxurious carriage moved on across the square and the Admiral smiled a trifle uncertainly at his wife. "A very good fellow, Melgund—but he talks too much."

Augusta Hazard did not return his smile. "He seems to be extremely well informed—much better than we are."

"In his job, he has to be—but he doesn't know it all, not by a long chalk. As he admitted himself, m'dear, a great many of these telegraphic reports are dictated by panic, especially the ones from India. You mustn't believe *all* he said or let it upset you."

"No." Feeling tears come to prick at her eyes, Augusta Hazard made a brave attempt to hide them. Head averted, she offered her arm. "It's *not* knowing that I find hard to bear, George. Not knowing what the girls are doing or even where they are with any certainty. The mails take so long. I ought to be used to it by now, I suppose—letters took long enough from the Crimea, heaven knows. But now I—"

"Neither of us is getting any younger, m'dear." The Admiral gently patted the hand he held. "It's harder to bear as one begins to feel the weight of one's years. But Graham will give us firsthand news—the *Lady Wellesley* should be in the Hoogly River by this time. He'll make enquiries about the girls in Calcutta and he'll write as soon as he can. He'll know we're anxious." He released her arm and gave a resounding pull on the door bell.

It was answered by their youngest daughter, Lucy, a pretty, blue-eyed seventeen-year-old, who was the apple of her father's eye. She was flushed with excitement and hugged them both enthusiastically as they entered the hall.

"Oh, Mamma, Papa, I've been longing for you to come back," she announced breathlessly. "There's a letter . . . look, on the hall table! It came just after you left for the Park and I've been burning to open it."

"A letter?" The Admiral peered short-sightedly at the little gate-legged table which stood in the centre of the entrance hall. "From Hattie or Lavinia? Or"—remembering his remarks a few moments earlier—"is it from Graham?"

Lucy shook her head. "No, from Phillip. Oh, please, Papa, read it aloud to us, will you not, before we have our luncheon?"

"Very well," her father agreed. "If your Mamma does not mind?" Receiving a nod of assent, he beamed, and went to pick up the letter. Augusta Hazard followed him, some of the tension draining out of her, and all three of them ascended the stairs to the second floor, where the Admiral had his sanctum.

Settled in his favourite chair, his spectacles perched comfortably on his long, high-bridged nose and a glass of the excellent Madeira he had offered Lord George Melgund in his hand, he started to read. The letter began with enquiries as to their health and well-being and then continued: *"By this time, no doubt, you will have heard of the loss of our beautiful* Raleigh *which—needless to tell you, Father—has broken Commodore Keppel's heart. It was no fault of his or, indeed, of any of her people—the culprit was a rock, uncharted and, as we afterwards ascertained, lying nine feet beneath the water, shaped like a sugarloaf and the top so small that a boat's anchor could not lie on it.*

"We sailed from Singapore with a supply of shot and shell for

conveyance to Hong Kong, having to beat up the coast against the monsoon—a weary business for the first few days of our passage. But on 14th April, a fine breeze was blowing and we were running close-hauled with land and islands all round us and Hong Kong barely 30 miles distant . . . and it was then that she struck. I was on deck and thought at first she had struck some heavy floating timber. Her bow lifted but it did not deaden her way—she heaved and passed on, and I heard the leadsman calling 'By the mark, seven!' Then came a report from the lower deck that daylight could be seen through a fifteen-foot rent in the ship's side.

"We beat to quarters and the first order was to sound the well—the carpenter reported ten feet of water. Rigging the pumps was a matter of minutes; I never saw men turn to their work in grander fashion. Off came their frocks; they stripped to flannels and hove round with a will but the water steadily gained on us. Keppel decided to try to ground the ship in shoal water. The wind was easterly and every sort of sail was improvised, even to setting the sails of boats hanging at the davits, and the Commodore himself took charge of the conning of the ship.

"Then one of our large chain pumps broke down. Just at that moment, a ship was reported at anchor off Macao and, with a glass, I made her out to be a frigate flying the French Admiral's flag. Keppel—this was typical of his splendid spirit—ordered me to lower the fore-royal, hoist the French flag, and fire a salute. Our foremost maindeck guns had been run aft to prevent the ship settling forward but they were already loaded, in preparation for saluting our own Flag, and most of our after-ports had more than one muzzle protruding. A boat was seen coming from the French ship but there was nothing to show that we were in distress apart from our ensign at the peak, hoisted Union Jack downwards, and this was hidden from the Frenchman by our studding sails. A few

minutes after firing our salute, our poor Raleigh *grounded on the mudbank between Roko and Typa Islands and the officer commanding the boat, learning what had occurred, returned at once to his ship, the* Virginie, *to inform his Admiral.*

"Rear-Admiral Guérin came in person to offer us any help we needed. Keppel received him at the gangway and the Frenchman embraced him, exclaiming again and again, 'A British frigate saluting the French flag while she is sinking . . . c'est magnifique!' *If we had been French, we could not have been given more kindly assistance. Keppel landed marines to clear the nearest island of Chinese and then, with the assistance of our allies, we put most of the ship's company ashore, with their hammocks and bags, stores, and the ship's sails. The Commodore remained, on an improvised bridge set up before the mizzenmast and over the wheel, with a small guard of seamen and marines throughout the night, and sent our First Lieutenant, Jim Goodenough, to Hong Kong in the French gunboat* Catinat, *to report to Admiral Seymour.*

"The after part of the lower deck was still dry up to nine o'clock, so that most of us were able to get to our cabins to salvage our clothes and personal possessions, but after that, the ship settled considerably and at 5 a.m., when it was still dark, we were called upon to man the boats and land. The Frenchman sent us boats at daylight and helped us all that day to get stores and provisions ashore. Admiral Seymour sent the Bittern *to our assistance and came himself on 16th, the* Nankin *and* Inflexible *standing by as we hoisted our guns out and loaded them into lighters sent from Hong Kong.*

"The poor Commodore was, as I told you, heartbroken. He only left the ship when all hope for her had to be abandoned and, even then, he insisted on dismantling her, hoisting out lower masts with the aid of our spars only . . . quite a task, as you well know,

Father! I think he hoped, if we cleared her even to the ballast, that it might be possible to refloat her but, I regret to say, the Admiral has decided against it.

"Keppel, and the Master, Mr Williams, are to be tried by court martial early in June but the verdict, of course, is a foregone conclusion, since no blame can be attached to either of them. In the meantime, preparations are being made for an attack on the Chinese Fleet, which we hope will not be long delayed. It will be a boat attack, since all the war junks are dispersed up rivers and creeks, and Keppel, as senior Commodore, has been made senior officer in the Canton River and second-in-command of the Fleet. His broad pennant was hoisted on board the old Alligator—*you will remember her in '42, Father—now a hospital ship and, after ten days of hard work and exposure on our desert island, the rest of us followed him to Hong Kong.*

"I am fortunate in being appointed temporarily to the river steamer Hong Kong, *in which Keppel plans to lead the attack. She is useful, being of fair speed and very light draught. She is armed with a long thirty-two-pounder, and a few brass guns and rocket-tubes are being put into her—the latter splendid weapons with which to deal with the bamboo stockades we shall encounter up river. With me are Jim Goodenough, Prince Victor Hohenlohe, and three of the* Raleigh's *mids, Scott, Montagu, and Keppel's nephew, Harry Stephenson. And, by a happy coincidence, a young gentleman named Lightfoot, who was with me briefly in the* Huntress *until, if you remember, he broke his leg in a fall from the rigging. He is now a husky sixteen-year-old and bears no sign of his injury. The other* Raleigh *officers are divided between ships of the fleet and the Macao Fort but we shall all be reunited when we rendezvous off the Bogue Forts . . . Keppel has promised us command of our own* Raleigh *men and boats and will, being the*

man he is, keep his word whatever contrary plans the Admiral may have made!

"I must close now, as the mail is leaving this forenoon, but will write again as soon as I can to keep you informed of our doings and, God willing, to send you news of our victory over the China Fleet . . ."

The Admiral's voice faded into silence and Lucy exclaimed eagerly, "They *were* victorious, weren't they, Papa?"

"Yes, child," her father confirmed. He smiled and quoted, still smiling, "And 'twas a famous victory as I don't doubt time will prove. But"—he removed his glasses and, meeting his wife's anxious gaze, permitted himself a sigh—"what good will come of it against a nation like the Chinese remains to be seen, alas. We shall have to wait for the arrival of the official mail to tell us. However, let us drink to it . . . and to Phillip and his gallant comrades!" He raised his glass of Madeira.

Lady Hazard followed suit. "To Phillip!" she whispered softly. "May God preserve him in victory or defeat . . ."

CHAPTER ONE

In the cramped cabin of the old frigate HMS *Alligator,* serving as depot flagship for the Canton River Fleet, Commodore the Honourable Henry Keppel issued final orders to his divisional Commanders. Initially he read from a paper in his hand, prefaced by the information that he was quoting from the General Order of Battle sent out under the hand of the Commander-in-Chief, Rear-Admiral Sir Michael Seymour.

"Having determined on attacking the junk fleet above Hyacinth Island, in the Fatshan Creek," the Commodore read, *"the whole of the ships' boats, manned and armed, are to be ready at three-thirty o'clock on Monday morning, June the first, the crews having previously breakfasted and been victualled for two days . . ."* There was an eager lilt to his voice, Phillip Hazard heard with relief, as he went into details. Meeting the eye of his fellow Commander from the *Raleigh,* Edward Turnour, he grinned. It was good to see their gallant little Commodore in a happy and optimistic mood once more—the tragic loss of his beautiful sailing frigate had deeply distressed him, and, try as they might, his officers had despaired of bringing a smile back to his face. But it was there now, oddly and incongruously boyish among the greying red whiskers—at the prospect of action, Henry Keppel was, as always, in his element, and he had not earned the reputation of being the bravest officer in the British Navy for nothing.

"The movement will commence," Keppel went on, *"by the Hornet, Haughty, and Coromandel—the last named flying the Commander-in-Chief's flag—moving up to a berth as close to Hyacinth Island as depth of water will permit, and convenient for landing the seamen and Royal Marines told off for the attack on the fort and covering guns."* He paused, looking about him. "The attack on the fort will be led by Commodore Elliott, gentlemen, and I have no doubt that it will be successful. The Commodore has already shown us how such an attack ought to be made when he captured or destroyed 27 war junks of Sonhay's squadron in Escape Creek last week, bringing out ten as prizes . . . and all with the loss of only two men wounded!"

He paused again, blue eyes twinkling, and Phillip saw the expression on Commodore Charles Elliott's face undergo a swift change. Elliott had been resentful of his supersession in command of the Canton River and, for days now, had made no secret of his resentment, scarcely exchanging a word with the man who had replaced him. Now, however, finding himself the object of such unstinted praise, he reddened and then managed an answering smile.

"Thank you," he acknowledged. "We were fortunate, of course, and only about forty junks opposed us. There are at least three times that number defending Fatshan Creek."

"In the region of a hundred and seventy," Henry Keppel told him. "As nearly as the Admiral and I could ascertain from the top of a pagoda, after Divine Service this morning. Seventy of them form the first division, moored in line abreast across the two creeks, with their bow-guns ranged so as to cover both channels. Autey's made copies of my sketch—pass them round, Matt, if you please." He added, as his secretary obediently handed out the sketch-maps, "There is a six-gun battery mounted opposite the fort, Commodore Elliott, and you'll have about twenty ranged against you in the fort itself."

"I had observed that," Elliott returned, with a hint of asperity. "Don't worry, my dear Keppel—we shan't permit you to be held up."

Phillip again exchanged glances with Edward Turnour but neither spoke and Commodore Keppel, still with a smile playing about his lips, continued to read his orders. "The Commander-in-Chief objects to long-range firing and, in the advance, the return of the Chinese fire is to be regulated by the officer commanding the leading division. The all-important object is to reach the junks through narrow and shallow water, requiring attention to navigation, which should not be diverted by a too hasty discharge of guns." His smile widened. "You have been warned, gentlemen! For the rest, Admiral Seymour wishes it to be clearly understood that, if any impediments exist to the steam gunboats' progress up the creek, it is not to delay the prompt advance of the oared boats. All casualties for hospital treatment are ultimately to be conveyed to the *Inflexible* for passage to Hong Kong. And finally, the Admiral wishes me to impress upon all Officers the necessity of restraining their men from attacking unarmed people, confining operations to those directed against the war junks and troops, and they are strictly to respect and protect the persons and property of the peaceable inhabitants. I trust that is clear to you all?" There was a murmur of assent from the assembled officers. The attacking force had been divided into four divisions and individual commands and stations had already been allocated so that, when the Commodore invited questions, only Elliott responded.

"I understand that it will be left to my discretion whether— having taken possession of the fort and outworks—I advance by land with my division or re-embark in the boats, to unite with the other divisional attacks on the junk forces." It was more a statement than a question and Keppel nodded. Clearly,

Phillip thought, Commodore Elliott had no intention of being omitted from the main attack, merely because, as a necessary prelude to it, he was required to storm a fort defended by twenty heavy guns. This attitude was understandable; he had been involved from the outset in the tortuous negotiations with Commissioner Yeh, had captured a Chinese brig in retaliation for the seizure of the nominally British *lorcha,* the *Arrow*—which had initiated hostilities—and he had led the attacks on the Bogue Forts and Dutch Folly the previous year.

The Canton River had been, until Keppel's arrival, his happy hunting ground. With Captain Hall, of the flagship *Calcutta,* and Commanders Bate and Fortescue, Charles Elliott had been at the right hand of both the British Plenipotentiary, Sir John Bowring, and his own Commander-in-Chief, Rear-Admiral Sir Michael Seymour. He had assisted the Consul, Harry S. Parkes, the American Commissioner, Dr Parker, and the French Chargé d'Affaires, Count de Courcy, in their dealings with the Chinese and, in liasion with the French Admiral, Guérin, and the American Commander-in-Chief, Commodore Armstrong, had carried out the capture and destruction of the four Barrier Forts and the bombardment of the Government buildings in the city of Canton, at the end of November, 1856.

Since then, however, there had been changes, Phillip was aware. The French struck their Consular flag in Canton and removed their subjects from the factories, withdrawing their naval force from the river; the Americans, whilst continuing to demand assurances for future adherence to the Treaty, and respect for their flag, desisted from the use of force and, early in December, resumed diplomatic negotiations with the Chinese Viceroy. Commodore Elliott was by no means the only man to find himself superseded; Sir John Bowring had informed the British government in January that, before the negotiations could be opened with the Chinese in Peking or elsewhere with any prospect of success, it was essential to capture and occupy the city of Canton. On the advice of Admiral Seymour, he had asked for military aid to enable him to achieve this objective, advocating that a force of five thousand men, with artillery, should be supplied from India.

He had the full support of the American and French Plenipotentiaries. In April he, Dr Parker for the United States, and M. de Bourboulon, the French Minister, signed a Memorandum of Agreement, pledging the co-operation of their naval forces for the reduction of the city of Canton as a necessary preliminary to further negotiation. The British Government, however, wanted pressure brought upon the Chinese by a naval blockade of the Yangtze and Peiho Rivers and Sir John Bowring's proceedings in Canton had come under strong criticism in the Commons. The Foreign Office, displaying its traditional reluctance to trust to the judgement of the man on the spot, announced the appointment of the Earl of Elgin— previously Governor-General of Canada—as High Commissioner and Plenipotentiary. Bowring was directed to serve under him as Minister and was informed that Lord Elgin, who was to travel overland to Singapore, might be expected in Hong Kong aboard the fifty-gun steam frigate *Shannon* early in July, together with a military force of fifteen hundred men.

The French also decided to replace their Plenipotentiary, appointing Baron de Gros in place of de Bourboulon, and Dr Parker, although he had signed the Agreement on behalf of the United States in April, had received no further instructions from his Government since then and he, too, was anticipating his replacement and recall. In these circumstances, neither Minister considered that he had the power to involve his country's naval forces in aggressive action and, without their support, a blockade of China's major rivers by the British alone was clearly out of the question.

Diplomatic activity continued unabated, particularly on the part of the French and a report concerning the arrival of a Russian emissary in the Peiho added to the uncertainty. As Admiral Seymour had wryly put it, when endeavouring to explain the complexities of the present situation to a gathering of his senior officers, Phillip recalled: "We're on our own, with our feathers clipped, gentlemen . . . but at least we shall maintain control of the Canton River. Mainly, of course, in the belief that, on his arrival here, Lord Elgin will see the wisdom of the measures Sir John Bowring has advocated and permit us to enter the city of Canton. In addition, we must ensure that no foreign diplomats, with bribes in their hands, are in a position to tempt Imperial Viceroy Yeh to grant them trade concessions to the exclusion of ourselves. We'll hold what we have fought for and leave Yeh in no doubt that we mean business!"

The order for an attack on the Chinese war junks followed shortly afterwards and had been greeted enthusiastically by both officers and men of the British naval squadron. The arrival of the frigates *Tribune* and *Amethyst* had provided adequate reinforcements; that of the battleship *Sanspareil,* with 300 Royal Marines on board, was expected and a total force of nineteen hundred seamen and marines was now gathered below Hyacinth Island, some two miles from the entrance to Fatshan Creek and about halfway to Canton itself. A miscellaneous fleet of oared boats had been towed into position by steam gunboats and corvettes, each division having its own towing craft which, tomorrow—as Commodore Keppel had outlined—would take it as far as the depth of water permitted.

As he listened to Keppel, with his irresistible charm, continuing the discussion on tactics with his fellow Commodore,

Phillip let his own thoughts wander. The attack would have its perils, he knew; the Chinese fought well and their guns were well served and accurately ranged but, like everyone else in the crowded cabin, he was eager for action . . . and boat actions smacked of Nelson's day—of seamen, armed with cutlasses, boarding enemy ships and fighting for their possession at close quarters, on decks slippery with blood. He smiled at his romanticised picture. It would not be like that tomorrow, of course. Initially it would be fought out with guns; the Chinese thirty-two-pounders and "stink-pots" and their gingalls —those curious, breech-loading firearms which required two men and a rest to fire their four- to eight-ounce balls—pitted against British ships' guns and rockets, and Minié or Enfield rifles. Only later would it come to hand-to-hand combat—and only then if the junks weren't set ablaze by British rockets.

For the moment, Phillip found himself pitying their primitively armed opponents; then, recalling the sickening eyewitness accounts he had heard of Commissioner Yeh's wholesale executions, his resolution hardened. Yeh was a brutal tyrant, who had put down the rebellion of the so-called Taiping Celestial Dynasty with an iron hand, reputedly beheading three thousand whom he had taken prisoner. He had incited his people to murder British subjects by offering a substantial reward for their severed heads, conniving at attacks on their persons and an attempt to poison those resident in Hong Kong by the addition of arsenic to flour supplied for making bread in the Colony. And he had, of course, burnt down the trading factories and sought, in every way he could, to deny to "foreign barbarians" the rights they had been granted under the Treaty of Nanking—clearly, he had to be stopped. He . . . Edward Turnour laid a hand on his arm.

"Time to be on our way, Phillip. Our revered Chief has

worked his usual miracle and charmed Elliott out of his sulks. Look, he's actually smiling! You'd think, to look at him now, that he'd chosen his role for tomorrow himself, instead of having it forced upon him. Keppel, I swear, could charm the birds off the trees if he set his mind to it."

Phillip laughed. In common with virtually every officer and seaman who had served with him, he had become a devoted admirer of the diminutive Henry Keppel. His admiration dated from his midshipman days, when both he and Turnour had served under Keppel's command in the frigate *Maeander*—an eventful, three-year commission, which had taken them to the Far East and Australia between 1848–51. His boyish hero-worship had been in no wise diminished when he had again found himself under his old Commander in the Naval Brigade in the Crimea. Indeed, it was largely thanks to Henry Keppel, he reflected gratefully, that he had lived down the stigma of his court martial and the bitter self-doubt which dismissal from command of the *Huntress* had engendered in him. On the rocky Heights above Sebastopol, when his whole career had been in jeopardy, Keppel had given him more than friendship; where another Commander might have ignored the torment he was enduring, Keppel had recognised it and offered him the chance to redeem himself. The little Commodore's charm was proverbial but there was a great deal more to him than charm. A very great deal more.

Commodore Elliott departed in his gig for the steam paddle gunboat *Coromandel,* at anchor with her string of oared boats a mile ahead of them and, with his departure, Commodore Keppel relaxed his earlier formality. He was in high good humour, joking and laughing, the keen blue eyes holding their familiar twinkle as he wished each one of them well. "No racing me tomorrow, Cochrane," he warned the *Niger*'s Captain. "Have proper respect for my grey hairs!"

"When have I not, sir?" Cochrane challenged, smiling. His gig, handled more smartly than Elliott's, went skimming up river and Keppel watched it, eyes momentarily narrowed.

"Get as much sleep as you can, my boys," he advised, when the more junior of his officers filed past him in their turn. "You'll need all the stamina you've got tomorrow—and all the guts! Don't underrate John Chinaman simply because his junks look a trifle antiquated—they're ideal for navigating this river and he handles them expertly. If you've never encountered them before, you'll be astonished at the punch they pack and the speed at which they can travel, under sail or oars." He laid a hand on Phillip's arm. "Ah, my dear boy—the Admiral was talking about you this morning."

"*Was* he, sir?" Phillip eyed him uncertainly.

"Indeed he was. We shall shortly have three holders of the Victoria Cross on this station—Captain Peel and Midshipman Daniels, when *Shannon* joins, and yourself," Keppel said. "Her Majesty is to present the first Crosses to sixty-two officers and men at a special parade to inaugurate the award, in Hyde Park on the twenty-sixth of June. Their Lordships have informed the Commander-in-Chief that your three Crosses are to be sent out here and he's been instructed to arrange for their presentation . . . in the latter part of July, very probably. I thought you would like to know."

"Thank you, sir," Phillip acknowledged, without noticeable pleasure. Keppel should have been given a Cross, he thought rebelliously, instead of the penny-pinching C.B. with which the First Lord had sought to fob him off. He . . .

"You'll be in excellent company," the Commodore reminded him. "Well, I'll see you first thing in the morning. You're commanding *Raleigh*'s cutter, Edward, are you not?" Turnour nodded. "Then be a good fellow and make sure that Spurrier has a length of blue bunting to serve as my broad pennant when I leave *Hong Kong,* would you? I intend to lead the attack in my galley and it's important that the third and fourth divisions should be able to see exactly where I am."

"Very good, sir, I'll attend to it," Edward Turnour promised.

"And," Keppel added, as an afterthought struck him, "tell Spurrier also that he's to leave my dog Mike behind—there's no space for it in any of the boats."

Turnour contrived to keep a straight face. Spurrier, the Commodore's coxswain, had served with him for so long that he regarded certain privileges as his right and the dog, Mike— an intelligent little terrier—had adopted him and was his constant shadow, to whose presence the *Raleigh*'s officers usually turned a blind eye. "I'll tell him, of course, sir. But he maintains that Mike won't leave him and—"

"Be damned to that for an unlikely yarn!" Keppel retorted. "He's my dog, isn't he? Well, he can be tied up here in my cabin."

"Aye, aye, sir," Turnour acknowledged.

Phillip, also careful to conceal his amusement, put in diffidently, "Mike *is* quite good for morale, sir. The younger men regard him as a mascot, I fancy and—"

"Mascot indeed! Since when have seamen of Her Majesty's Navy required a mascot?" Keppel demanded. But his lower lip had a suspicious tremor and he said, with well-simulated gruffness, "All right but it's pure superstitious poppycock, you know. If Spurrier must bring the unfortunate animal into battle with him, he'd better keep it out of my sight. If he gets it killed, he'll have only himself to blame . . . and what price his mascot then, eh?"

"I'll warn him, sir," Turnour assured him.

"Yes, you do that, my dear boy," Keppel agreed. The tremor became a smile. "I'll have a quiet word with him when he picks me up in the morning. *I'm* going to make sure of a comfortable night—I'm sleeping here, in my own cabin, and the Admiral's dining with me. Rank has its advantages sometimes, has it not? I wish you both joy of the *Hong Kong*'s deck!"

The *Hong Kong*, when they returned on board, was in a state of organised chaos, her boats, like those of the other steamers—strung out astern of her and her decks crowded with seamen and marines. Edward Turnour went in search of the Commodore's coxswain to discharge his errand and Phillip, after inspecting his own command—the *Raleigh*'s launch—partook of a frugal supper and then lay down as best he could in the sternsheets of the launch, his long legs tucked uncomfortably beneath him and his head resting on the gunwhale. It was a calm, warm night; the hum of men's voices and the croaking of frogs on the river bank the only sounds he could hear and, accustomed to snatch a brief nap at sea, whenever the opportunity offered, he dozed off undisturbed by the men talking on either side of him.

Young Lightfoot, his boat's midshipman—whom he had sent to the *Hong Kong* for what remained of the night—wakened him well before first light, bringing with him the rest of the launch's crew and the news that Commodore Keppel had come aboard the gunboat an hour before.

So much for the privileges of rank and the comfortable night he had promised himself, Phillip thought, and smiled in the warm darkness, remembering other nights in the Sebastopol batteries when Henry Keppel, supposedly sound asleep in his tent, had made his appearance just before an attack as if, by instinct, he had sensed the danger and knew that his mere presence would put heart into the men who had to face it.

"Shall I issue the rations, sir?" his coxswain asked and he

nodded. Breakfast, according to the Admiral's orders, was to be eaten before the advance began—ship's biscuit and the grog ration, sparse enough fare, but welcome as a distraction, if nothing else, from thoughts which at such a moment tended to be apprehensive ones. His own included . . . Phillip stretched his cramped limbs. It was nearly two years since he had been under fire from an enemy and he felt the familiar sick sensation in the pit of his stomach as he recalled details he had imagined long since forgotten. The face of a young soldier, newly dead, his rifle still clutched in his nerveless hands; the agonised sobbing of a gallant sergeant of the 88th whose legs had been carried away by a roundshot as he led the way into the Russian Redan. And—he drew in his breath sharply. The ghastly scene of carnage inside the fort itself, when he had finally entered it with the survivors of his ladder party and the Engineer officer, Ranken, to find the Russians, secure behind their embrasures, mowing down their attackers in a terrible cross-fire of grape and canister and ball.

That attack had heralded the end of the siege of Sebastopol. During the night, the Russians had withdrawn their troops from the city and its surrounding forts and bastions, leaving the harbour a wilderness of burnt-out, sinking ships and blazing buildings. But for the Allies, faced with an appalling butcher's bill, there had been little joy in the victory. How much joy, Phillip wondered glumly, as he poured a lavish tot from his flask for Midshipman Lightfoot, how much joy would there be today?

"Mix that with lemon juice," he cautioned. "And drink it slowly, Mr Lightfoot." The boy, he realised, was shaking with excitement, eager as a puppy, but he managed a dutiful acknowledgement although, in fact, he had swallowed most of his shared portion at a single gulp. It was too dark to see his face clearly but he appeared to be grinning and Coxswain O'Brien, working dexterously with his measure by the dim glow of the boat's lantern, passed out the last of the men's grog ration and observed dryly, "Wonderful to be young, sir, is it not?"

He was a small, spare man of indeterminate age, who had joined in the *Raleigh*'s launch as a volunteer from the 84-gun flagship *Calcutta* which, on account of her size, had remained at the Hong Kong anchorage. He had only joined the previous day, as replacement for the launch's regular coxswain, who had gone down with fever, and Phillip asked him, curious as to his antecedents, "How much service have you put in, Cox'n?"

O'Brien looked surprised. "Eighteen years, sir." His voice was educated, with no trace of accent. "I should have known better, shouldn't I? Never volunteer—that's not a bad motto in the Navy!"

"Well, why *did* you volunteer?"

The coxswain shrugged. "I served here in '42 in the *Dido*, sir, under Captain Keppel, and I thought I'd like to see him in action again. It's a rare sight, I can tell you." He shifted the plug of tobacco in his mouth from one side to the other, muttered a "beg pardon" and spat expertly over the gunwhale into the murky water below him. "I was in Sarawak with him too, sir—with him and Rajah Brooke. Those were the days! We were never out of action and we revelled in it, chasing pirates and Dyak headhunters by boat up the river. And as for Captain Keppel, why there wasn't a Captain afloat that could touch him. I remember once he . . ." His reminiscing was cut short by a flashing light signal from the *Coromandel*, upstream and to port, a signal that was repeated by her next in line, *Haughty*, and then by *Starling* and *Hornet*. The first two weighed anchor and, paddle-wheels clanking, could just be seen as dark shapes, starkly silhouetted against the glow of the lightening sky.

Conscious of a quickening of his pulse, Phillip watched them, as they started to forge ahead in the direction of the island and the as yet unseen fort which was their objective.

It would be the turn of the second division next; there was activity on the *Hong Kong*'s deck as her duty watch prepared to weigh anchor and a rocket rose from the fort to hurtle skywards in hissing proof that the Chinese were aware of the impending British attack.

"Out pipes, my lads," Phillip ordered. "Gun's crew close up." He felt the tow rope go taut and the bowman called out, "The *Hong Kong*'s under way, sir!" a slight tremor in his voice. Day dawned with the startling suddenness of the East; the shower of rockets which had been rising from the walls of the fort abruptly ceased and, glass to his eye, Phillip saw the *Coromandel,* with the Admiral's flag at the foremast, alter course, evidently to avoid some obstacle. She was within about two thousand yards of her objective, smoke belching from her two squat funnels as she increased speed but, a few minutes later, Midshipman Lightfoot, squatting behind the bow-gun, let out a yell of dismay.

"The *Coromandel*'s grounded, sir!"

Phillip raised the Dollond again. The flagship was held fast on some submerged barrier but Commodore Elliott, he saw, was wasting no time—already his landing parties were piling into their boats. The fort opened fire; roundshot and grape peppered the water all round the racing boats but all fell short and the *Haughty,* holding to her original course and beautifully handled, supplied effective covering fire when the boats were beached and the first wave of scarlet-coated marines leapt ashore on the shelving river bank.

The *Coromandel* had brought two of her three guns to bear now and her gunners were pitching shot and shell into the fort with admirable speed and accuracy. The landing party of seamen and marines, with Commodore Elliott well to the fore, charged up the steep hill with bayonets fixed, cheering as they ran. The position was a formidable one and, Phillip thought, as he watched, a body of resolute troops could have made a hard fight of it. The Chinese, however, unnerved by the heavy fire from the gunboats, after firing a few more shots, abandoned their stronghold and their guns to flee in wild disorder across the paddy fields to their rear.

They were not pursued but, within minutes of the British party's entry into the fort, several of its guns were turned on the line of junks moored in an adjacent creek, upon which they got out their sweeps and started to make off. The *Haughty*'s boats, which had landed a reserve party of marines, were seen to be re-embarking some of them and, the first phase of the attack successfully completed, Commodore Keppel signalled the remainder of his flotilla to advance up the channel on the east side of Hyacinth Island, himself leading the advance in the *Hong Kong*.

CHAPTER TWO

They *made good progress* at first, on the rising tide, but then the river began to shoal and, one after another, the gunboats grounded. The *Hong Kong,* with her light draught, got within sight of the first division of junks before she, too, was brought abruptly to a standstill in the shallow water and Commodore Keppel could be seen entering his six-oared galley and waving to the other boats to cast off their tow-ropes and follow him.

"Right, my boys, this is it," Phillip sang out. "Out oars and give way together!"

His crew needed no urging. Pulling with a will, they sent the heavy launch skimming through the water, making a race of it with the *Starling*'s pinnace. It was tiring work, with the sun now hot on their backs and a heavy fire of grape from a gun battery, masked by trees on shore, falling about them like rain. The first division of junks, numbering twenty or so, were moored in a compact line and positioned so as to bring the enfilading fire of their guns on the attacking force. They presented an awesome spectacle from the approaching boats, high, square-prowed craft painted in garish colours, each with an eye depicted on the headboards, their upper decks swarming with men and brass cannon bristling from their lower deck ports. Apart from a few sighting shots, they held their fire until the leading British boats were within 600 yards and then they opened with devastating effect.

Keppel's galley sustained at least one hit before it vanished from sight in the smoke of battle, but the heavier boats were now within range and returned the fire with their bow-guns, Phillip's among them. Led by Edward Turnour's cutter and that of the *Hornet,* the rocket-boats sent a shower of incendiaries into the close-packed junks, which set first one and then another ablaze, the flames spreading rapidly from adjoining, tinder-dry decks and matting sails. The first line disintegrated in a series of fires and explosions, spars and timbers hurtling skywards as stored powder blew up and, with little conscious recollection of how they had got there, Phillip realised that his boat had passed through the once-formidable line and was faced with a second, moored at right angles which, as they approached it, met them with a hail of missiles from gingalls and cannon.

Some of the gunboats had evidently come up, for heavier fire than could have been sustained by the oared boats was opened on the second fleet of junks, which brought a brief but timely respite and enabled the leading boats to close with their opponents. Twice Phillip took his launch alongside a junk with the intention of boarding but each time the crew abandoned ship with scant ceremony and, adhering to his orders, he left the third and fourth divisions to take what prizes they could and continued upstream. As the smoke cleared he could see, a mile or so ahead, the flag-draped mastheads and red and green prows of yet another line of moored junks.

Keppel's galley, flying his pennant of blue bunting, was making towards them, the rowers straining at their oars and several light gigs and pinnaces close astern in support. With the *Sybille*'s launch and the *Calcutta*'s black pinnace to starboard and just ahead of him, Phillip urged his own men to redouble their efforts and, aided by the now strongly flowing tide, they managed to reduce the distance separating them from the leading boats. But then both launches and one of the rocket-boats grounded off the southern side of a small, flat island. When they finally refloated, they were a hundred yards astern of the Commodore's gig which, with only four boats in support, was receiving terrible punishment.

"Come on, lads!" Phillip yelled hoarsely. "A strong pull does it! Fire as you bear, Gunner's Mate!"

The junks, he saw, were so placed as to present a front of their heavy thirty-twos; their fire was as rapid and accurate as if they formed the broadside of a frigate, and the two launches, with the *Hornet*'s rocket-boat fractionally ahead, emerging into the main channel north of the island, found the water alive with ricocheting shot. Phillip's bow-gun engaged in a brief duel with one of the junks and then was put out of action by a roundshot, which struck with such force that the gun was dismounted, crashing backwards and pinning the gun-captain's legs beneath it. Whilst they were struggling to drag the injured man clear, a second shot took his head from his body and, continuing on its deadly way, wounded two of the midships oarsmen.

All about them, Phillip could see foundering boats, some with whole sides of oars shot away. He went to the aid of one but succeeded in rescuing only four of the crew, the rest being dead and, through a momentary gap in the swirling gunsmoke saw, to his dismay, that Keppel's gig was sinking, the Commodore himself standing ankle-deep in water on one of the thwarts. He yelled to Lightfoot to steer towards the stricken gig but the *Calcutta*'s black pinnace was before him. Keppel, his Flag-Lieutenant, Prince Victor of Hohenlohe, and two others—

both obviously wounded—managed to scramble aboard the pinnace only seconds before the gig submerged. The Chinese, sensing victory, sent salvo after salvo into the scattered boat flotilla but they were not having it all their own way—several of the junks were sinking, others on fire, and two, at least, had their sweeps out, preparatory to taking flight. Obstinately determined to reply to their fire, Phillip scrambled forward to assist the two surviving members of his gun's crew to right their weapon, but the task was beyond their strength and their frantic efforts came near to swamping the launch.

"Sir . . . sir!" Lightfoot was at his side, mouthing something at him which he could not hear. But the boy was pointing and he saw that the *Calcutta*'s barge, with Keppel in the stern-sheets, was coming towards them, her Commander waving to them to retire, and he gave the order thankfully. Rowing back against the tide, with the men gasping and close to collapse at the oars and a disabled gig in tow, they had to run the gauntlet of the junks' fire but, miraculously, the launch was not hit. The *Hong Kong* and *Starling,* floated by the rising tide, had come up two miles from Hyacinth Island and the boats of Keppel's division reformed abreast of the *Hong Kong*. The gunboats were under very heavy fire, which was now concentrated on them and, although they replied with spirit, the *Hong Kong,* her decks crowded with wounded men from the boats, was hulled a dozen times in as many minutes and Keppel, standing on her sponson, his glass to his eye, gave the signal to retire out of range.

The deeper-draught steamers, led by the *Haughty,* with the third and fourth divisions of boats, could be seen coming up, and, clear of the worst of the enemy fire, the *Hong Kong* dropped anchor to await the arrival of much-needed reinforcements. Phillip transferred his wounded, numbering four, to her surgeon's care, replaced them with volunteers from the gig they had rescued and, with their aid, managed to remount his battered brass gun. The order came to serve out quinine and biscuit to the exhausted boats' crews and this was being obeyed when Commodore Keppel, still keeping the junk fleet under observation from his vantage point on the *Hong Kong*'s paddle-box, suddenly gave vent to a stentorian bellow.

"The rascals are making off!" A small, unmistakable figure in his white pith hat, he shook his fist in the air. "You rascals— I'll pay you off for this! Man the boats, my boys! Man the boats!"

Not everyone had heard his order but his meaning was clear as he was seen to go over the side into the *Raleigh*'s cutter, commanded by Edward Turnour, the faithful Spurrier at his heels with his length of blue bunting, the dog, Mike, clutched under his left arm. A cheer went up from the *Hong Kong*'s deck, which was taken up and echoed resoundingly by the boats' crews. The newly arrived third and fourth divisions cast off their tow-ropes and raced after those of the now-depleted first division, all of them somehow finding the heart and energy to join in the cheering. For all the world like boats at a peacetime regatta, the whole flotilla made straight for the junks which, evidently taken by surprise at this sudden turn of events, slackened their fire. Oars out, they broke their hitherto compact line and started to retreat up river, several hoisting their sails.

The manoeuvre, Phillip saw, was performed in beautiful order, the outermost moving off first and the rest continuing to fire at their on-coming attackers. But now, lacking their earlier cohesion and fire power, they were vulnerable and the British shot began to tell, particularly that of the *Hong Kong.* She steamed after the boats for a considerable distance, her bottom scraping mud, until once again the water shoaled and her progress was halted. She kept up her fire, however, scoring hit after hit with roundshot and rockets.

One of the junks, bearing a baleful red and yellow eye painted on her bow, received a hit which smashed most of her port-side oars to matchwood and Captain Cochrane yelled out an order to head and take her. Phillip's boat won the race, his men pulling their hearts out in their efforts, and he came alongside with a jolting crash among the shattered oars, seeing above his head the junk's lower gun-ports open yet robbed of menace, since the angle was now too steep for the gun muzzles to be depressed so as to bear on the launch. A frantic pounding of bare feet on the main deck told him that her crew were about to abandon her and, seizing a dangling rope, he led the rush to board her.

It was—as he had earlier imagined it would be—a novel and exhilarating experience to leap on to the deck of an enemy ship, cutlass in hand and six eager seamen at his back, all cheering wildly as they prepared to secure their prize. But . . . He drew in his breath sharply. Not all her crew had sought refuge in flight. Three or four were grouped round a swivel-mounted gingall, feverishly trying to slew it inboard to ward off the attackers, and a huge fellow with a pock-marked face, armed with a sword, rallied some of his people about him with the clear intention of making a fight of it.

Thankful that he had left young Lightfoot in charge of the boat, Phillip made for the big Chinaman, ducking a vicious slash from his sword and only dimly conscious of the shots whistling above his head as the crew of the gingall brought their cumbersome weapon into action at last. His pock-marked opponent parried his thrust and struck at him again but this time he went in under the man's guard, warding him off with jabbing blows as the Chinese attempted to kick the blade from his grasp. He was surprised and not a little disappointed when his adversary screeched something in his own language and, turning swiftly, dived over the junk's wooden guardrail into the river. The remaining members of his crew instantly followed his example, leaving their weapons behind them, and Phillip halted, breathless.

"Sir!" O'Brien seized his arm. "Watch out!" He pointed to a train of greyish-black powder laid along the deck. It had been ignited but hastily laid and Phillip could hear it hissing—or imagined he could—just behind him and there was scarcely need to look to ascertain in which direction it led. He yelled to his boarding party to get back to their boat and, fearing that they would not make it before the spluttering powder train reached its destination, started desperately trying to stamp it out. O'Brien joined him and he had barely time to repeat his order to return to the boat when the junk's magazine exploded with a dull roar. The force of the explosion flung both of them off their feet. Phillip picked himself up, bruised and shaken. With water pouring into her shattered hull, the junk took on a heavy list and, the deck canting steeply under his feet, he went in search of his coxswain, groping blindly in the black, choking smoke which, now ominously tinged with flames, was rising from the lower deck.

He had almost given up hope of finding the missing seaman when he stumbled over the prostrate body and heard O'Brien cursing dazedly. He dragged him up and together they staggered to the rail. The launch was below them, the boarding party safely inboard, and Lightfoot was standing up, waving furiously.

"Jump!" he managed thickly and, to his relief, O'Brien did so. Minutes later, the boat's crew picked both of them out of the water, O'Brien shocked into full consciousness by his immersion and swimming strongly. They paddled clear of the junk before she sank in a welter of smoke and flames.

"We're licking them, sir," Midshipman Lightfoot offered consolingly, as Phillip slumped down beside him on the stern-sheets, dripping and breathing hard. "Just look, sir—they're all on the run! And the Commodore's not going to let any of them get away. He's signalling for a chase, sir!"

The boy was right, Phillip saw. The majority of the junks had been taken or run ashore; some, abandoned in midstream, were on fire as their lost prize had been, their crews adding to the hundreds of bobbing heads on the wreckage-strewn surface of the water. But some twenty or thirty had contrived to make their escape and it was these the Commodore was after, heading the chase in Edward Turnour's cutter. Only seven or eight boats followed him, for the flotilla had taken savage punishment, some hulled and barely afloat, others disabled by casualties and capable of doing no more than paddle slowly to the rescue of sinking comrades. Keppel, he knew, was not the man to quit when there was still fighting to be done and he would need all the support available . . . He glanced at O'Brien. The coxswain, reading his thoughts, gave him a grin.

"I'm all right, sir," he asserted.

"Very good," Phillip said. "Obey the Commodore's signal, Mr Lightfoot."

"Aye, aye, sir," Lightfoot acknowledged happily. He gave a shrill-voiced order and the men bent to their oars.

The fleeing junks were well commanded and, even in defeat, they fought back bravely. Some were headed and taken, several blew up or ran aground, but the remainder continued the running battle, hotly pursued by Keppel's boats. For mile after mile they pulled, the rowers half-blinded by sweat and suffering casualties from the persistent fire of the Chinese stern-guns and gingalls. As a wounded oarsman slumped across his thwart, his place was taken by an officer or a marine and the chase continued, with only six boats in it now, two badly disabled by the enemy's fire.

Phillip, serving the battered brass gun in the bow of his launch, realised suddenly that he could see the red roofs of the city of Fatshan coming steadily nearer and found himself wondering whether the Commodore knew how small their force was and, if he did, whether it was his intention to attempt the capture of the city with his half-dozen boats. That the inhabitants feared an attack became evident, a few minutes later, when several hundred of them sallied forth in martial array, ringing bells and beating gongs, their waving banners and brandished swords clearly visible from the river.

A few shots from Minié rifles and a shower of grape from the bow-gun of the cutter commanded by Captain Cochrane soon scattered them and they retired in undignified haste to the city. Three of the leading junks took advantage of their appearance to make their own escape but five others were caught up with and captured intact, and Commodore Keppel, his coxswain Spurrier lying severely wounded beside him and his boats' crews exhausted, finally gave the signal to break off.

"Well done, my brave boys!" he called out, as the boats clustered about him. "I wish I could lead you into the city—with the support you've all given me today, I fancy it would be in our hands by nightfall. But never mind . . ." He shook his fist in the direction of the retreating Fatshan soldiery and added, with a laugh, "We'll be back, you rascals—and very soon!"

The men, spent and weary though they were, somehow found the energy to respond with a cheer.

"Do what you can for the wounded," the Commodore

ordered. "And then we'll take our prizes back with us." He looked down at the injured Spurrier, whose hand was clasped in his own, and the flush of elation faded from his cheeks. "Only three of them got away from us . . . we must have polished off most of their fleet and that's a good day's work, by any standard. But now there's the butcher's bill to be paid, more's the pity . . . still, we saved your dog for you, Spurrier my lad. Although I shall never know how!"

The little terrier, crouched by the coxswain's side, wagged his stump of a tail, and Edward Turnour said smiling, "We told you he was our mascot, sir. He didn't do his job badly, did he?"

The wounded attended to, the five lately captured junks were taken in tow and the boats paddled slowly but triumphantly down river to where, nearly a mile below the island on which the boom boats had earlier grounded, the *Hong Kong* and the *Starling* were waiting at anchor. Phillip supervised the transfer of his two slightly wounded gunners to the *Hong Kong* and then he and Lightfoot went aboard. It was 3:30 in the afternoon, he realised with some surprise—they had been hard at it for over twelve hours and they were suffering the pangs of hunger and thirst, as well as intense fatigue. But the needs of the wounded had to come first—there were some seventy of them, lying wherever space could be found on the steamer's deck and below, on the mess deck and in officers' cabins, many enduring the appalling agony of burns caused by exploding powder in their boats' magazines. These cases were wrapped in wadding, in the hope of lessening their pain and, on the surgeons' insistence that to move them to another ship would endanger their lives, the *Hong Kong*—despite the fact that she had suffered severely from the Chinese roundshot and was in a perilously leaky state—was ordered to convey them posthaste to the Naval Hospital at Victoria.

Hasty repairs were made and most of the holes plugged and covered with planking but, as she started down river, the vibration of her engines caused some of the plugs below the waterline to work loose and the pumps had to be kept going continuously. Phillip, relieved of responsibility for navigation by the Master of the *Encounter*—an experienced river pilot who had volunteered his services—managed a glass of lukewarm beer and an attempt at a wash and then, startled by the sound of gunfire, rushed back on deck, expecting to find the ship again under attack.

In fact she was, but no living gunners fired the shots which sent her reeling; ironically, as she passed through the wilderness of wrecked junks taken during the first attack, it was to find them in flames, their magazines exploding and their guns, which had been left fully loaded, going off spontaneously as they became heated.

There was no way of avoiding them. The pilot set his teeth and asked for all the speed the engineers could give him and, her paddles churning the flotsam-strewn water to foam, the little steamer ran the gauntlet of indiscriminate but deadly fire, her awning set alight by falling debris and her pumps fighting a losing battle against the water pouring in through her battered planking. Every man on deck, including the slightly wounded, turned-to in an attempt to spare their more helpless comrades from further suffering.

Phillip, aided by two of the watch, was endeavouring to cut away the blazing awning when a random charge of grape showered down on them from the blindly gaping muzzle of one of the junk's bow-guns, and he was conscious of a dull sensation of pain in his left arm and shoulder, as if both had been seared by a hot iron. He had stripped to his shirt and trousers and, looking down at his arm he saw—with more astonishment than alarm—that the once-white sleeve was saturated with blood. The pain was slight, the arm itself numb, and when the seaman who had been working beside him, observing his plight, moved to assist him, he shook his head.

"All right, lad, it's nothing—only a scratch. You carry on— that awning's got to come down."

"Aye, aye, sir." The man obediently returned to his task but he called out over his shoulder, "You ought to get attention, sir. You're bleedin' something chronic."

He was, Phillip realised ruefully but, with upwards of seventy other wounded men to attend to, the *Hong Kong*'s two surgeons had their work cut out, without his adding to the demands on their skill. He pulled back his sodden sleeve, and only when he saw a jagged end of bone protruding from the bloodstained flesh was it borne on him that his wound was a serious one. He cursed it savagely. Devil take the infernal thing . . . after coming unscathed through the day's action, it was infuriating to receive a wound which would render him *hors de combat,* perhaps for weeks, long after the action had been concluded!

Jim Goodenough, the *Raleigh*'s First Lieutenant, who had been commanding the *Hong Kong* during the attack on the junks, came to his side.

"We're through the worst of it now, I think," he said. "But the blasted water's gaining on us and . . ." He broke off, staring with red-rimmed eyes at Phillip's arm. "Good God, Phillip . . . you look as if you've caught it and no mistake!" He assisted in stopping the bleeding, using his own smoke-grimed neck-cloth as a tourniquet. "Sorry if I hurt you—I'm no surgeon, I'm afraid. Were you hit just now?"

"Yes," Phillip confirmed bitterly. "I was."

"Infernal bad luck," Goodenough sympathised. "I wonder

who gave the order to burn those junks—our people or the Chinese? Whoever it was, they could hardly have chosen a more inopportune moment, could they? While it lasted, that was the heaviest fire we've been under all day." He mopped his brow, adding wearily, "I'd better relieve the men at the pumps or we'll never make it to Hong Kong. The last report I had was that the water had almost risen to the stokehold fire-pits—God help us if it does, because we're leaking like a sieve. You'll get a surgeon to look at that arm, won't you? The tourniquet's a bit amateurish and it ought to be loosened after twenty minutes or so, I believe."

"Don't worry, I'll attend to it," Phillip assured him. "You carry on and thanks for your help, my dear fellow."

It was an hour before he found a surgeon free at last of his more pressing duties. Unshaven and dropping with weariness, the doctor subjected the arm to a cursory examination, shook his head glumly and instructed the young assistant who was with him to dress and splint it.

"You may lose this arm, Commander," he warned, with brusque honesty. "It's a nasty fracture. But all amputations will have to wait until we can get our wounded to the hospital ship—they can't be done aboard this leaking tub. You'll be transferred of course, and we'll see how it is then. Your name is . . . ?"

"Hazard, Doctor—of the *Raleigh*."

The surgeon noted the name on his pad. "I'll try and see you again if I can, Commander Hazard. You'll be a bit more comfortable once the splint is on—I should try to get some sleep, if you can find space to lie down."

The arm was still numb, the splinting, even so, agonising enough, although the young surgeon's mate did his work with skill and deftness, and Phillip was glad, when it was over, to find room to seat himself cross-legged on the forward part of the deck, his back propped up against the rail. He felt oddly light-headed and apathetic. Although he had heard, he had not really taken in the surgeon's grim warning concerning the possibility that he might lose his arm—that was something for the future and decision would, in any event, be postponed until a proper examination could be made, so there was little to be gained by thinking about it now. There were wounded men all round him, worse off than he, some crying out in delirium, others too far gone even to raise their voices, and one or two—wadding-wrapped burn cases—whose torment was such that they moaned ceaselessly, making sleep impossible for those in their vicinity.

Phillip did what he could for them. His flask was empty but he shared his slender stock of cigars with those who could smoke and tried to talk to some of the others. Sleep was out of the question, as his earlier apathy was succeeded by anxiety for the safety of the ship, his mind and ears tuned to the shouted orders of Lieutenant Goodenough and the pilot, and to the laboured clanking of the pumps. He was aware from his interpretation of these sounds, that the little steamer was frequently in difficulties and, at times, in actual danger of foundering but, with the coming of dawn, the pumps finally got the better of the inrushing water. More repairs were made, as soon as it was light enough to see where patching was required and, by sunrise, to his infinite relief, the pumps were operating to a more normal rhythm and the ship proceeding steadily on her way.

A strange silence fell over the crowded deck, as death or merciful unconsciousness brought peace to many whose suffering had become unendurable. Josiah Thompson, the *Raleigh*'s chaplain, who had worked indefatigably throughout the night, found time to pause for a cheerful word with the less seriously injured, and the off-duty officers and men of the watch below, relieved of anxiety for the ship, came on deck with drinking water and flasks of whisky or brandy for the wounded. The *Hong Kong* did not carry provisions for the number of men now crowded on board and her cooking fires—extinguished when she had cleared for action—had not been relighted, but her hard-worked crew did the best they could in the circumstances. Pipe tobacco and cigars were handed out and a welcome issue of grog was made, which raised flagging spirits and started the men talking. Wry, foul-mouthed jokes were exchanged, as those who had survived the long ordeal of the night found renewed cause for optimism in the fact that they were still alive and the ordeal almost over, with the white-painted houses and landscaped gardens of Hong Kong's British residents in sight on the tree-clad hills.

Phillip, his own supply long since exhausted, gratefully inhaled smoke from a black cheroot of doubtful origin, pressed on him by one of *Raleigh*'s midshipmen, and broke his long fast with a handful of ship's biscuit, which young Lightfoot had thoughtfully soaked in cold coffee, left over from the previous morning's brew.

"You must eat, sir," the youngster advised earnestly. "To keep up your strength." He eyed Phillip's arm, swollen and throbbing unpleasantly under its blood-caked dressing, and added, full of concern, "I hope the surgeons can save your arm for you, sir. If you remember, my right leg was broken in two places when I fell from the *Huntress*'s rigging off Sebastopol in the winter of 'fifty-five. Surgeon Fraser told me it might have to come off but he set it—and my arm, too—and look at me now, sir!"

"You look a pretty healthy specimen, Mr Lightfoot," Phillip agreed.

"Yes, sir, I am. Some more biscuit, sir?" The boy offered the bowl of sodden mush, smiling. "Of course I owe it to Surgeon Fraser—he made a wonderful job of setting the bones—but I owe a lot to that steward of yours, sir. He was Irish and he'd lost most of his teeth . . . I don't remember his name but he was quite a character."

"O'Leary," Phillip supplied. "Joseph Aloysius O'Leary." Memories came flooding back. O'Leary had always had the name of a "Queen's Hard Bargain" and, when he had come to the *Trojan,* under Captain North's taut command, it had been as an able-seaman with eighteen years' service, whose punishment sheet and crime record ran into several pages and effectively debarred him from promotion. But like many of his kind, O'Leary was a fine seaman, at his best when in a tight corner or when there was fighting to be done and the end of the *Huntress*'s commission with the Black Sea Fleet had seen him holding—and fully meriting—the warrant rank of Gunner. He had gone home to Ireland on leave after the *Huntress* paid off and they had lost touch, Phillip recalled, but . . .

"O'Leary," Midshipman Lightfoot went on, "stole the best part of a bottle of whisky from the wardroom and poured it over the dressing on my leg, sir. He swore it would cure me and prevent gangrene! Certainly something did. I . . ." He paused, eyes bright, "Sir, would you like me to see if I can find some whisky for you? It *might* help and O'Leary did swear by it, sir. And he was a better hand at surgeon's mate than that fellow Brown."

Phillip shook his head. The Russian army surgeon who had treated him at Odessa and later at Yenikale had shared

O'Leary's faith in the efficacy of raw spirit as a guard against infected wounds, he remembered wryly, but all the same . . . He sighed. "I shouldn't imagine there's a drop of whisky left on board, Mr Lightfoot, so don't trouble yourself. I'll be all right."

"It's no trouble, sir," Lightfoot assured him cheerfully. "I think Padre Thompson has some. I'll go and ask him." He scuttled off, ignoring Phillip's half-hearted protests, to return just as the ship was coming to anchor in Hong Kong harbour, triumphantly clutching a silver-stoppered flask.

"There's not much left, sir," he announced breathlessly. "But it might do the trick and the padre says you're welcome to it." He removed the stopper. "Where's the bone actually broken, sir?"

Phillip indicated his forearm and braced himself as the boy emptied the contents of the borrowed flask on to his already sodden dressing. The pain was excruciating for a moment or two and he was hard put to bite back the anguished expletive which rose to his lips, but then it faded to a dull ache and he was able to voice his thanks with appropriate restraint.

Three hours later, he was lying on one of the busy operating tables aboard the hospital ship, again being offered whisky but this time in a china mug, held to his lips by Dr John Crawford, the *Raleigh*'s competent Scottish surgeon.

"Dr Anderson fears you'll need to lose this arm, Commander Hazard," the surgeon said, as Phillip gulped down the undiluted spirit, wretchedly aware of what, in these circumstances, its consumption portended. "But needless to tell you, I shall save it if I can. Right . . . over on to your face, if you please, and let's take a look at you. Easy does it, we're not in a rush now."

His assistant cut away the dressing carefully and Phillip waited in an agony of suspense, as Crawford's strong fingers probed and palpated. Finally he said, "Well, you've quite a variety of Chinese ironmongery embedded in the flesh of your upper arm and shoulder but I can remove most of it easily enough. In addition you have an open fracture of the radius and normally that would call for amputation. But the wound is clean . . . in heaven's name, what did you use to cleanse it?" He bent closer, wrinkling his nose suspiciously. "Whisky, eh? Well, it seems to have done no harm and the bone's not splintered—indeed, it's gone back into place quite nicely. I think we've a better than even chance of saving your arm, Commander. I'm prepared to take it, if you are."

"Most certainly I am," Phillip returned, without hesitation. He breathed a silent prayer of thankfulness, blessing both Lightfoot and O'Leary in his relief. "That's the best news you could possibly have given me, Doctor—believe me."

"It will take time," the surgeon warned. "Time and patience. You'll not be following Commodore Keppel up the Canton River for a good few weeks and nor will the brave Cox'n Spurrier. But I managed to patch him up—and God knows, when I first saw the state he was in, I had my doubts. So maybe I'll be equally lucky with this arm of yours. We'll give it a damned good try, anyway. Hang on, now—this will hurt but I'll be as quick as I can."

His probe bit deep and Phillip winced involuntarily. But it was a small price to pay, he thought—a very small part of the butcher's bill of which his Chief had spoken with so much feeling. And they had won a victory which might well bring the treacherous Yeh to terms, they . . . even the double tot of whisky he had swallowed could not dull the pain of the cuts

Crawford was making but he gritted his teeth and bore it some-how, the sweat streaming in rivulets from every pore in his tortured body. For God's sake, he . . .

"He's fainted, Doctor," the assistant said.

"Good," Dr Crawford grunted. "Now we can set the broken bone." He worked swiftly and expertly, head on one side and eyes narrowed as he studied the position of the fractured arm. "Just a wee stretch will do it, I think . . . this lad's been wounded before. D'you see his other arm?" Bone grated on bone and both surgeons were sweating now. "That's enough, Andy . . . hold it so while I get the splints on . . . fine. He'll do. Mind, I'm not saying that either he or Spurrier will be as good as new—that would be too much to hope for. But given time and the devil of a lot of luck and by heaven, they won't be far off it!"

CHAPTER THREE

Phillip's arm healed slowly but, until the splints were removed, no one could forecast the degree of mobility with which he was likely to be left. Dr Crawford's warning that it would take time and patience had, he came to realise, been no idle one and he fretted increasingly at his continued and enforced inaction.

Following the successful attack on the Chinese war junks in Fatshan Creek, Commodore Keppel consolidated his position by taking the fort at Chuenpee. With seventeen ships, the Royal Navy now controlled the Canton River from the Macao Fort to the newly captured stronghold—a distance of forty miles—with all intervening forts disarmed or destroyed. Apart from the occasional chase after isolated junks, there was little to be done until such time as operations could be undertaken against Canton itself. Of this, Phillip was repeatedly told by his various visitors, there was no prospect until the arrival of Lord Elgin, the British Plenipotentiary, which was expected early in July.

"You're not missing anything," Jim Goodenough assured him. "Except heat and flies. We had a brush with a pirate the other day—she was a beautiful fast boat, with twenty-six oars, mounting two 32-pounders and gingalls on swivels. But she only put up a token resistance and when young Montagu boarded her, with six men, her entire crew bolted! Still, that was fun while it lasted and I won't pretend I'm not enjoying being in command of the *Hong Kong* in your absence." The *Raleigh*'s former First Lieutenant grinned at him happily. "Although Chuenpee was a washout. The Chief was hoping for a good scrap but the Chinese just let us walk in. They've learnt their lesson, I suppose, after the drubbing we gave them at Fatshan and in Escape Creek. Perhaps they'll defend Canton, though—*if* we ever attack the place."

"Don't you think we will?" Phillip asked eagerly.

Goodenough shrugged. "The Chief's afraid we won't for political reasons, unless the other Treaty Powers back us up. You'll have heard, no doubt, that he and the Master stood trial for the loss of *Raleigh*—last Friday, on board the *Sybille?* They were both honourably acquitted, of course, and the Chief put up a capital show . . . attended in immaculate full dress, wearing every Order and medal he possesses and made a most impressive and dignified speech, in which he never once alluded to himself. The Court were almost apologetic when they returned his sword to him . . . you should have seen Elliott's face! Our Commodore is the hero of the hour and yet—" Goodenough's face clouded over—"and yet he talks of going home."

"Going home? For heaven's sake, Jim, why?" Phillip was stunned.

"He hasn't taken me into his confidence," his visitor confessed. "But I gather that, for some reason the First Lord has expressed official disapproval of his being appointed Second-in-Command—and I believe the loss of our poor *Raleigh* is being made the excuse. She's been written off, you know—the Admiral felt he couldn't accept any tender to raise her."

"But if the court martial exonerated Keppel—" Phillip began indignantly, "Then surely—"

"Quite so, Phillip." Goodenough's tone was dry. "But it seems the First Lord didn't wait for the findings of the court martial. I could be wrong, of course, but during the past few days I've had the impression that the Chief had made up his mind that he intends to throw his hand in out here. He obviously can't serve under Elliott—he's the senior Captain on the Navy List, due for his step up to Flag-rank . . . unless the First Lord queers his pitch."

"Perhaps he feels he'll have a better chance of setting matters to rights if he goes home. Or he may regard it as the honourable thing to do—you know what he's like on the subject of honour."

Lieutenant Goodenough nodded. "Indeed I do. And he *is* being stabbed in the back. I—" he hesitated. "Strictly between ourselves, Phillip, it did occur to me to wonder whether Elliott might have put his oar in . . . what do you think?"

Phillip considered the question, frowning. Commodore Elliott certainly hadn't liked relinquishing his command but . . . He shook his head decisively. "I'm quite sure he wouldn't stoop to such tactics. In any case, Jim, our Chief and Admiral Seymour have been friends all their lives—their families too. The Admiral wouldn't allow it and I don't imagine *he* wants Keppel to go home."

"No, he doesn't, that's very true. You should have seen the letter he wrote the Chief after the Fatshan affair. It was positively glowing! And immediately after the court martial, he left Keppel in command of the Canton River, when he came back here to consult with Sir John Bowring and Consul Parkes."

"Then the back-stabbing is being done at home," Phillip asserted.

"It does look that way," Goodenough agreed regretfully. "And if it means the Chief really is going then I, for one, won't feel much like staying, I can tell you. Perhaps, if this trouble in India gets worse, we may have the chance to volunteer for service there. Or even—"

Phillip stared at him blankly. "Trouble in India—*what* trouble in India, Jim?"

"You haven't heard?"

"No—for God's sake, one hears nothing incarcerated in this blasted sick bay! Tell me about it, please."

"There's not a lot to tell," Jim Goodenough confessed. "But rumour is rife—how reliable it is I have no idea. From what I can gather, the sepoys in the Bengal Army are threatening mutiny—some regiments have had to be disbanded and some, it appears, have actually murdered their officers and attacked British stations. They—"

"In Oudh?" Phillip put in sharply.

"I don't know about Oudh, Phillip. You have married sisters there, haven't you?"

"Yes, two. They're both in Lucknow, I believe."

Goodenough eyed him sympathetically. "I've heard nothing specific about Lucknow. The most alarming news—which *has* been confirmed—is that Delhi was seized nearly a month ago by mutineers from Meerut, joined by the native garrison, and that they've restored the old Mogul Emperor to his throne . . ." He gave what details he could and Phillip listened with shocked dismay.

"Surely our people are making every effort to recapture Delhi? They *must* be!"

"Yes, I think they are. There's been mention of a column on its way from the hills but European troops are very thin on the ground and India, as you know, is a pretty vast country. That's why—" again Jim Goodenough hesitated. "Well, that's why I thought there might be something doing there for us. Especially if the rumour—that troops intended for China, are to be diverted to India—proves to be true. It's a very persistent rumour, Phillip, so it may well be true and if it is, it'll mean that our operations here will be virtually at a standstill. We can't take—and certainly can't hold—Canton without troops, can we?"

"No, I don't suppose we can." Phillip's brain was racing. He had heard nothing from either Harriet or Lavinia since his arrival on the China Station—they probably did not know where he was and would not know, until his mother or the old Admiral wrote to tell them.

In the last letter he had received from home—written seven weeks ago—his mother had mentioned that Lavinia hoped to accompany her husband and his regiment to Lucknow, and that Harriet planned to join them there, with the children, as soon as she could. But such plans might have had to be abandoned or changed under the threat of mutiny by the Company's sepoys. Harriet's husband had been promoted to command of his Native Infantry regiment and posted to one of the many isolated Oudh out-stations, some distance from Lucknow—a station with an entirely native garrison. God only knew what the consequences would be, if the sepoys there rose in mutiny . . . He expelled his breath in a sigh of frustration, inwardly cursing his own helplessness and the wound which had incapacitated him. Tom's was a Queen's regiment, of course, so that Lucknow should be reasonably safe . . . pray heaven that Harriet and her family *had* taken refuge there, if there were any danger of the mutiny becoming widespread.

"Jim," he demanded urgently. "Have you heard anything definite about naval ships being sent to India from here?"

Jim Goodenough shook his head. "Nothing, I'm afraid. There's talk of it, of course, but it's all very vague and we don't know for certain yet whether troops *are* to be diverted to India.

I imagine decision will be postponed until Lord Elgin gets here, don't you? The *Shannon's* to bring him from Singapore and presumably she'll bring the mail from India as well. Then we may know how bad the situation really is." He rose to take his leave. "Well, duty calls—it's back up the river with the Commodore tonight for us. I hope that arm of yours will heal soon, Phillip—and without ill-effects. How much longer are they keeping you here, have you any notion?"

"Crawford won't commit himself. But he's promised to permit me to go to Macao to convalesce as soon as he's satisfied that the arm won't have to come off. A wealthy British merchant here, whose name is Dent, has apparently offered his house in Macao for the use of wounded officers. The air there is supposed to be more salubrious than it is here. I can hardly wait to sample it! Thanks for coming to see me, Jim, and for bringing me up to date with the news." Phillip wrung his visitor's hand. "Good luck up river . . . and please convey my respectful greetings to the Chief. And to Turnour and the others, if you see them."

During the next two weeks, Phillip—although his arm continued to heal much to Surgeon Crawford's satisfaction—found the time hanging very heavily, with anxiety added to his earlier frustration. The wildest rumours concerning the trouble in India were bandied about and, although many were subsequently discounted, the rest, received from more reliable sources, were alarming enough. Cawnpore was reported under siege by mutineers; troops from Persia and Burma were being recalled for the purpose, it was said, not only of going to the aid of beleagured up-country garrisons, but of defending Calcutta itself, and Sir Henry Lawrence, Chief Commissioner of Oudh, was believed to be making preparations to hold Lucknow against an overwhelming rebel force.

The mail from England—even that sent by the overland route—was weeks out of date and of little help in sifting fact from panic fears. Phillip had letters from his father and mother but these told him nothing, and a brief missive from Graham, written on his way out to India and posted in Capetown, gave details only of his pleasure in his new command and of his eagerness to reach his destination, so that he might purchase a house in Calcutta and, with Catriona, settle down to "regular married life."

On 28th June, thankful to be free, at last, of medical supervision and the soul-destroying routine and restrictions of the sick bay, Phillip crossed to Macao with two other convalescent officers from the naval hospital to occupy the comfortable quarters put at their disposal by the generous Mr Dent. Thanks to the connivance of Surgeon Crawford, they took Spurrier with them—officially as their steward and accompanied, as always, by the little terrier, Mike—and the change, both of air and of the surroundings, did them all good. The foreign residents of Macao offered them hospitality and a warm welcome; they were showered with invitations to luncheons, dinners, and receptions, and Phillip would have enjoyed himself had it not been for the anxiety which plagued him and the dearth of reliable information as to what was happening in India.

The steam frigate *Shannon* entered Hong Kong Harbour on the evening of 2nd July, her guns booming out in salute and, within half an hour of her arrival, Admiral Seymour went on board to greet the new British plenipotentiary. In addition to the Earl of Elgin and his suite, she brought mail and the latest news from Calcutta. The news, as Phillip had feared it would be, was bad and it travelled fast. Over dinner at the sumptuous residence of one of Mr Dent's associates, he listened to a horrifying account of the rebels' seizure of Delhi where, it seemed, mutinous sepoys and the King's retainers had led the scum of the native bazaars in an orgy of murder and arson. No mercy had been shown, even to the helpless; women and children had been savagely done to death, hundreds of native, as well as white, Christians had been slaughtered, and the Commissioner shot down when attempting to reason with the mob.

Elsewhere in India, after a brief period of uncertainty, the pattern was being repeated, as regiment after regiment throughout the Bengal Presidency broke out in open revolt. There were fears now for Allahabad and Benares, as well as for Lucknow and Cawnpore, and troops sent to their relief were being delayed by lack of transport and supplies, and by the need to put down uprisings in towns and villages along their route.

"India is denuded of European troops," Phillip heard his host say gravely. "My information is that there are fewer than forty thousand in the whole country, including the Company's regiments—and the sepoys in the three Presidency armies number over three hundred thousand, with most of the artillery in their hands. So far, I understand, the Madras and Bombay armies have remained loyal, for which we can only thank God . . . and pray that the Sikhs follow their example, because if the Punjab rises, India will be lost." He spread his hands in a despairing gesture. "The lives of thousands of our countrymen—and of their wives and families—are at stake, I fear. In view of which, our war here will have to take second place, so far as demands for troops and supplies are concerned . . . India must come first. Even if we lose face as a result of our failure to attack and occupy Canton, this need not, in the long run, have any serious effect on our position here. The Chinese are accustomed to prolonged negotiation and endless discussion and bargaining, it's the breath of life to them. We've proved we *can* enter the city and, thanks to the Royal Navy's brilliant actions at Fatshan and Escape Creeks, gentlemen"—he beamed at his three naval guests—"we control the Canton River. That, by itself, must have given Commissioner Yeh cause for thought; he's lost his fleet and with it more face than we're likely to lose, if operations have to be postponed."

"Do you suppose, sir," Lieutenant Beamish asked diffidently, "that Lord Elgin will agree to the troops he's been promised being diverted to India?"

"He's done so already, my dear boy," his host assured him. "And with the full concurrence of General Ashburnham, I'm given to understand. He sent the troopship *Simoon* to Calcutta with the Fifth Regiment. They were in Singapore, waiting to come on here. But His Lordship will, I am sure, consult with your Admiral and with Sir John Bowring and Consul Parkes before reaching a final decision. He will find the merchants of Hong Kong behind him to a man if he decides to put India's very urgent claims before all others."

"Have you heard whether there is a prospect of any naval ships being sent from here to Calcutta, sir?" Phillip enquired but, to his disappointment, the merchant shook his head.

"It is too early to say, my young friend. But—as an inspired guess only—I believe it possible that one or two may be sent, probably for a limited period, until the crisis is over. A warship or two in the Hoogly might be all that is required to ensure the safety of Calcutta." He sighed, glancing across at a tall, grey-bearded man, who was also his guest but whose name Phillip had not caught when being introduced. "What's your opinion, Hamish?"

The stranger smiled. "It concurs with yours, Henry. We must act and act at once if we're not to lose India. Here we have plenty of time. If we take any more drastic action than we have already taken—entry into Canton or a blockade of the Peiho—it must be with the agreement and support of the other Treaty Powers. Since Baron de Gros is travelling via the Cape, he isn't likely to arrive until sometime in September and, in the meantime, de Bourboulon considers that he has no power to act on behalf of the French Government. The same applies to the Americans—Dr and Mrs Parker are making plans to return home, although his replacement as Plenipotentiary, Mr William Reed, has not yet left the United States or so he told me a few days ago. I would say, therefore, that we are in a position of stalemate for the next two or even three months, and for us to hold troops or ships here—when India is in desperate need of both—would be neither wise nor necessary."

Henry Jardine extinguished his cigar and rose. "Let us join the ladies, shall we?" he suggested. "And endeavour to forget our troubles for a little while, at least. Our naval friends are here to recuperate . . . does a hand or two of Whist appeal to you, Commander Hazard? Or perhaps you would enjoy a little music . . . Mrs Chesterfield has promised to regale us with some songs from her repertoire and she has a truly fine voice."

Phillip murmured a polite rejoinder but even the charms of Mr Jardine's three attractive daughters and the accomplished singing of Mrs Chesterfield failed to distract him from his own anxious thoughts. Next day he returned to Hong Kong, called at the naval Agent's for mail and coming away empty-handed, hailed a rickshaw to take him to the waterfront, with the intention of going out to the *Shannon*'s anchorage by sampan. One of the frigate's boats was, however, tied up at the quay and the midshipman in charge, a slim, good-looking youngster of sixteen or seventeen, after eyeing him uncertainly for a moment, saluted and greeted him by name.

"Are you seeking passage to the *Shannon*, sir?" he enquired. Phillip returned his salute. "Yes," he answered, "I am. But . . . you have the advantage of me, I'm afraid. Your name is . . . ?"

"Edward Daniels, sir." The boy smiled. "I don't suppose you'll remember but we rode up to the Naval Brigade camp from Balaclava together a few days before the battle. And we met Lord Cardigan on his way back to his yacht for dinner— he was somewhat scathing about sailors on horseback and the quality of our mounts. I remember that because it rankled rather—I was proud of my pony. I'd just paid a fiver for it."

The young mid on the white pony, Phillip recalled, who had talked of his fears and hopes, his opinion of the Army and then, in a burst of frankness, had admitted that he doubted his ability to live up to the high standard of courage and leadership set by his present Captain, William Peel, to whom he had then just been appointed as aide-de-camp. The over-imaginative fourteen-year-old who had confessed, almost apologetically, that he hated to see men killed in battle but who—when the real test came during the abortive June assault on the Redan—had saved Peel's life under fire and been awarded the Victoria Cross for his gallantry. Edward St John Daniels had filled out and added several inches to his height but the same intelligent blue eyes met his and Phillip echoed the midshipman's smile and held out his hand, genuinely pleased to see him again.

"Good Lord—I hardly recognised you! But I remember you very well, Mr Daniels . . . and the illuminating conversation we had on our way to Kadikoi when, if my memory isn't at fault, we agreed that our Service was vastly superior to the Army. You had strong views on the subject—sparked off, I fancy by Lord Cardigan's appearance. You asked me, I think, how His Lordship could command a brigade of cavalry from a yacht."

Daniels reddened. "I expressed my opinions rather too freely, sir. I was a bit damp behind the ears in those days and didn't know when to shut up. All the same"—his smile returned—"I *still* don't see how 'The Noble Yachtsman'—that's what we used to call Lord Cardigan—managed to get away with it. He wouldn't have, in the Navy, would he, sir? I mean, sir, Captain Peel and Admiral Lushington *could* have lived aboard the *Diamond* in Balaclava Harbour if they'd had Cardigan's mentality but they didn't, of course—they roughed it in camp with the rest of us. And so did Commodore Keppel, when he took over command of the Naval Brigade."

"True," Phillip agreed. He nodded in the direction of the waiting boat. "Who have you come to collect, Mr Daniels?"

"Our First Lieutenant, Mr Vaughan, sir, and some of our other officers. Lord Elgin invited them to take luncheon with him on shore. We gave His Excellency passage from Singapore, as you probably know, and it was, well, a sort of return of hospitality. Captain Peel was invited also but he had to call on the Commander-in-Chief."

"Then he's not on board? I was hoping to see him."

"Oh, you will, sir," Edward Daniels asserted. "I saw his gig leave the *Calcutta* ten minutes ago." He consulted his pocket watch. "Our fellows shouldn't be long now and I'm sure the Captain will be delighted to see you, sir." He hesitated and then gestured to Phillip's heavily bandaged arm. "Excuse my asking, Commander Hazard but—did you get that in the Fatshan boat action?"

"After it, to be strictly accurate," Phillip admitted. He explained the circumstances and saw the midshipman's eyes widen in astonishment. "Good heavens! I never imagined

anything like *that* happening. What a rum business and awfully
bad luck—for you, I mean, sir. And to think we were kicking
ourselves for missing Fatshan! There's nothing much going on
up river now, I believe."

"Not a great deal, they tell me, no."

"We aren't likely to get there in any case," Daniels said.
"There's a rumour that we and possibly the *Pearl* will be
ordered to Calcutta but—" He broke off, as half a dozen rick-
shaws came to a halt on the quay, to decant the same number of immaculately uniformed officers from their curtained
interiors. "Here are our fellows at last, sir. I'll inform the First
Lieutenant that you're here." He performed the introductions
punctiliously. "Lieutenant Vaughan, sir—Commander Hazard,
late of the *Raleigh,* sir. Lieutenant Salmon—Lieutenant Lind of
the Swedish Navy, sir, on attached service. Our Surgeon, Dr
Flanagan. And Mr Garvey and Lord Arthur Clinton, mess-
mates of mine."

Vaughan was a tall, thin man of about his own age, Phillip
observed, who gave him a firm and friendly handshake.
Salmon was younger, fit and athletic, the Swedish officer a
blond young giant with a humorous quirk to his mouth, and
the surgeon—just as typical of his race as the Swede—the old-
est of the six. Of the two midshipmen, Garvey was dark and
well built, Clinton fair and frail, with almost effeminate good
looks—a younger son, as Phillip later learnt, of no less a per-
sonage than the Duke of Newcastle.

They boarded the boat—Vaughan giving him precedence—
the bowman cast off, and the crew gave way smartly together.
During the ten-minute pull to the *Shannon*'s anchorage,
Lieutenant Vaughan questioned him minutely as to the present situation in the Canton River and the effect and nature of
the recent actions there. Phillip did his best to answer the

stream of questions, aware that the others were listening with equal interest and—on the part of Salmon and Lind—undisguised envy. Both had apparently served in the Baltic Fleet throughout the Russian War, where opportunities for action had been fewer and less glorious than in the Crimean theatre and Black Sea, and both looked frankly disappointed when Phillip repeated the gist of what his host of the previous evening had told him.

"Then it looks as if we shall be ordered to Calcutta," Salmon said resignedly. "Not that it's likely to be any more exciting for us than this place. We'll be stuck in the Hoogly, I expect, defending Calcutta with the mere threat of our guns! We probably shan't even get ashore."

"You think there really is a chance of your being sent to India?" Phillip asked Vaughan.

The First Lieutenant shrugged. "If there isn't going to be anything doing here for the next month or two, then it's certainly on the cards. Lord Elgin said at luncheon today that he's seriously considering the advisability of going there, in order to confer with Lord Canning and to see for himself how bad the situation is. From all accounts, it's pretty bad . . . and it could get a great deal worse. If His Excellency does decide to go, we shall take him."

They were approaching the *Shannon* now and Phillip studied her with appreciative eyes as her First Lieutenant proudly listed her virtues. She had been built only two years previously, as the first of a new and very powerful class of steam-screw frigates, designed to obtain great speed under either steam or sail and to carry very heavy armament. Of 600 horsepower and 2,667 tons, she carried 51 guns, Lieutenant Vaughan stated—twenty 56 cwt. 32-pounders on the upper deck, one 95 cwt. 68-pounder on the forecastle, and thirty 65 cwt. 8-inch guns on the main deck.

"We've had twelve knots with the screw, Commander Hazard. And after we left Simon's Bay, in a strong nor'-westerly gale, under double reefed tops'ls, courses, and reefed fore-topmast stuns'ls, she averaged between fourteen and fifteen knots. During one squall, when the log was hove, she was going at 15.8. Not bad, eh?"

"Not bad at all," Phillip agreed. He thought nostalgically of the beautiful *Raleigh,* without steam-power, one of the last of her kind. Commodore Keppel had brought her out of Portsmouth Harbour under studding-sails, scorning the assistance of the tugs standing by to take her in tow, and she had made a record passage from South America to the Cape, averaging 275 miles a day for six days under sail alone. But now . . . He sighed and said nothing and, as Midshipman Daniels brought his boat alongside the *Shannon's* accommodation ladder, Lieutenant Vaughan asked courteously, "Is yours a social call, sir, or do you wish to see the Captain?"

"My call is on the Captain but he's not expecting me, Mr Vaughan, so perhaps you'll be so good as to ascertain if it is convenient to receive me."

"I'm sure it will be, sir. But I'll ascertain of course. You knew him in the Crimea, didn't you?"

Phillip nodded. The First Lieutenant escorted him to the Captain's day cabin, knocked on the door and, being given permission to enter, opened the cabin door and announced him by name. "Go in, sir," he invited. "Captain Peel says he'll be delighted to see you . . . Commander Hazard, sir, of the *Raleigh.*"

"Late of the *Raleigh,* to my sorrow, is it not, Phillip?" William Peel rose and came to meet him, his hand outstretched, He had changed little since Phillip had last seen him. At thirty, Peel had been the youngest Post-Captain in the Navy, with a brilliant record, which service with the Naval Brigade in the

Crimea had enhanced. Now, at thirty-three, he still looked as youthful as he always had, a smile of singular warmth lighting his pale and rather austere face, as he ushered his guest to a chair and went to pour drinks for them both.

He was of no more than medium height, slightly built and cleanshaven, his brown hair—worn a trifle longer than current fashion decreed—luxuriant and curling, despite the severity with which it was dressed. He had, Phillip thought, many of the qualities which distinguished Commodore Keppel—breeding, personal courage, and a fine brain, coupled with exceptional powers of leadership. Like Keppel, he was immensely popular with the officers and men he commanded, and his meteoric rise to his present rank had won him more friends than enemies. There were a few, of course—mostly his contemporaries, men with less brilliant records than he—who professed mistrust of Peel's volatile temperament and keen intelligence, maintaining that his rapid promotion had been due rather to the influence of his father, the late Sir Robert Peel, than to his own merit. But he had confounded his critics in the Crimea and won the wholehearted approval of Their Lordships and no one in naval circles doubted that he was destined for further advancement in the near future—in spite of his age.

"I was truly distressed to hear about the *Raleigh*," he went on, passing Phillip a glass and courteously raising his own. "Good health! Because we're not likely to see her like again in naval service, are we? Even this ship, although she's the first of her class, is really a compromise. With the development and perfection of the marine engine, it won't be long before we dispense with sail altogether and that will indeed be a sad day."

"It will," Phillip agreed, with feeling. Peel questioned him about the circumstances of the *Raleigh*'s loss and then said, gesturing to his arm, "I see you've been winged, my dear fellow . . . is it bad?"

"No, it's healing nicely. But I was lucky not to lose it." In response to Peel's prompting, he supplied a condensed account of the Fatshan action, ending wryly, "I got this when we were coming down river in the *Hong Kong,* after it was all over. The junks we had taken in the early morning attack had been set on fire and abandoned so hastily that their guns were still loaded and, of course, they were going off in the heat. A charge of grape hit us and I, like an idiot, failed to duck."

"I'm glad the wound's healing. Mine took a very long time, as you may have heard . . . oddly enough, it was also my left arm. By what I now regard as a curious coincidence, some of my officers were arguing, the night before the assault on the Redan"—Peel smiled reminiscently—"as to which limb they could best spare, if one had to be lost. Dayell and young Wood both agreed on the left arm but I said that arms were more useful for sailors than legs. They talked me round eventually by suggesting that a one-legged man would probably become very stout and next day, believe it or not, all three of us were hit in the left arm! Poor Dayell lost his, Wood and I were more fortunate, although I almost certainly wouldn't have been if my other A.D.C., Edward Daniels, hadn't come to my aid so promptly. Fine boys those, Phillip . . . Daniels, as you probably noticed, is with me still. He was the only one, out of seven officers, who wasn't hit that day. Wood, incidentally, obtained a cornet's commission in the Cavalary. He's now in India with the Seventeenth Lancers, in Bombay, I believe."

"Talking of India, sir . . ." Phillip began. "I . . ."

"Don't tell me," William Peel put in, his smile widening. "There's nothing likely to be doing here for the next two or three months and you've heard the rumour that we may be ordered to convey Lord Elgin to Calcutta. You've also heard that India is threatened with a sepoy revolt and you've come to ask if the *Shannon* has any vacancies for officers. Am I right?"

"Yes," Phillip admitted. "But how did you guess?"

"You are now the fourth officer to approach me on the same errand today, my dear fellow," the *Shannon*'s Captain returned dryly. "The other three buttonholed me aboard the Commander-in-Chief's flagship this morning, all of them convinced that the *Shannon*'s departure for Calcutta is imminent and drawing the inference that, if *I'm* in command, a Naval Brigade is bound to be formed and sent up country to assist in quelling the mutiny!"

Even the possibility of such an outcome rekindled Phillip's hopes and he asked, unable to hide his eagerness, "Is there any chance of that happening, sir?"

"For God's sake, Phillip, I don't know! I don't even know as yet whether Lord Elgin intends to pay a visit to Calcutta. He's mentioned it, certainly, but nothing's been decided. Elgin's only been here a few days—he hasn't had time to reach a decision." Peel spread his hands in a resigned gesture. "He has to consult with Sir John Bowring and Parkes and the other Plenipotentiaries, as well as with the Admirals—ours and the French and the United States Commodore. I don't suppose he's had time to read all his mail from England yet—there was a stack of it waiting for him when he arrived."

"Yes, but—"

"All I can tell you is that the situation in India is giving cause for grave anxiety, Phillip. But how much help we can give from here doesn't depend on me."

"I realise that, sir. But didn't the Admiral say anything?" Phillip persisted. "I mean, if there's no prospect of our attacking

Canton for the next two or three months, surely he doesn't need to retain a large fleet here?"

William Peel shook his head. "No, but he could say nothing definite. Lord Elgin is the one who will have to decide, I tell you. Dear God, have you become a glory hunter? I should have thought that you'd have had enough action to last you for a while, after Fatshan . . . but you can't wait to get into the thick of it, can you?"

His tone, if not quite censorious, was critical and Phillip stared at him in surprise. "You misunderstand me, Captain Peel," he defended stiffly. "I'm not looking for glory, I assure you. I—"

"Then why all this damned eagerness to get to India? That's what you're after, is it not? It's why you've come to see me, in spite of having one arm in a sling and—"

"I have two sisters in Lucknow, sir. My damned eagerness is prompted by fears for their safety," Phillip returned, still stiff. "If you imagine that I—"

"I'm sorry, my dear fellow." Peel laid a hand on his arm. "I didn't realise. In Lucknow, you say—both of them?"

Phillip nodded. "As far as I know they are but there's been no recent news of them. One is married to a subaltern of the Queen's 32nd and, when my parents last heard from her, she and her husband were in Cawnpore, expecting to follow the regiment to Lucknow. My elder sister, Harriet, was in Sitapur, which is an out-station about forty or fifty miles north of Lucknow. She assured my mother that there was no likelihood of their sepoy regiments joining the mutiny but, if they did, it had been decided to send the women and children to seek refuge with Sir Henry Lawrence's British garrison at the Lucknow Residency. I can only pray they got there safely . . . Harriet has three small children, the youngest less than a year old." He had a mental vision of his sister Harriet's pretty, smiling face. He had not seen her since her marriage, seven years previously, to Major James—Jemmy—Dorling, but as a boy, she had been his favourite sister, an affectionate, gentle person, who had frequently defended him from his father's wrath and whom he had loved deeply. He looked up to meet Peel's gaze and added quietly, "If there's any chance at all of a Naval Brigade being sent up country, sir, I'd . . . dear heaven, I'd give my right arm, as well as this one, to be able to go with them! In any capacity—as a volunteer, if necessary, without pay. I can't stay here, kicking my heels when they . . . I must do something and I'd esteem it a favour if you could make any use of my services, Captain Peel."

"This puts a different complexion on the matter," Peel said. "I understand how you feel but . . ." He was frowning. "*If* we're ordered to India—and there's no guarantee that we shall be—I could probably give you passage, Phillip. As a volunteer or in a supernumerary capacity. All the *Raleighs* will have to be reappointed to other ships, obviously, and I'm sure you know that nothing would please me more than to have you appointed to the *Shannon*—but your rank raises a problem. I have my full complement of officers and my First Lieutenant, Jim Vaughan, is junior to you, although I think he has a couple of years' more service. It would hardly be fair to put you over his head, would it?"

"No, no, of course not. I wouldn't expect you to do anything of the kind, sir."

"And what about that arm? It is really healing?"

Phillip reddened. "It is, I promise you. Your Surgeon can examine it, if you wish."

Peel smiled. "Nonsense, I'll take your word for it, my dear fellow. Failing all else, it might serve as a valid reason for you to apply for sick leave and take a cruise to Calcutta with us to recuperate."

"I hadn't thought of that," Phillip confessed.

"Then think about it," William Peel advised. "You said it was immaterial in what capacity you joined us, did you not?" He rose, holding out his hand for his visitor's glass. "Let me replenish that for you." Busy with the selection of bottles on his sideboard, he went on, "You could also make a formal request to the Admiral, you know—or ask your Chief to do so on your behalf. Commodore Keppel's very persuasive and you do have good reason for wishing to go to India. He'll be sympathetic, will he not?"

"Oh, yes—he's the kindest, most generous man in the world. But—" Phillip hesitated. "He has troubles of his own at present, as you may have heard."

"Yes, the Admiral mentioned it." William Peel passed him a brimming glass and resumed his own seat. "He seems to think Keppel will go home."

"Jim Goodenough, our ex-First Lieutenant, is with the Commodore up river, and he said that it was a strong possibility. I was hoping it wasn't true." Phillip sighed. "If he *is* going, then it's a damnable shame! He was cleared of all responsibility for the loss of the *Raleigh* and rightly so, since he was in no way to blame . . ." He went into details and Peel listened gravely.

"Keppel deserves better of Their Lordships, Phillip—by God he does! I'm told he was simply magnificent at Fatshan."

"He was—and equally so, when the *Raleigh* went down."

"I fear that the underlying reasons for Their Lordships' actions are political . . . and personal. Or so the Admiral hinted. *He* doesn't want Keppel to leave the station and, like you, he's hoping it won't come to that. However"—Peel's tone was dry—

"if you want a barometer with which to measure the situation here, Phillip, I fancy the Commodore will provide one."

"What do you mean, sir?"

Peel's laugh was devoid of amusement. "Well, if there's any possibility of an attack on Canton within the next two months, your esteemed Chief won't throw his hand in—whatever the First Lord writes or says or does. Not until it's over, anyway. So if he takes passage home, the chances are that we shall be ordered to take Lord Elgin to Calcutta . . . and you'd be well advised to make your application for extended sick leave and come with us."

They talked for another twenty minutes about the mutiny in India, Peel supplying what information he could, and then Phillip drained his glass and got to his feet.

"I won't take up any more of your time, Captain Peel," he said. "Thank you for seeing me and I'm more grateful than I can begin to tell you for affording me the opportunity to join your ship's company if you are ordered to India. Indeed, sir, you—"

Peel cut him short. "Say no more, my dear Phillip—you'll be worth your weight in gold to me if I *am* called upon to form a Naval Brigade. Won't you dine with me? I've some of the *Calcutta*'s officers coming and Commander Sotheby of the *Pearl,* who may or may not be known to you."

"I haven't had the pleasure of meeting him. But—"

"Then stay," William Peel urged. "We can find you a cabin on board and you can return to Macao with the *Firmée* in the morning. Make a night of it and get to know your shipmates, it'll do you good. For a start, let Jim Vaughan show off the ship to you . . . He's as proud of her as if he'd designed her himself and it gives him enormous pleasure to demonstrate her refinements to an appreciative audience."

It was an invitation to put himself on good terms with the one man who might resent his joining, Phillip realised, and he accepted it gratefully, liking Peel the more for having issued it. The *Shannon,* he quickly learnt—whilst the First Lieutenant was demonstrating her refinements to him—was a happy ship, her company efficient and well disciplined. A number of her seamen and virtually all her officers had served under William Peel before and were united in their admiration for him, particularly those who were veterans of the Crimean Naval Brigade, and they included one or two whom Phillip recognised as "Queen's Hard Bargains" of the O'Leary stamp. He spent a pleasant evening on board the frigate, finding the wardroom officers friendly and hospitable and her Commander's table predictably excellent. He departed next morning to resume his convalescence in Macao, submitted a formal request for sick leave and, a week later, was summoned to Hong Kong to attend a medical board.

Dr Crawford, who was a member of the board, supported his request, it was granted and Phillip readily obtained permission to join the *Shannon* for a recuperative cruise, the Admiral giving official approval to his appointment in a supernumerary capacity—which, he thought, would set Jim Vaughan's mind at rest.

The *Shannon,* the Admiral's Secretary informed him, when he called to pay his formal respects, was under orders to sail for Calcutta within the next few days. "Lord Elgin has decided— in view of the gravity of the crisis in India—that a consultation between the Governor-General and himself is imperative. So you'll be embarking His Excellency with his staff, Commander, and the *Pearl* will accompany you, as well as three hundred Royal Marines from this station. And there's talk of a Naval Brigade being formed . . ." Abandoning formality, the Secretary added, with feeling, "I must confess I envy you, sir—I really do! I'd give a year's pay to have a crack at those damned mutineers. The tales one hears of what they're doing to defenceless British women and children make one's blood boil!"

He knew nothing specific, however; the tales were mostly rumour and all that Phillip was able to glean from him was confirmation that both Cawnpore and Lucknow were under siege. Troops and a Brigadier-General named Havelock—recalled from Persia—were being sent to their aid but it was not yet known whether they had left Calcutta.

On board the hospital ship, when he went to take leave of Dr Crawford and the rest of the medical staff, he heard the same rumours repeated, many obviously exaggerated and without foundation, but all of them an alarming indication of how grave the situation in India had become.

"Your two ships may be the means of saving Calcutta itself from anarchy, if even half these terrible tales are true," Crawford said grimly, when they had discussed the spate of rumour and conjecture at some length. "Please God they are not! It's an appalling thing when women and children are in the forefront of the battle and when that battle is being fought in India, at the height of summer and against a merciless foe, their suffering doesn't bear thinking about, does it? And if the stories *are* true, God help the poor souls!"

"Amen to that," Phillip said, his voice flat.

Crawford eyed him searchingly. "Do you have loved ones out there? Relatives, friends?"

"Two of my sisters, Doctor. I believe they are in Lucknow but I don't know—there's been no news of them."

"I see. Well, if you are pinning your hopes on joining a relief force to go up country, you will have to take care of that arm, Commander Hazard," the surgeon warned. "There's no infection, the bone is knitting very nicely, but you'll not be able to dispense with the splints for another week or two."

He offered advice and Phillip said wryly, "And if I obey your instructions to the letter, Doctor, what then?"

Dr Crawford smiled. "Then you should be as fit as the next man by the time you reach Calcutta, apart from muscle weakness in your left arm."

Phillip started to thank him but Crawford brushed his thanks aside. "It's a pity we've all to go our separate ways now," he observed, with genuine regret. "The padre, our good Josiah Thompson, was here yesterday from the front. He told me that the Commodore will probably go home. He's still up river but Josiah says he's only waiting for the next English mail. If Their Lordships don't relent, he'll go back by mail steamer and the padre and Spurrier will go with him."

William Peel's barometer, Phillip thought, conscious of an inner anger directed against those on the Board of Admiralty who had—for personal and political reasons, Peel claimed—treated Keppel so scurvily. Did they not realise what he had achieved out here in the few short weeks since his arrival? Did they not understand that victory at Fatshan had been won because of Keppel's courageous leadership, his ability to inspire the men he commanded to a valour almost matching his own? The destruction of the Chinese war fleet by a handful of British seamen in ships' boats had made it possible for the Canton River to be controlled by that same handful and a few small gunboats and, as a result, Lord Elgin was in a position to send aid to India. For God's sake, how could the loss of *Raleigh* be measured, to Keppel's detriment, against Fatshan?

"Poor young Foster died of his wounds on board *Fury,* off the Macao Fort," Surgeon Crawford was saying. "But your friend Commander Turnour is doing great things in the *Bittern.*

He took five pirate junks the other day, it seems, and Josiah Thompson tells me that the C-in-C has recommended him for immediate promotion. His brother Nicholas, whom you probably know, is here now, with the *Pearl* . . ." He mentioned other *Raleigh* officers and men and Phillip made an effort to listen, still conscious of the bitter anger burning inside him.

"The youngsters have all got other ships," Dr Crawford went on. "Johnny Lightfoot and Mark Kerr will be joining you in the *Shannon*. Charlie Scott, Victor Montagu, and Harry Stephenson have been appointed to *Pearl,* so no doubt you'll see something of them . . . and *we* may yet run across each other in India, if fate so decrees."

"We, Doctor?" Phillip echoed. "Do you mean that you—"

"Oh, I'm not aiming to join the Naval Brigade," Crawford answered, with more than a hint of bitterness. "I'm being invalided, alas. But I have a brother in Madras, so I thought I'd take my sick leave with him. Stay a while, perhaps, just in case there's anything a crocked naval surgeon can do." He did not offer any explanation and Phillip did not press him for one, sensing that his own ill-health was not a subject he wanted to discuss.

John Crawford was in his late forties and now he looked every year of his age, wan and tired, his cheeks hollow, as if it had been a long time since he had slept. His skill had saved a great many lives and he had never spared himself but now, it seemed, Their Lordships had no further use for him—for him or for Keppel . . .

"It is a case of 'physician, heal thyself,' is it not, Commander Hazard? Well, I'm going to have a damned good try to do just that and confound them! Godspeed, good luck, and I hope we'll meet again. My prayers, for what they are worth, will be for all of you." He held out his hand and Phillip wrung it, his throat tight.

He joined the *Shannon* that evening; next day the Marines from the *Sanspareil* were transferred. On the morning of 16th July, having embarked the Earl of Elgin and his staff, *Shannon* and *Pearl* weighed anchor and set course for Singapore, which was reached on the 28th. Two days later, having completed with coal and taken on board a company of the 90th Light Infantry—shipwrecked in the transport *Transit* off the Malayan coast—the two frigates proceeded on their voyage to India.

CHAPTER FOUR

Mutiny came to Sitapur, with horrifying violence, on the morning of Wednesday, 3rd June. To the British civil and military officers and their wives, the outbreak came as no surprise but rather as a nightmare ending to the weeks of tension and uncertainty which had preceded it.

Crouching now in a jungle clearing, as merciful darkness descended upon her, Harriet Dorling unbuttoned the front of her torn and bloodstained dress and holding her baby son to her breast, thankfully gave him suck. His feeble whimpering stilled at last and the other two children falling into an exhausted sleep beside her, she forced her mind back into the past, reliving the nightmare of the last 24 hours.

They had expected a mutiny but had sought, all of them, to avert it by remaining at their posts and showing no outward signs of fear. Perhaps they had been wrong, Harriet thought— perhaps *she* had been wrong to insist on staying at Jemmy's side, instead of taking the opportunity, when it had been offered to her, of going under escort to Lucknow with her children. But very few of the other wives had accepted it; some because, like herself, they were reluctant to leave their husbands, and others, on their own admission, because they feared that their escort—sepoys of the 41st Native Infantry— might betray them. Their commanding officer, Colonel Birch,

had continued to the last to trust them and, in proof of his
confidence in their fidelity, had sent his own wife and daughter with them, but no one knew whether or not the small party
had reached Lucknow safely. And . . . Harriet bit back a sob.
One of his own sepoys had, that morning, shot the poor
Colonel in the back, without warning and seemingly without
compunction. Just as they . . . The baby stirred restlessly and,
releasing her nipple from his flaccid lips, she lifted him gently on to her shoulder to caress the wind he had sucked in
from his small, distended stomach, glad that, in this emer-
gency, she had suckled him herself from birth, instead of
employing a wet nurse. At least now—for as long as she was
alive—she could sustain his precious life and perhaps Ayah
would keep her promise and return to them from her village,
with food for the other two.

The baby relieved, she placed him on her other breast and
again forced herself to look back, trying to place, in their
proper order, the events which had led to her presence here
and to . . . tears welled unbidden into her eyes, ached in her
throat. To darling Jemmy's . . . death.

Ever since mid-May, when the news of Delhi's capture by
the mutineers from Meerut had reached them, the native
troops on the station had been showing increasing signs of
disaffection. Priests and holy men had paid secret visits to
the Native Lines, preaching *jehad,* urging the sepoys to betray
the Company's salt and it had been impossible to deny them
entry. By the end of the month, two of the four regimental
Commanders had been compelled to warn the Commissioner,
George Christian, that no reliance could be placed on their
regiments' continued loyalty. It had almost broken Jemmy's
heart to make such an admission, Harriet recalled with bitterness. Jemmy was of the old school, a commanding officer

who regarded his men as his children and who, all his service life, had made their welfare his first concern. He had always had their respect and their personal devotion and, in return, had loved them and taken an intense pride in everything they did. His house, as well as his office, had been open to any and all of them; every man, from his Subedar down to the newest recruit, had been known to him by name and could count on a sympathetic hearing in time of trouble. Dear heaven, he had spent more time with his sepoys than he had with his own family and yet, in spite of it, they had betrayed him. They . . . Harriet laid the baby, sleeping now, across her knees and, with a trembling hand, wiped the tears from her eyes.

How, oh how, could the betrayal have been avoided? The Commissioner, God rest his soul, had taken what steps he could to meet the expected outbreak. Since so few of the British wives and families had left the station, he had decided that the first step was to arrange for their protection and had, accordingly, set about the task of provisioning and fortifying his bungalow. The Residency bungalow stood in a large, open compound, on two sides of which flowed the Sureyan River and from it, access to the Lucknow road could only be gained by passing through the military cantonment and Native Infantry Lines. This made it far from ideal as a defensive position but it was large enough to accommodate the majority of those who were likely to seek refuge with the Commissioner and he had issued instructions that, at the first sign of trouble, the British families were to gather there, each family bringing with them whatever transport they possessed, in case evacuation became necessary.

The 2nd Regiment of Military Police, commanded by Captain John Hearsey, had continued to obey orders and had expressed their intention to remain loyal and, in the belief that they, at least, could be trusted, George Christian had called upon them to guard the Residency. But, Harriet recalled wearily, in the end even they had betrayed their trust and joined the rest in a savage orgy of slaughter, shooting down poor George Christian, with his wife and younger child, and putting to the sword all those who had fled, in terror, from the building they had been pledged to defend. A few, like herself, had managed to make their escape but . . . She drew a long, shuddering breath. Like herself, all were now hunted fugitives in a trackless, inhospitable jungle, without food or water or weapons, their lives in danger both from pursuing sepoys and the wild animals by which it was infested.

Her own ordeal had begun before the police guards had joined the sepoys in their attack on the Christians' bungalow. She had wakened before dawn to find her husband hurriedly donning his uniform by the light of a single candle and he had told her, she remembered, that the Havildar-Major had summoned him to the Lines in the hope that, by his presence, he might prevent the hotheads from breaking out.

"I must go, darling," he had told her. "It's my duty to do what I can. And they may listen if I appeal to them . . . they're not all affected by this madness. Burnes is coming with me and I've sent a *chitti* to Dick Snell to tell him to escort you and the children, with his own wife and child, to the Residency or to the Lucknow road, as he thinks best. The servants are putting the horses into the buggy now—it will be waiting for you by the time you're dressed—but please, don't waste any time."

She had protested, of course, Harriet thought dully, had begged him not to go, not to risk his life by attempting to reason with his men.

"They're beyond reason now, Jemmy," she had said. "And we need you, the children and I."

"I'm in no danger from my own sepoys," Jemmy had assured her. "From the others, perhaps, but not from my men. And I owe it to them to try to stop them, Harriet." Buckling on his sword, he had promised that it would not take long, that he would come back for her. "I'll find you wherever you are, my love—at the Christians' or on the road. Dick Snell will look after you and I'm leaving Sita Ram with you, too—both will be armed." He had kissed her, held her to him for a moment, and then vanished into the early morning mist, a tall, ramrod-stiff figure, bent only on saving his wayward sepoy-children from the consequences of their own folly, the stout Havildar-Major, respectful as ever, trotting at his heels.

Oh, Jemmy, Harriet's heart cried in silent agony, *did you not know what they would do? Had you no inkling of the treachery they planned, the cruel betrayal? Had you no suspicion at all that they intended to take from you the life you had already given them a hundred times before?*

No answer came from the humid darkness and, careful not to disturb the sleeping baby on her lap, Harriet drew her shawl more closely about her, shivering as the terrible, searing memories returned. She had done as Jemmy had bade her; had sent Ayah to rouse and dress the children and hastened to dress herself. The bearer brought tea and told her that the buggy was harnessed and ready; she had drunk the tea, she recalled, and waited for the Snells. A little later Sita Ram—Jemmy's orderly, a bemedalled veteran who had served him for fifteen years—had presented himself, smartly uniformed as always and his musket slung from his shoulder, to be greeted eagerly by the five-year-old Phillip, whose favourite companion he was.

"Is Sita Ram coming with us, Mamma?" the little boy had asked, eyes bright with expectation. "Can't we go soon?" And then, slipping easily into the vernacular, "May I ride with you, Sita Ram, on your horse, instead of in the buggy?"

Beaming, the orderly had hoisted him on to his shoulder, setting down the musket and then, just as she had been about to chide Phillip for his impatience, a terrible, ear-piercing scream had come from the Snell's bungalow opposite, followed by a fusillade of shots and the sound of running feet. When she could nerve herself to go out on to the verandah, Harriet had seen smoke rising slowly from the rear of the Snell's bungalow and the old bearer came, the breath rasping in his throat, to tell her brokenly that some sepoys had run amuck and she must go at once, whilst there was yet time to save herself and the *baba-log*.

"Snell Sahib is dead, his *mem* and the *baba* also. Delay no longer, Memsahib, for surely they will come here."

"What Sepoys are they?" she had demanded, not realising the futility of her question until after she had asked it . . . or had she, perhaps, been as anxious as Jemmy to absolve his men from blame? *Those* men . . . oh, God!

The bearer had shaken his head helplessly and again begged her to flee her home, a note of panic in his quavering voice. When Sita Ram had made the same plea, she had agreed. With Ayah carrying the baby, she had taken Phillip and little Augusta each by the hand and led them, chattering excitedly in their innocence, out to the waiting carriage, Sita Ram bringing up the rear, his musket at the ready.

The coachman, standing by the horses' heads, looked panic-stricken and ready to take to his heels but, forcing herself to speak calmly, she had ordered him to drive to the Commissioner Sahib's bungalow and he had salaamed and climbed back on to his box. She had been in the act of entering the carriage, Harriet remembered, when the sound of galloping hooves had reached her, coming from the direction of the Lines. Turning her head swiftly, she had seen a horseman approaching, with four or five others some distance behind and it was a second or so before she recognised the leading rider as Jemmy—capless, his thick dark hair blowing wildly in the breeze—and realised, with an acute sense of shock, that those behind him were pursuing, not riding after him. From the rear of the Snells' blazing bungalow a mob of men on foot emerged—some sepoys, in uniform, the rest townsfolk—and, in response to yells from Jemmy's pursuers, half a dozen of the sepoys dashed out to spread themselves across the road and bar his way.

Shots were fired but the aim was poor and Jemmy came on, his right arm holding a drawn sword, which he was waving frantically above his head—waving to her to make her escape, she had sensed, although she could not hear, above the tumult of other voices, the words he was trying to say to her. And she had stood there, frozen, unable to bring herself to desert him in order to save her own life or even those of the children . . . She had stood there watching him, praying for him, willing him to reach the carriage so that they might escape together. Or die together . . . Harriet caught her breath on a sob.

He had so nearly succeeded in reaching her, scattering the sepoys on the road before most of them had had time to recharge their muskets, when a shot, fired by a bazaar *budmash* in a white robe, seemingly at random, brought his horse crashing to the ground. Jemmy was flung forward heavily, the animal rolled over, legs threshing, pinning him beneath its heaving body and he had scarcely struggled free of it when his pursuers were upon him. Harriet recognised all of them as native officers of his regiment, saw the stout Havildar-Major strike the first savage blow, his dark face contorted with hate as Jemmy parried his cut and ran him through the arm with his own weapon.

But they had been too many for him and when the sepoys from the road ran to join the mounted officers, Harriet had turned her head away, knowing that it was over. Even then she had made no attempt to escape. Numb with shock, she had simply stood beside the carriage, having in her immobility a dignity of which she had been quite unaware. The children were sobbing in Ayah's arms but she was, in that moment, as deaf to their frightened cries as she was to Sita Ram's pleas that she enter the carriage and seek safety in flight. Flight was, in any case, impossible—the road was the only way to the Commissioner's bungalow and to reach it, the carriage would have to pass through the mob of sepoys and bazaar riff-raff gathering in search of plunder.

"Memsahib . . ." She had heard Sita Ram's voice then, realised that he had come to stand at her side, ready to protect her. "Memsahib, they are coming."

"Go," she had bade him, with weary resignation. "Save yourself, Sita Ram—you have done all you can. They will kill you, too, if you remain. Take Ayah with you."

"They bring the Colonel Sahib's body, Memsahib," the orderly had whispered. "That is all. They intend you no harm."

Incredulously, her heart pounding in her breast, she had watched them approach, two of them bearing Jemmy's lifeless body, Subedar Bihari Lal at their head. In silence they laid the bleeding, barely recognisable corpse of her husband at her feet and Bihari Lal had saluted, stony-faced, and told her that she was free to go, with her children.

"We will give you escort to the Lucknow road, Memsahib. The Colonel Sahib's body shall be placed in his own house and we will set it on fire, so that his soul may find release."

In vain she had protested, Harriet remembered, saying that she wished to go to the Residency but, pointing to a column of smoke drifting skywards beyond the trees to their left, the Subedar had told her that the Christians and those who had taken shelter with them were either dead or fleeing for their lives. "The Police sowars attacked them, Memsahib, vowing to show them no mercy. But we do not make war on *mems* and *baba-log,* as do those dogs of Muslims. We will set you on the road to Lucknow."

She had been compelled to agree, since they had left her with no choice, and they had kept their word. An old havildar had taken the place of her terrified coachman on the box and, with Bihari Lal and a dozen others as escort, the buggy had been driven unmolested through the Lines and for over two miles along the Lucknow road. She had looked back only once, Harriet recalled bitterly, to see flames rising from the bungalow that had been her home and which, by some strange logic she did not understand, his sepoys had selected to serve as their Colonel's funeral pyre.

"The Colonel Sahib was a good man," Subedar Bihari Lal had told her, when they reached the parting of their ways and came to a halt in the shade of a roadside mango *tope.* "We besought him to remain as our Colonel and lead us to Delhi, forsaking the Company's service. But he refused, so we were forced to put him to death. It was not the wish of all of us that he should die, Memsahib . . . least of all was it mine. But now"—he glanced unhappily at the Havildar-Major—"we serve new masters and must obey their commands."

The stout Havildar-Major, unlike his military superior, was of Brahmin caste, Harriet knew; he had addressed no word to her and, with the memory still etched in her mind of the bitter hatred in his face as he had struck at Jemmy, she was thankful that he had not. Clearly, he was one of the ringleaders in the mutiny and, as such, even the Subedar feared him. And yet, only a few short weeks ago, at Jemmy's instigation, he had begun to give little Phillip his first riding lessons, displaying a gentle patience towards the boy that had completely won her heart. Had it all been false, she wondered dully; had his protestations of affection for Phillip, his promises of loyalty to Jemmy been deliberately intended to deceive? She shivered again. If he had hated Jemmy, enough to override the other native officers and demand his death, why had he spared Jemmy's children, his wife? Was it, perhaps, because he had condemned them to a slower but no less certain death in the jungle, unarmed and unprotected?

The answer to her unvoiced questions had not been long in coming. They had taken Sita Ram and the carriage with them when they left her at the roadside, with the warning, offered by the Subedar, that she should hide until the mutineers' fury had abated and the regiments set off on the long march all were pledged to make, in order to join forces with their comrades in Delhi.

Poor Sita Ram had wept when taking leave of her. "I am ordered to go with my *paltan,* Memsahib," he had whispered brokenly. "And I dare not refuse. Seek shelter and concealment in the jungle when we have gone, you and the *babas,* for the sepoys of other *paltans* will hunt for you and kill you if they find you. I will come back if it is possible."

She had clasped his hand, Harriet recalled, feeling it cold in hers, feeling it tremble. She had longed to reward his loyalty but knew that, if she were to give him money, he might be made to suffer for it—at best, the mutineers would take it from him. She had a ring on her finger—a single small pearl, set in chip diamonds—and, careful that none of the others saw her do so, she slipped it off and let it slide into the orderly's brown palm. He bent over her hand, as if to touch his brow to it and said, very softly, "No, Memsahib, give that to Ayah. She may be trusted . . . send her to her village to ask for shelter. It is nearby—her people will help you."

He had straightened to attention, leaving the ring in her hand, salaamed, and marched woodenly off with the others and that had been the last she had seen of them . . . and of Ayah. No sooner had she followed Sita Ram's advice and given her the ring than the woman, thrusting the baby into her arms, had made off through the trees at a shambling run, calling out over her shoulder that the village was further away than the orderly had suggested and, if she were to reach it before nightfall, no time must be lost.

"You will come back!" Harriet had called after her, trying to keep the despair she felt from sounding in her voice. "Ayah, you will bring help—food for the little ones, if you can—and ask your headman to give us shelter!"

"*Achcha,* Memsahib." The Ayah's tone had been sullen, her acknowledgement automatic. It was possible that she would do as she had been asked but more likely, alas, that fear would hold her silent when she reached her village. She had been a good servant, devoted to all three children, and had entered Harriet's service five years ago, when little Phillip was born. Five years of exemplary service was no guarantee of fidelity now, though, Harriet reflected wryly—and Ayah had been frightened out of her wits, cowering down in the carriage during the drive to the Lucknow road, in the evident hope that her presence would go unnoticed by the mutineers, until a chance of escape should present itself.

As . . . She bit back a sigh. As it had when the sepoys had

abandoned them by the roadside. No doubt it had been a mistake to give her the ring there and then—she should have waited, should have promised the trinket as reward, when the woman had kept her part of the bargain and returned with help. As it was, they had agreed no rendezvous—Ayah, to whom this area was familiar, had offered no guidance, and yet must have overheard the Subedar's injunction to her mistress to seek a temporary hiding place, even if she had not heard Sita Ram's. Knowing the danger, would the badly frightened woman make any attempt to find her erstwhile charges, when to do so would bring her no further reward and might be to risk her life?

It was too much to expect, Harriet told herself despondently. To Ayah, that small ring would be riches; she would be tempted to keep it and say nothing, but even if she did deliver her message, rescue was still uncertain. It would depend on the goodwill of the headman and on the attitude of the villagers whether a party was sent to search for the fugitives or whether they were left to fend for themselves as best they might. So far, she had managed tolerably well. Despite the baby's weight and the bemused state of shock to which their father's murder had reduced her two elder children, she had led them to this clearing—which she judged to be at least two miles from the road—without mishap. But the heat had exacted a heavy toll of them all and it had taken them almost until nightfall to get here, resting at frequent intervals.

They had encountered only one other human being on their weary, difficult journey—a wounded Eurasian clerk on a jaded horse, who had paused only long enough to gasp out a horrifying account of the attack on the Residency and had then ridden on, refusing Harriet's offer to attend to his wounds. The death of Colonel Birch—shot down with two of his officers by his own Treasury guard—had apparently been the signal for a general uprising. The clerk had witnessed this and had fled in terror to the Residency with the news. His account of subsequent events had confirmed, in blood-chilling detail, the Subedar's claim that virtually all those who had taken shelter with the Christians had been killed and the bungalow burnt to the ground. The few who had escaped had done so by wading or swimming across the shallow river, as he himself had done, or on horseback from cantonments, braving vicious musketry fire. He had found the horse wandering loose in the jungle, the clerk had explained, its rider lying dead nearby, and had taken it, hoping that the animal would carry him to Lucknow.

"I will send back help to you when I get there," he had promised but the promise had been half-hearted, his concern solely for himself, and Harriet had watched him go, neither believing that he would keep his word nor that he would reach his destination, for his wounds were severe and he was losing blood as he talked to her. But he had named several of those who had contrived to cross the river and her sad heart had lifted a little with the realisation that some, at least, of her friends might still be alive. Captain Hearsey, who had been saved but held prisoner for a time by his treacherous Police; Madelaine Jackson and her brother Mountstewart, the Assistant-Commissioner; Jemmy's adjutant George Burns; and two other young women the clerk knew only by sight, one of whom had been carrying a little girl.

"Where are they now?" Harriet had asked and, kicking his weary horse into motion, the Eurasian had waved vaguely behind him.

"They may come this way," he had suggested and, buoyed up by the hope that he was right and she might sooner or later encounter them, she had struggled on, her first concern to find a safe hiding place where, with the children, she could wait and watch for their coming. But the way was rough, the path they followed—an animal track—frequently overgrown with thorny brushwood and their progress became slower with each passing hour. Finally, her hands and arms lacerated and bleeding and the two older children, parched and breathless, clinging to her skirts and pleading with her to let them rest, she had been compelled to halt in the clearing in which they now were. It was by no means the safe refuge she had been searching for but it was hemmed in by trees, the approaches to it used, as far as she could judge, only by animals and, as the moon rose, she realised that, crouched in the shadows, she and the children would probably not be seen by an intruder— or, if they were, not before that intruder had made his presence known to her, both by sight and sound. But there was no water, the trees were not of the fruit-bearing variety and, by daylight—whilst she might assuage the baby's hunger—Phillip and Augusta would be famished and she would have no means of satisfying either of them.

Water was a vital necessity for them all; they would have to find it or die, Harriet thought despairingly, which meant that they could not remain here after the new day dawned, in the hope that some of the other fugitives would catch up with them or that the people from Ayah's village would track them to their hiding place, bringing the help she had requested. She dared not count on either of these possibilities; the other fugitives might be dead or in the hands of mutineers and Ayah's people—if they came—would not attempt to search for her until it was light. With her children's lives in the balance, she had to depend on her own efforts and must plan accordingly. She . . . Somewhere, frighteningly near at hand,

an animal squealed and went crashing through the under-
brush, emitting grunts and more squeals. A wild pig, she
decided, her heart thudding, one of the most dangerous animals in the jungle, Jemmy had told her which, if startled,
would attack human beings on foot without provocation.
Instinctively, she clasped the baby to her, and he wakened,
whimpering plaintively. She rocked him to and fro, fearful lest
Phillip and Augusta should waken also and be afraid but, to her
relief, both slept on, and she glimpsed the pig—a formidable-
looking boar—as it crossed the clearing and then vanished into
the shadows at its far end.

With its going, Harriet's heart resumed its normal rhythm;
the baby quietened and she laid him, very gently, on the
ground beside her, cautiously stretching her cramped limbs.
She must conserve her strength, she knew; must rest when
she could—although she dared not sleep in this all-too vulnerable refuge—and, however desperate their need for water,
she and the children must travel only in the cool of the early
morning and late evening. To do as they had yesterday—
attempt to fight their way through the jungle, blindly and without direction, in the full heat of the sun—was to dissipate what
little stamina they possessed and to no purpose.

She would get her bearings from the sun and go south,
making her first objective the river, which could not be more
than a mile distant and, although all Indian rivers were con-
taminated and dangerous for Europeans to drink from, this
was a chance that she and the children would have to take.
Any water was preferable to the risk of dehydration, and the
awful torment of unassuaged thirst, she decided, and the only
alternative water supply was that to be found in village wells,
to approach which, in her present circumstances, would be
dangerous . . . the villagers could as well attack as give her

aid. Besides, if any of the other fugitives had survived, they would undoubtedly make for Lucknow, as the wounded clerk had done, and her best chance of encountering them would be if she, too, attempted to head in that direction, with the river as guide. Lucknow lay forty daunting miles to the south but the Sureyan was a tributary of the River Goomtee, which flowed through the centre of Lucknow, passing within sight of Sir Henry Lawrence's Residency . . . Harriet sat up, conscious of renewed hope.

Why, she asked herself dazedly, had she not thought of the river before? If she could procure a boat and a native boatman willing to row herself and the children down river for the promise, on arrival in Lucknow, of a substantial reward, then the forty miles which now separated her from her goal need not be quite so daunting as she had initially supposed. The road was out of the question—it would be teeming with mutinous sepoys, the out-stations it served, Khyrabad and Muhona, probably in the same state of anarchy as Sitapur—and clearly to attempt to make the journey on foot through the jungle, with three helpless children, would be beyond her strength. But the river offered hope and . . . She caught her breath on a sob. In Lucknow, God willing, Lavinia and Tom would be waiting—anxiously, no doubt—for her arrival. She and the children would have a roof over their heads—the quarters Lavinia had invited her, weeks ago, to share—they would be with their own kith and kin, guarded by British soldiers of Tom's regiment, who would protect them, if the mutineers should grow bold enough to launch an attack on Lucknow itself. Sir Henry Lawrence, wise and farsighted man, had provisioned his Residency for a siege . . .

Almost with impatience, Harriet waited for the dawn. When it came, she roused the two older children and, promising that they should have the water they craved if they helped her to find the river, she set off, careful to keep the newly lighted eastern sky always to her left. At first, refreshed by their sleep, Phillip and Augusta ran ahead of her, the little boy manfully trying to open a path for her through the tangled undergrowth, but after an hour, both became weary and Augusta started to wail that she was thirsty and could go no further. Fearful that the child's loud sobs might lead to their discovery, Harriet chided her sharply, her own hopes sadly dashed and her energy flagging.

"Where *is* the river, Mamma?" Phillip asked. "Do you know where it is?"

"It's only a little further," Harriet told him, without conviction. "Take Augusta's hand, darling, and help her along. We'll find it soon . . . you must be brave, both of you. It's just that it's difficult to see exactly where it is, with all these trees getting in the way."

It was more than difficult, she thought grimly; not only did the trees obscure their view but there was a sameness about the whole landscape which rendered it well nigh impossible for her to be certain that they were going in the right direction. A huge, gnarled banyan tree, which she had taken as a landmark to gauge their progress, was echoed by one exactly similar in shape and size only twenty yards further on and she had to look back to the first before she could be sure that it was not the same. And the sun was rising higher, brazen and pitiless; soon, she knew, they would have to find shelter from its powerful rays and wait, still tormented by thirst, until it sank and permitted them to continue their search. If they did not find the river by nightfall, their chances of survival would be slight . . .

"Oh, God," she prayed silently. "Help us . . . do not abandon us here. These are Thy children, Thine own little ones . . . didst Thou not say that Thou would'st answer prayers offered in their name?"

"Mamma . . ." Phillip said, his lower lip trembling, his small face bloated and blistered beneath the useless little sailor cap he wore, "Mamma, I'm so tired—please may I stop? Augusta won't walk, I have to drag her and one of her shoes has come off."

He sounded so lost and defeated that Harriet's heart went out to him in helpless pity. "All right, darling," she said, making a great effort to hide her own feelings, as she pointed to the nearer of the giant banyan trees. "Lie down there, under the roots of that tree, both of you. I'll go and look for Augusta's shoe." As an afterthought, she laid the baby under the twisting roots between them, noticing with dismay as she did so that Augusta's shoeless foot was badly swollen, the child white with pain. "Tie her poor little foot in this," she instructed, giving Phillip her scarf. "In case I can't find her shoe. And—look after Baby for me, won't you?"

Relieved of the baby's weight, she retraced her steps at a brisker pace than she had hitherto managed to keep up, and found the shoe beneath a clump of thorny brushwood about two hundred yards from where she had left the exhausted children. It was as she knelt to pick it up that she heard Ayah's voice, calling her by name, and stumbling to her feet with a strangled cry of thankfulness, saw the woman coming towards her. Ayah was not alone; there were three men with her, rough looking *ryots* in ragged cotton *dhotis*, one of whom was armed with a matchlock of ancient pattern, which he held somewhat uncertainly in front of him, its muzzle pointed towards herself. But Harriet had no eyes for his weapon; her gaze went to the earthenware *chatti* which Ayah bore on her shoulder and she said, making no attempt to disguise her relief and gratitude, "Oh, Ayah—you came! I cannot thank you enough, I . . ." She had spoken in English and then, seeing the look of suspicion in the face of the villager with the matchlock, repeated her greeting in fluent Hindustani. "Have you brought us water? The little ones are in sore need of it."

"I have brought water," Ayah confirmed. "Also *chapattis.*" She indicated a bundle, tied up in a dirty white cloth. This was welcome news but Harriet hesitated. There was an odd note in Ayah's voice, a subtle change in her manner which, if not insolent, was bordering on it . . . and she had not made the customary salaam.

"Is there anything wrong, Ayah?" she asked.

Ayah shook her head. "I came, as the Memsahib asked, bringing food and water. Where are the *baba-log?*"

"They are nearby resting." Knowing with what joy the children would greet their Ayah, Harriet was about to lead her to their hiding place when one of the men said, in a harsh whisper, "Tell the Mem our price."

"Your *price?*" Harriet echoed bitterly, scarcely able to believe the evidence of her own ears. "Is there a price for helping us, then?"

"We are poor people," the man said sullenly. "And we take great risks to bring you this food. Our brothers of the Company Army would punish us if they knew. Our price is fifty rupees— give it to us and we will leave the food and water and return to our village."

She had little more than the fifty rupees he had demanded on her, Harriet thought, and she had hoped to use most of the money as advance payment to a boatman, when they reached the river. Her heart sinking, she asked quietly, addressing her question to the Ayah, "Does this mean that you will not give us shelter in your village, as I had also asked?"

Ayah was silent, avoiding her gaze and the man with the matchlock said harshly, "We cannot—the risk is too great. The sepoys are everywhere, hunting for the *sahib-log*—they come from Khyrabad as well as from Sitapur, and the word is that they have risen also in Shahjehanpur, throwing off the Company's yoke and killing all, *mems* and *babas,* as well as the sahibs who commanded them. Soon they will rise in Cawnpore and even in Lucknow. The Company's *Raj* is ended, Memsahib."

"No!" Harriet protested. "You are wrong—you listen to lies."

The man smiled thinly. "We see what is happening with our own eyes. Today you beg us for help—yesterday you would have driven past us in your carriage without sparing us a glance, without observing that we are in rags and our children's bellies empty. Now *you* are in rags and it is *your* children who cry out for food and drink." He spat his contempt in the dust at Harriet's feet. "Pay us and we will go. We will do you no harm . . . but the price is fifty rupees."

"That is all the money I have with me." Harriet told him. It went against the grain to plead with such a man but, for her children's sake, she knew that she had to try. "I had hoped to use the money for the hire of a boat to take us to Lucknow. I will give you ten—or fifty if you will shelter us and help us on our way to Lucknow."

"You will not find a boatman willing to accept your hire," the man retorted impatiently. "Nor a village where they will give you shelter . . . rather will any you approach betray you to the sepoys. But we will not betray you if you pay us what we ask."

His words struck a chill to Harriet's heart. Were they, she wondered aghast, could they *possibly* be true? Her hands trembling, she felt for the small bag of money, which she had placed in the bosom of her tattered dress for safety on leaving the carriage. "I will pay you twenty-five. That is all I—"

"Fifty," the *ryot* countered, his expression suddenly ugly. He motioned Ayah to set down her water *chatti* and, raising his matchlock to his shoulder, took aim at the *chatti*. "I will shoot if you do not pay, Memsahib, and then you will have no water for your little ones."

Ayah muttered a protest, tears starting to her eyes but the man ignored her and Harriet reluctantly counted out fifty rupees into the outheld hands of one of the other men. The owner of the matchlock lowered his weapon and gave her a mock salaam. "Eat well, Memsahib," he bade her cynically. "And drink your fill." He signed to his companions to follow him but Ayah, moved to pity, lingered for a moment at Harriet's side.

"Take this, Memsahib," she whispered. "For the boat." The little pearl ring was restored to Harriet's finger. "The river is not in the direction you were going, it is behind you. Walk back—there is a cart-track not very far away, which will lead you to the river. Do not delay—go there as soon as you and the little ones have eaten. Seek an old man named Mahee Singe; he will help you. He—" One of the men called out to her to hurry and Ayah laid the cloth-covered bundle of *chapattis* at Harriet's feet and, without a backward glance, ran off to catch up with her companions.

Her fifty rupees seemed to Harriet well spent when she rejoined the children with the provisions they had bought. The water, stale and luke warm though it was, tasted like nectar to her parched lips; Phillip and Augusta took on a fresh lease of life when, at last, their thirst abated. They fell upon the *cha-pattis* with exclamations of delight and the baby lay gurgling on her lap after she had fed him and sponged his tortured little body with a handkerchief, wrung out in a little of the precious liquid. They set off for the river, finding the cart-track Ayah had indicated with little difficulty but the sun was now almost at its zenith and, remembering the toll it had taken of them the previous day, Harriet stifled her impatience and deliberately set a slow pace, pausing every fifteen or twenty minutes to rest. It was afternoon when suddenly, to her heartfelt joy, she glimpsed the sun-bright water of her goal a hundred yards or so ahead of them, at a bend in the track. There was a village, many of the houses built on stilts over the water, about the same distance to her right, she saw, and she halted, bidding the two older children keep out of sight until she could reconnoitre it.

Leaving them to crouch obediently in the shade of a clump of trees, she moved forward with the caution which bitter experience had taught her, and subjected the village to a careful scrutiny, shading her eyes with her free hand. There were boats drawn up on the muddy bank, some fashioned from hollowed-out tree trunks, the rest of more conventional construction and one—a squat, high-prowed sailing vessel, ideal for the purpose she had in mind—lay anchored in shallow water on the far side of a line of rush-thatched houses. Apart from half a dozen women, spreading their washing on the ground for the sun to bleach, she could detect no signs of undue activity and, after a while, she saw the women, their task completed, make a leisurely return to the village, whose other occupants were seemingly following the usual village practice and sleeping through the heat of the day.

It looked safe enough, Harriett thought, yet still she

hesitated, remembering what the *ryot* with the matchlock rifle had said earlier that day. *"You will not find a boatman willing to accept your hire nor a village where they will give you shelter. Rather will any you approach betray you to the sepoys . . ."* Dear heaven, was he right, she wondered, could people like these change overnight from docile peasants to enemies, ready to betray and steal, perhaps even to kill those who had previously been their rulers? Or were the people of Ayah's village the exception, motivated more by fear than by hatred?

Ayah had returned her ring, it was true, but in pity, not in gratitude or love and she had gone without even a farewell to the white children to whom, it had always seemed, she was devoted . . . Harriet bit back a sigh. There was no understanding what had happened, no reason within her comprehension which could explain why Jemmy's sepoys had murdered him in front of his wife and children.

She moved forward slowly, tears blinding her. She would go to this village, would ask for Mahee Singe; even if they refused to allow her to stay, at least they would direct her to the man she sought—the old man whom Ayah said she could depend on for help. He might be in the village, a fisherman, perhaps, or—since Ayah had seemed confident of his loyalty—a Government pensioner. Regretting now that she had not asked Ayah for more precise details concerning Mahee Singe, she stumbled on, her baby on her hip, the tears flowing unchecked down her flushed and dusty cheeks.

She was almost within hailing distance of the village when she saw the bodies and halted, numb with shock. There were four of them—three men and a woman, all of whom were known to her—and there was a dead horse lying nearby. All had been shot and . . . She turned her head away, fighting down nausea. All had been hideously mutilated, the woman with such bestial savagery that Harriet could not bring herself to look a second time. Less than a week ago, she thought, her mind rebelling against the memory, Mrs Gowan and her husband—the Commanding Officer of the 9th Oudh Irregulars—had dined with Jemmy and herself. So, too, had the young Assistant-Surgeon, John Hill, and Lieutenant Greene and his wife. Now four of their five guests lay . . . *there,* unburied, exposed for any passing *ryot* to gloat over, until the jungle scavangers should complete the work they had already begun. And she, fool that she was, *she* had been about to enter the village to plead for help . . . Choking uncontrollably, Harriet began to run, the baby almost falling from her arms and setting up a thin, protesting wail which she was forced to stifle, a hand over his mouth.

"Dear God," she prayed. "Oh merciful Father in Heaven . . . don't let them find us! Don't let them hear!"

She regained the track, her heart pounding, and paused there for a moment to get her breath, listening fearfully, every sense alert, for sounds of pursuit. None came and she staggered on towards the clump of trees where she had left Phillip and Augusta, the baby's weight almost more than she could sustain. And then she saw them coming to meet her, two small, wobegone figures in their filthy, tattered clothes, each holding the hand of a white-bearded old native. They were chattering to him trustingly in their fluent, chirping Hindustani, and he was answering them, laughing with them, encouraging them to go with him to . . . what? To the death meted out to the Gowans and poor young Greene and the doctor? Oh, God in Heaven, not to that, not to . . . The river was preferable. It was near enough. If she called to them and they ran, all three of them together . . . God would give her strength to carry her baby those last few desperate yards and . . .

Harriet's lips moved but no sound came from them. The children saw her and called out to her joyfully. She took two swaying paces towards them and then the bright sunlight faded and she was in darkness, falling into a deep abyss to which, it seemed, there was no bottom and no end . . .

When she recovered consciousness, the white-bearded old man was kneeling beside her, holding a cup of water to her lips and little Phillip clumsily dabbed at her face with a cloth wrung out in water, calling to her anxiously, begging her to wake up.

"Do not be afraid, Memsahib," the old native bade her gently in English. "We will not harm you or your little ones. We are friends here."

"Friends?" Harriet echoed bitterly. "Are those—are the bodies of my people evidence of your friendship?" She sat up, horrified to see that a crowd of villagers had gathered about herself and her children, hemming them in, cutting off their escape to the river.

"You saw them?" the old man said. "I am sorry that you did. But we did not kill them, I swear to you, Memsahib. That was the work of the sepoys who betrayed their allegiance— we were powerless to prevent it. The sepoys commanded us to leave the bodies exposed but when the sun goes down, we will bury them—as Christians are buried, with a cross above each one."

His tone, as much as his words, carried conviction and Harriet's fears began at last to fade. One of the women, she saw, was nursing the baby, cradling him in her arms and crooning to him softly; another had little Augusta on her knee—they would not do that, she thought thankfully, if there were murder in their hearts. Feeling tears of relief in her eyes, she looked up into the old man's dark lined face and asked hesitantly, "Are you . . . are you Mahee Singe?"

He smiled. "*Ji-han,* Memsahib, that is my name. Your Ayah, Sunda Dass, sent word to me that you were in need of help and I went in search of you, finding the two little ones before I saw you."

"Why should you help us?" Harriet questioned. "When others refuse?"

"For seventeen years I served as *chuprassi* to the British Resident at the Court of the King of Oudh," Mahee Singe told her proudly. "When Outram Sahib left, he rewarded me with the *tessaildarship* of two villages—this and another—and I live here in retirement. I will not betray my salt, Memsahib, nor will my people. Trust us—we will protect you and, if need be, hide you from the treacherous dogs of sepoys, who rebel against the Company's *Raj.*" He sighed. "When the other *sahiblog* came, with the sepoy curs howling at their heels, we were unprepared, taken by surprise, and we could not save them. But now we are armed and ready. We will give you food and shelter and, when it is safe to do so, we will take you to Lucknow."

Harriet wept as she thanked him. For the next ten days, she and the children stayed in the village, treated with respect and touching kindness by Mahee Singe and his people. On several occasions, marauding sepoys entered the area but no word of the presence of the fugitives was allowed to reach their ears and, true to his promise, the old *tessaildar* had the bodies of their murdered victims buried a little distance away, with a roughly fashioned wooden cross to mark each grave. On the evening of the ninth day, to Harriet's joy, some fishermen brought Sita Ram to the village. The orderly was in peasant dress, his uniform discarded; he had managed to desert from his regiment, he said, on the eve of its departure with several others for Delhi and, on his advice, it was decided to make an attempt to reach Lucknow under his escort the following day.

They left at dawn by boat, dressed in native clothing— Mahee Singe and some of the village boatmen volunteering to accompany them—and a little while before their departure, a Eurasian clerk named Dudman—who, with his wife and two children, had been sheltering in a neighbouring village—came to join them in their flight. The river was low, their progress tedious, but they were unmolested and, despite the heat and the somewhat overcrowded conditions caused by the arrival of the four Dudmans, they suffered only minor discomfort. On the outskirts of Lucknow, Mahee Singe hired bullock carts to which, under cover of darkness, all the fugitives were transferred, together with the sacks of grain and baskets of dried fish that had formed the boat's cargo.

With the white-bearded *tessaildar* acting as driver of the leading cart and Sita Ram crouched beside the pile of sacks which gave them concealment, Harriet and her children completed their long journey, to receive a warm welcome from the people in the Residency, and the offer of hospitality from Mr Martin Gubbins, the Financial Commissioner. In his large, two-storey house—which formed part of the newly completed defensive perimeter south-west of the Residency—she found Colonel Birch's widow and only daughter, and Mrs Apthorp and her three children, who had been escorted in by a company of the 41st Native Infantry, commanded by Major Apthorp, before the outbreak of the Mutiny in Sitapur. The entire party was safe, Mrs Apthorp told her, the other ladies being accommodated in the house of the Judicial Commissioner, Mr Ommaney, but her husband's company had since left Lucknow, with the avowed intention of joining their comrades in the mutiny.

"And that, after being rewarded most lavishly for having saved our lives!" Mary Apthorp said bitterly. "There is no understanding them, is there?" She drew Harriet aside and lowered her voice, so that the other occupants of the room might not overhear. "Poor dear Mrs Birch is quite heartbroken by her husband's death . . . as, indeed, you must be, Mrs Dorling. We heard the terrible news of what happened in Sitapur, after our departure, from Lieutenant Lester, who managed to reach here about a week ago. Like you and your sweet, brave children, he was helped and given shelter by friendly villagers but many others, alas, were not so fortunate."

Thinking of the four crudely marked graves she had left behind her at the river's edge, forty miles away, Harriet's throat ached with tears, but she said nothing. Only to Martin Gubbins did she reveal the fate of those who now rested beneath the small wooden crosses and he, patting her hand sympathetically, advised silence. "There is enough sadness and anxiety here already, my dear lady, and—as no doubt you will have observed—our turn is coming. We shall defend ourselves, of course, have no fear of that. Our preparations to do so are almost completed."

He was kindness itself, advancing Harriet a loan to enable her to give a generous reward to Mahee Singe before he returned to his village, and sending a servant with a note to the quarters of Colonel Inglis, the Commanding Officer of the Queen's 32nd Regiment, asking him to inform her sister and brother-in-law of her safe arrival.

"I believe they are here," Harriet said, gratefully sipping a glass of sherry which, when the note had been dispatched, her kindly host had poured for her. "The last time I heard from my sister, they were both in Cawnpore but expecting to remove here as soon as Tom—my brother-in-law, Tom Hill—had recovered from a bout of fever. My sister is expecting to be delivered of her first child . . ." She hesitated, seeing a frown crease Martin Gubbins's smooth brow, and then asked, filled with sudden fear, "Mr Gubbins, is it true that Cawnpore is under siege?"

He nodded, his frown deepening, "Yes, it's true, I'm sorry to say. The garrison was attacked on the sixth of June by mutinous native troops, commanded by the one man in whom poor old General Wheeler reposed implicit trust . . . the Nana of Bithur. They have held out with great gallantry in a mud-walled entrenchment—scarcely worthy of the name—on the south side of the city, the sole advantage of which appears to be that it is situated close to the Allahabad road. Pray God they will continue to hold out!"

"Don't you think they will?" Harriet asked. Again the Financial Commissioner hesitated, as if reluctant to distress her, and she said quietly, "Nothing can shock me now, Mr Gubbins, and I should be grateful if you would tell me the truth."

He sighed. "The latest news—a message from General Wheeler, delivered by *cossid* yesterday—warned that their losses have been heavy and cruel. The General has begged us for aid which, alas, Sir Henry Lawrence feels he dare not give, lest he weaken our own position irreparably. I, on the other hand, would send aid, no matter what the cost but . . . I am not in command. So I can only pray that the relief column from Calcutta will reach them in time. A column is on its way, commanded by Colonel Neill, but it consists of a single European regiment—the Madras Fusiliers—and it has been held up by outbreaks in Benares and Allahabad, according to the news we've had by electric telegraph. That is the truth, Mrs

Dorling." He shrugged disconsolately. "If that column doesn't get through, the consequences—both to General Wheeler's garrison and ourselves—don't bear thinking about . . ." He talked on, at times more to himself than to her, and Harriet finally left him with a heavy heart, to dress in a borrowed gown for a dinner, served in incongruous state, for which she had no appetite.

Mrs Case, wife of the second-in-command of the 32nd, called to see her when the lengthy and elaborate meal was over and Harriet sensed, from the look on her face, that the news she brought was the reverse of that for which she had hoped.

"Colonel Inglis asked me to call on you, Mrs Dorling, after he received the note concerning your sister from Mr Gubbins. I'm afraid that neither your sister nor her husband are here, with the regiment. They . . ." She paused, pity in her eyes, and Harriet said flatly, knowing the answer, "They're in Cawnpore?"

"Yes, my dear, I'm sorry to say they are. Captain and Mrs Moore, and Lieutenant and Mrs Wainwright are also there, with about seventy of our invalid men. But there is hope . . . they are still holding out and, as I'm sure Mr Gubbins will have told you, a relief force is trying to reach them. A European regiment, the Madras Fusiliers, commanded by Colonel James Neill, has got as far as Allahabad, and more troops—recalled from Burma and Persia—are being sent up country with all possible speed to join them. If General Wheeler can just hold out for another week or ten days, they will be saved."

"Yes," Harriet agreed but without conviction, feeling her control begin to slip. She had told Mr Gubbins that nothing could shock her now but this . . . She bit her lower lip, vainly attempting to still its trembling. Lavinia was so young, hardly more than a child herself, and she had been waiting so eagerly for the arrival of her baby . . . Oh, God, let them be saved, she prayed silently. All those poor, brave souls in their—what had Mr Gubbins called it? Their mud-walled entrenchment, scarcely worthy of the name . . . She remembered Jemmy and the others and shivered. Spare them that, at least, dear merciful God, spare them the fears and the horrors that I endured, spare my sister the death that poor Mrs Gowan suffered at the hands of men we trusted, who are now turned into fiends . . .

Mrs Case took a letter from her reticule. "This came— miraculously—by *dawk* from Calcutta. It is addressed to you *and* Mrs Hill, so Colonel Inglis thought you should be given it." She smiled, holding out her hand. "I'll leave you in peace to read it. If you want to reply, Captain Wilson, Sir Henry's Military Secretary, has arranged for a *cossid* to take letters to Benares. They must be *very* brief and sent to Captain Wilson's office by midnight and, as you'll understand, I'm sure, there's no certainty that they will reach their destination. Good night, Mrs Dorling, I do hope you'll sleep well and that you won't be too overcrowded and uncomfortable. If there's anything you need, such as clothing, for yourself or the children, you have only to make your needs known to me or to Mrs Gubbins."

Harriet thanked her. The letter, she saw, was from Graham. It consisted of only a few lines, announcing his arrival in command of the *Lady Wellesley* and informing her that Phillip was in China. "*There is something of a panic here in Calcutta,*" her brother had written. "*The news of mutiny in Meerut and the fall of Delhi to the mutinous regiments has caused considerable alarm among the people here. But Catriona and I have not changed our plans—we intend to take up residence and we are looking for a house of sufficient size to enable us to invite you both here, with your children, dearest Harriet and, we both hope, your new arrival, dearest Lavinia.*

"Come at once, if you can and the state of the country permits. Jemmy and Tom will, of course, have to remain at their posts—they are soldiers and will want to play their part in quelling the insurrection. But I do urge both of you to join us, if it is possible, without delay. If I am required to transport troops or supplies—as I well may be—Catriona will accompany me but the house will be yours. You have only to contact the shipping agents.

"Come, I beg you—the storm is gathering, without any doubt. Come before it breaks."

The storm *had* broken, Harriet thought, with infinite sadness; it had broken, in all its hideous violence, a few days after Graham had written his invitation. It had imprisoned her here, just as—she choked on a sob—just as it had imprisoned Lavinia and Tom in Cawnpore, and there would be no escape for any of them until it was over.

With borrowed pen and paper, she wrote a short reply, gave it, with the others, into the keeping of Captain Wilson's *chuprassi* and then, with the other occupants of the house, attended Evening Prayer in the garden.

There were daily services held in the various larger buildings in which women and children from cantonments and those who had fled from Oudh out-stations were housed and, each day, special prayers were said for the Cawnpore garrison. Harriet, with her two older children, joined fervently in them all but hope began to fade when it was learnt that General Wheeler had decided that further resistance was beyond the strength of his severely depleted garrison and that he was, in consequence, about to treat with the Nana Sahib of Bithur, who had offered terms for their surrender. No relief had reached them from Allahabad, all save two of their nine light-calibre guns had been put out of action, their supplies were all but exhausted, their crumbling breastwork, defended by sick and wounded soldiers, could no longer withstand assaults of the mutineers. Of close on a thousand souls—400 of them women and children—who had crowded into the entrenchment at the beginning of June, only 437 still survived, more than half incapacitated by wounds or fever.

One letter, written by Colonel Wiggins of the 53rd Native Infantry, reached Lucknow, and described the suffering endured by the garrison as "beyond anything ever written in history," adding that, with the temperature soaring to 130° and the larger of their two brick buildings destroyed by fire, the sun had been their greatest enemy. A second—a mere scrap of paper, dated 25th June and written by Lieutenant George Master of the same regiment to his father, a Colonel serving in the Lucknow garrison—also reached its destination. It read: *"We have held out now for 21 days, under a tremendous fire. The Rajah of Bithur has offered to forward us in safety by river to Allahabad and the General has accepted his terms. I have been twice wounded but am all right . . . I'll write from Allahabad. God bless you!"*

Ironically, on the same date, Sir Henry Lawrence received two dispatches from Colonel Neill, stating that—order having been restored in Allahabad and their lines of communication with Calcutta secured—an advance force of 400 European Fusiliers of his regiment, 300 Sikhs, and two guns was about to leave for Cawnpore. A further reinforcement of troops returned from Persia, under Brigadier-General Havelock, was hourly expected in Allahabad, also intended for the relief of Cawnpore.

This was good news and Lawrence immediately sent a

cossid to Cawnpore, urging General Wheeler to hold out and warning him, in a tersely worded postscript, written partly in French, *"You cannot rely on the Nana's promises. Il a tué beaucoup de prisonniers."* The message was never delivered. On 28th June, the native messenger returned with a companion and both were closeted for a long time with Martin Gubbins and Captain Hawes; after reporting to Sir Henry Lawrence, Martin Gubbins sadly informed the members of his household that no hope could now be entertained for General Wheeler's garrison. As Henry Lawrence had feared, the Nana had betrayed them. They had been promised honourable surrender and boats to convey them to Allahabad, but no sooner had they entered the boats than a savage attack had been launched on them, by armed sepoys and guns hidden among the trees above the landing stage, which had showered them with grape.

"My *cossids* witnessed this terrible massacre," Gubbins said, his voice harsh with pain. "And I have, alas, no reason to doubt that the account they have given me is true. The few women and children who survived the Nana's treacherous attack on their boats are being held prisoner in Cawnpore, near the Nana's encampment—perhaps as hostages. I have dispatched a *cossid* to Allahabad with this news. We must pray that the relief force will be in time to save the poor, unhappy souls."

Harriet heard him; her heart turned to stone, her grief too deep even for the relief of tears. That evening her baby was taken ill with colic and, on the advice of the Civil Surgeon, Dr Fayrer, she removed into his house with all three children, joining ten other ladies and seven children. Cholera had broken out among the European soldiers and two of the ladies lodging in the Residency were said to be dying of the disease. Although the kindly Dr Fayrer assured her that her baby's illness was not unduly serious, she watched over the poor mite anxiously, going without sleep in order to be on hand, day or night, should he need her. To while away the long hours of inactivity, she began a letter, in the form of a diary and, after earnest heart-searching, addressed her epistle to her brother Phillip who would, she knew, delete any upsetting details before passing the contents on to their parents.

At first, the letter was a catalogue of heartbreaking casualties among friends and acquaintances in Cawnpore and other neighbouring stations, as news of these filtered through, brought in by native *cossids* and spies. Every native regiment in Oudh and the Upper Provinces appeared to have risen in revolt and there was increasing concern in Lucknow itself, lest those in the garrison who continued to affirm their loyalty— in particular the Sikhs—should, in the end, betray Sir Henry Lawrence's trust in them. They were put to the test on 30th June, under which date Harriet recorded:

"At first light this morning, we were startled by the sound of guns passing this house. I learnt from Dr Partridge (a friend of Dr Fayrer's and one of the seven gentlemen who are quartered in his house) that, having received intelligence of a force of some four or five thousand rebels advancing to attack us, Sir Henry Lawrence was sending a detachment of three hundred of the 32nd, with the Volunteer and Sikh Cavalry, two hundred loyal sepoys, and seven guns to meet and, it was hoped, drive them back.

"You may imagine with what consternation we awaited news and, when it came, it filled us with despair. Sir Henry led our detachment himself and, it is now said that he ordered it out against his own better judgement, being taunted for want of spirit by some of his advisers when, initially, he objected to the proposal. When they reached the village of Chinhat, about six miles from the city, they found—instead of the small advance guard they

had expected to engage—a rebel army of between twelve and fourteen thousand, with thirty guns and a large force of cavalry awaiting them.

"Our poor soldiers of the 32nd had marched without breakfast, the last few miles under a blazing sun, no supplies of water or reserve ammunition came up—the natives in charge of the waggons having bolted with them—and to make matters worse, many of their muskets proved unserviceable through lack of use and would not fire. In spite of this, they fought gallantly and have over a hundred killed, wounded or missing, including poor Colonel Case (whose wife was so kind to me when I first reached here) and four other officers killed. The native gunners deserted to the enemy, many of the wretches making off with the gun ammunition, and the big howitzer, of which much had been hoped, was put out of action before it could open fire, and later taken by the rebels, with two or three others manned by golandazes.

"Sir Henry had no choice but to order a retreat. They fought their way back, under a hot pursuit, many of our poor 32nd collapsing from sunstroke and being cut to pieces as they fell. The pursuers were only halted at the Iron Bridge over the Goomtee by fire from gun batteries within the Residency defences, and by the valiant efforts of the Volunteer Cavalry—of whom there are only 36—and Captain Hardinge's Sikhs, who repeatedly charged the advancing mass of the enemy. On gaining the bridge some of the field-guns were placed across it—empty, for their ammunition was exhausted—but the gunners stood by them with lighted portfires and the rebels, who are arrant cowards, did not dare approach them.

"They could not be prevented from entering the city, however, and by nine o'clock we were in a state of siege and tremendous firing commenced, a fierce attack being launched on the Bailey Guard Gate, at the back of this house. We got a cup of tea and *breakfasted as well as we could, sitting behind walls to escape the firing . . ."*

By nightfall, the Residency perimeter was completely invested, the city in the mutineers' hands, and there was a wholesale desertion of native servants and of the hundreds of coolies who had been employed in the construction of earthworks and gun emplacements. But the work was virtually complete and, with an irregular cluster of houses and gardens, covering an area of 33 acres and with the three-storeyed Residency in the centre, the Lucknow garrison began the long ordeal of the siege.

Their fighting strength consisted of the Queen's 32nd—535 strong, before the Chinhat casualties had been accounted for— 50 men of the Queen's 84th, 89 European artillerymen, 105 British officers from mutinied native regiments, 153 clerks and male civilians capable of bearing arms, and 750 loyal sepoys and native pensioners. The loyal sepoys were mainly from the 13th Native Infantry and the Sikhs of the garrison, among them Hardinge's 86 cavalry sowars. The non-combatants included over 600 British women and children and already the hospital—a two-storey building near the Bailey Guard Gate— was crowded with wounded, sick, and dying men. The rest, many of them spent and weary after their fighting retreat from Chinhat, spread themselves out to defend their perimeter of trenches and earthworks and loopholed houses, and to man the batteries of light guns which had been set up at regular intervals along each front. Dr Fayrer's house became a miniature fortress, under the command of Captain Weston of the Police, with an officer and twenty soldiers of the Queen's 84th, and a mixed party of Europeans and native pensioners to work the 18- and 19-pounder guns mounted in the compound.

The women and children were sent for safety to an underground room called the Tye Khana of which Harriet wrote: *"It is damp, dark, and as gloomy as a vault . . . and excessively dirty. Here we sit all day, feeling too anxious, miserable, and terrified to speak and here, also, we are compelled to sleep, with our bedding spread on the floor. The first night we spent there, the house was under a very heavy fire. I was so worried about poor Baby and— although so far they are keeping well—about Augusta and little Phillip, that I was almost beside myself and did not close my eyes. Bless them, both the children are obedient and well-behaved and they do all in their power to help me care for Baby. Phillip even feeds him spoonfuls of sugar and water when I doze off from sheer exhaustion, knowing that Dr Fayrer has ordered this—his sole refreshment—every hour. But he is so weak, my heart bleeds for him, poor little creature . . ."*

On the 2nd July the worst blow to morale the garrison had yet suffered fell without warning. Sir Henry Lawrence, whose staff had repeatedly begged him to remove to safer quarters, still occupied a room in the upper storey of the Residency which—only the previous day—had been damaged by a shell from the howitzer captured at Chinhat. He had promised to vacate the room but, on waking, was lying on his bed dictating orders to his military secretary, Captain Thomas Wilson, when a second shell entered the room and exploded there in a blinding sheet of flame. Wilson and Sir Henry's nephew, George, were both hurled to the floor beneath a cascade of shattered brickwork, where they lay stunned.

Wilson was the first to drag himself to his feet, dazed but uninjured, calling out frantically, "Sir Henry, are you hurt?" He called twice before Henry Lawrence answered him, in a low, shaken voice, "I am killed, Tom." Horrified, Wilson and George Lawrence groped their way through a pile of debris to the bed, glimpsing a slowly spreading crimson stain on the once-white sheet which covered its occupant. When the dust settled, they saw that his left leg had been smashed to pulp just below the hip and it was evident, before Sir Henry invited their confirmation, that his wound was mortal. He was moved to the verandah of Dr Fayrer's house, to die there thirty-six hours later.

Harriet, who had watched her poor baby die during the night, shared the vigil at Sir Henry's bedside with Dr Fayrer and the Chaplain, the Reverend James Harris, whose young wife alternated with her in such nursing duties as could be performed. Listening to the dying man's anguished screams, audible even above the incessant roar of the guns, she came closer to despair than she had ever been and, when Lawrence's long agony was over, she wrote sadly to Phillip:

"We have lost the brave, noble, and farsighted man who made our defence of this place possible because, months ago—whilst others procrastinated and did nothing, swearing that there was no danger—he planned and prepared for it. If any of us survive, it will be thanks to Sir Henry Lawrence, who died an hour ago.

"They carried him here, mortally wounded but fully conscious, and the Chaplain, the Reverend Harris, administered Holy Communion to him. Although in terrible pain, with his leg all but taken off at the thigh, he spoke for nearly an hour, quite calmly, expressing his last wishes regarding his children. He sent affectionate messages to them and to his brothers and sisters; he particularly mentioned the Lawrence Asylum and entreated that Government might be urged to give it support. He named Major Banks as his successor in chief authority here, and then he bade farewell to all the gentlemen who were standing about his bed and said a few words of advice and kindness to each. His nephew, Mr George Lawrence, he blessed most affectionately; and expressed the

deepest penitence and remorse for his own sins and the most per-
fect trust and faith in his Saviour.

"There was not a dry eye there; everyone was grieved and
affected by the loss of such a man, and we all felt as if our best
friend and staunchest support were being taken from us. I shall
never, as long as I live, forget the despair which seemed to take
possession of us, as if our last hope were gone.

"All day and all night he lingered in extreme suffering and the
screams and groans which were wrung from him were terrible to
hear. Save when under the influence of chloroform, he was in pos-
session of his senses to the last, and he frequently repeated the
words of the prayers and psalms the Chaplain read to him.
Throughout the day, the enemy directed their fire particularly at
this house, as if somehow they had learnt that Sir Henry had been
brought here, and several officers waiting on the verandah to pay
their last respects to him were shot and wounded. Among them
were his poor nephew, Mr George Lawrence, who was shot in the
shoulder, and Mr Ommaney, the Judicial Commissioner who, it is
feared, will not recover.

"I was not there when he died but Mrs Harris told me that
his end was peaceful. It came at a quarter past eight this morn-
ing—Saturday, 4th July—and his last words, uttered most urgently,
were, 'Entrench, entrench . . . let every man die at his post, but
never make terms!' After that, he spoke his wife's name, very softly,
and slipped into unconsciousness, a smile on his lips as, at last,
the terrible pain left him.

"He was buried after darkness fell but such was the combat
raging along every front of our defences that no officers could be
spared to attend him. Chaplain Harris and four soldiers of the
32nd carried him to his grave and Mr Harris told us, when he
returned, that Sir Henry had asked to be buried in a common

*grave, without fuss, with any others of the garrison who might die
during the day.*

*"My own poor Baby's loss pales into insignificance beside the
enormity of this one, yet both torment me sorely as, alas, does the
nightmare fear that our dearest Lavinia may be amongst those
poor hostages held prisoner by the treacherous Nana in Cawnpore.
We all feel sure that the Nana will not spare them—he and his
kind show mercy to none. If you ever read this letter, Phillip, spare
Mamma and Papa, what you can should the dreadful rumours of
their suffering, which reach us here, prove to be true."*

Harriet put down her pen, folded the pages she had
written and placed them carefully in the reticule Mrs Harris
had lent her. The guns were still thundering out their menace
as she lay down on the uneven floor of the Tye Khana beside
her two surviving children and closed her tired and red-
rimmed eyes.

For the first time in many years, she did not offer up her
nightly prayer—God, it seemed, had deserted them in their
hour of need and she no longer had the heart to call on Him
in vain. For Lavinia's sake—if the rumours which spies brought
back from Cawnpore were true—she could only pray that
death might be merciful and swift and this, as yet, she could
not bring herself to do . . .

It had come as a relief to Lavinia Hill when, after enduring a
prolonged and painful labour, the son to whom she had given
birth was stillborn. She had shed no tears for the poor mite—
had, indeed, envied it the oblivion it had found—and Captain
Moore's grieving widow, Caroline, when breaking the news,
had offered no words of commiseration for her loss.

Lavinia had expected none. Death, in its most hideous
and degrading guises, was no stranger to the Nana's unhappy

captives . . . already it had robbed the married women of their husbands, the children of their parents, and to many of the sickly, broken-hearted survivors of the British garrison of Cawnpore its advent was a welcome end to unendurable torment. True, their hopes had been briefly rekindled by the sound of heavy gunfire the previous evening, and the bolder spirits had cried out that, at long last, a relief column was on its way to effect their rescue, but the Commander of their sepoy guard had stoutly denied any such possibility and, after a few dispirited prayers, they had sunk again into the apathy induced by their state of near-starvation and the appalling heat.

There were over two hundred of them herded, like sheep, into the yellow-painted brick building, known as the Bibigarh, in the centre of Cawnpore's native city. It was flat-roofed and comprised two main rooms, each about twenty feet by ten feet, with four dark closets at the corners, less than ten feet square. The doors and windows, with the exception of the entrance, were secured by wooden bars and, in the walled courtyard which surrounded it, sepoy sentries patrolled, night and day, to ensure that none could escape. The bungalow had been built originally by a British officer for his native mistress, from whence the name—House of Women—had been derived. Hot and airless, lacking all save the most primitive of sanitary arrangements, the building had been used lately as a store for medical records and would scarcely have been adequate for the accommodation of a single family in normal conditions. As a prison for two hundred ailing European women and children, the Bibigarh was a torture chamber, adding degradation to the mental torment already inflicted upon them by their inhuman captors.

Deaths from cholera, dysentery, and wounds daily and inevitably reduced their number; a diet of husked grain, dried lentils and water left them with little resistance to infection, and the shock of seeing their loved ones butchered in front of them had robbed all but the most courageous of the will to live. A hundred and twenty-five of them had survived the massacre on the banks of the Ganges. When, at length, the Nana had called a halt to the savage slaughter, they had been driven at musket-point into a building near the river, the Savada Koti, which already housed a number of Eurasian families arrested in the city and forty fugitives from an up-river station, whose menfolk had also been massacred. There they had been left for 24 hours, without food, water, or medical aid, before being moved to their present quarters in bullock carts, jeered at and derided by mobs from the bazaars.

Clumsy and ungainly with the dead weight of the child she carried and stunned by the loss of her husband, who had been shot down at her side, Lavinia had prayed for death during that ghastly journey, expecting to meet it at the hands of their sepoy escort as they marched beside the slow-moving bullock carts, shrieking insults with the rest. But, strangely, in the Bibigarh a native doctor had been waiting and, to his eternal credit, he had done what he could for the sick and wounded. It was little enough—he was only one man, faced by a multitude of dazed and tormented souls—but Lavinia treasured the memory of the kindness he had shown her and the skill and gentleness he had displayed when her premature labour had begun.

Now, crouched in a corner of one of the dark, malodorous closets which opened off the main living room of their prison, she watched the dawn of the eighteenth day of their captivity, straining her ears for the sound of gunfire which, Caroline Moore had assured her when taking her leave the previous evening, they would hear at first light . . . if a relief column were indeed on its way to Cawnpore. But, as the sun rose, its rays slanting through the barred windows to herald the heat that was to come, she heard only the subdued murmurs of the sepoy guards and the shrilly raised voice of Hosainee Khanum—ayah to the Nana's courtesan—who had been put in charge of the prison servants. These—a *bhisti* and a motley gang of low caste sweepers—were supposed to supply the captives with water and keep the rooms they occupied swept and scoured but, in such over-crowded conditions, the task was beyond them. Of late they had done little more each morning than remove the bodies of any who died, depositing the meagre rations of the living on the dirty, neglected floor, where a horde of flies immediately settled on anything edible.

Two of their unpleasant servitors came shuffling into Lavinia's dark refuge, grumbling under the lash of Hosainee's tongue, to fling down a *chatti* of water and some parched grain and, after a cursory inspection of the sick women lying there, one called out sullenly that all were yet living and made to depart, ignoring Lavinia's plea that he place the water within reach of those who had not the strength to sit up.

"We shall die without water," she reproached him in halting, newly learnt Hindustani.

"You will all die before nightfall," the man retorted brutally. "You and the *feringhi* soldiers who seek to save you!"

Lavinia drew in her breath sharply. His was the first admission any of them had made of the presence of a relief column but, when she attempted to question him, the *mehtar* denied it.

"I know nothing, save that no British soldiers will reach here. The Nana Sahib's victorious army will destroy them when they approach the Panda Nudi River. Perhaps they are already destroyed."

One of the sick women raised herself on her elbow, her

thin, pale face suddenly alight with joy. "He is lying," she said. "Just listen, Mrs Hill—listen! The guns are firing again . . . oh, heaven be praised! Our troops are not destroyed—they are coming nearer!"

She was right, Lavinia realised, her heart quickening its beat. Faintly at first but steadily growing in volume, the roar of heavy guns could distinctly be heard and, throughout the morning, the sounds of battle continued to reach the prisoners in the Bibigarh, reviving their flagging spirits and putting new life even into those for whom, a few hours before, their native physician had held out little hope. He—the only one of their gaolers who had shown them pity or kindness—freely admitted that a British relief column was within less than a day's march of Cawnpore.

"They are few—not more than a handful—but they are led by a resolute General whose name, I am told, is Havelock, and they fight like tigers. Since leaving Allahabad just over a week ago, they have marched a hundred and twenty miles and have three times defeated the Nana Sahib's army . . . and now, I have just heard, they have fought their way across the Panda Nudi. The Nana's brother, Bala Bhat, was wounded in the battle and it is said that his General of Cavalry, Teeka Singh, had his elephant killed under him. Their troops flee the field like jackals as soon as General Havelock's redcoat soldiers are sighted. Soon, ladies, your countrymen will be here to set you free and your terrible ordeal will be over!"

They hung on his words, repeating them to each other again and again as the long day wore on, their hopes bolstered by the now almost ceaseless thunder of the guns, some of which, by their proximity to the city, they recognised as being the Nana's. Soon, Lavinia thought, soon they would be released from this awful place, they would be safe, guarded by British soldiers, their suffering at an end. Fighting off her weakness, she struggled to her feet to join those who waited by the door of their prison, eager to be among the first to greet their rescuers. They prayed, weeping, and sang hymns, their voices choked with tears, the sick, the wounded, and many of the children joining in.

It fell to Hosainee Khanum to shatter their brittle hopes of rescue. The woman had been absent for several hours; when she returned, one of the Eurasian captives abused her and rounding on her savagely, the ayah said with conscious malice that the Nana had ordered their execution.

"Pray rather that the *feringhi* soldiers never reach here, *mem!*" she added. "For you will die before the first *lal-kote* sets foot in the city!"

There was a stunned, unhappy silence; then, as the woman to whom she had spoken burst into a paroxysm of weeping, others passed on the brief and terrible words she had uttered and pandemonium ensued.

Caroline Moore restored them to calm. "I will ask the Jemadar of our guard," she volunteered. "If our execution has indeed been ordered, it is he who will have received the order. The Nana would not have given it to a serving woman . . . Hosainee must surely be lying in order to frighten us."

A number of them accompanied her to the barred window at the front of the building and Yusef Khan, the Jemadar, came in response to their cries. At first he denied all knowledge of the Nana's order but finally, with evident reluctance, admitted that Hosainee had brought him verbal instructions that the hostages were to be shot if the British column attempted to attack Cawnpore.

"You have nothing to fear at our hands," he assured his anxious questioners. "Without a written order."

"But our soldiers *will* attack," Caroline Moore stated with conviction. "Nothing is more certain. And when they do, then you—"

"If they do, Memsahib, they will be defeated," the native officer put in. "They are few and we are many and the Nana Sahib has placed great guns to cover the road." But he was plainly uneasy; head on one side he, too, was listening to the guns, affecting not to see Hosainee's angry attempts to attract his attention.

"If you preserve our lives, General Havelock will reward you," a Colonel's white-haired widow promised recklessly. Others reiterated this promise and the Jemadar hesitated, torn between fear and duty. Clearly he had heard of the Nana's defeat at the Panda Nudi, Lavinia thought and, in the hope of resolving his uncertainty, she said quietly, "If you take our lives and General Havelock's soldiers learn of it, they will not rest until retribution has been meted out to you. They may be few but they have been victorious whenever they have met the Nana's army in battle—and there will be more, many thousands more, following after them from Calcutta and from England itself."

Yusef Khan hesitated but, when Hosainee raised her voice in shrill protest, he silenced her with a contemptuous, "Your order will not be obeyed. Who are you to give orders? Bring me it in writing, under the Nana Sahib's signature and seal!" She flung away from him and the Jemadar went on, lowering his voice, "Do not fear, Memsahibs, we will not harm you. But so as not to incur the Nana's wrath, should the serving woman bring us a written order, we will fire through the windows into the walls and ceiling. If you lie down, our musket balls will not touch you."

The prisoners thanked him tearfully but Hosainee had

again vanished and, still apprehensive, at the suggestion of Mrs Tucker, the Colonel's widow, they tore strips from their dresses and petticoats, with which they endeavoured to secure the door. Exhausted by their efforts, they sank down behind it to join once again in prayer, mothers clasping their children to them in nameless fear when, from somewhere close at hand, they heard the crackle of musketry. Fear became panic when Yusef Khan shouted through the window that their kindly little doctor and the sweepers who had served them had been shot, on Hosainee Khanum's instructions.

"The woman comes back, Memsahibs!" he warned. "The time has come . . . lie down, that we may fire over your heads!"

In the gathering dusk, the terrified prisoners watched Hosainee's approach. With her were five men, one wearing the scarlet uniform of the Nana's bodyguard, the other four peasants of low caste, two, by their stained white robes, butchers from the Moslem bazaar. All were armed with hatchets and knives, the bodyguard with a *tulwar,* and they strode arrogantly past the sepoy guard who—having fired a ragged volley through the barred windows—stood helplessly by, as Hosainee waved a paper at the Jemadar.

"The order!" she sneered. "I bring the Nana Sahib's sealed order, Yusef Khan. March your men from the compound if they fear to carry it out!"

Crouched behind the door, Lavinia heard its timbers crack as the men outside put their shoulders to it. Within the dirty, littered room that had been their prison, the poor hostages waited petrified, the children wailing as, one by one, pathetic wisps of cloth which held the door shut burst from its hinges.

Aware that her last hour had come, Lavinia dragged herself to her feet. The Bible which Tom had given her on their wedding day was in her hands. Trembling uncontrollably, her voice a tiny whisper of sound inaudible above the shrieks and sobs which filled the room, she placed herself in front of two cowering children and began to read from the 23rd Psalm . . .

It was dark when Hosainee Khanum's butchers emerged from the Bibigarh and the heartrending cries which had issued from its shuttered windows faded at last to a deathly silence. Barely six miles away, the guns of General Havelock's relief force continued to fire, as the streets of Cawnpore started to echo to the running feet of fleeing mutineers and the Nana Sahib—himself a fugitive from the battle—prepared to follow his retreating army.

CHAPTER FIVE

On 6th August the *Shannon*, in company with the corvette *Pearl*, arrived off the mouth of the Ganges. Soundings were taken, the ship put under easy sail, and a jack hoisted for a pilot. Under his guidance, the frigate steamed through the dull and muddy waters to the mouth of the Hoogly and then up river, with thick, luxuriant jungle on either bank, broken only by mud flats and innumerable small islands which, with their tangled vegetation and basking crocodiles, looked anything but inviting.

On nearing Calcutta, the east bank of the river—called Garden Reach—became more attractive, with its well-kept gardens and pleasure grounds and white painted bungalows and, passing beneath the gun batteries and green slopes of Fort William, the *Shannon* was enthusiastically cheered. At five o'clock on the evening of 8th August, she dropped anchor off the Esplanade, firing a 19-gun salute. Lord Elgin disembarked at once and was driven to Government House to consult with the Governor-General, Lord Canning, and Captain Peel accompanied him.

Phillip also went ashore, anxious to find his brother Graham, only to learn that the *Lady Wellesley* had sailed over a week before for Mauritius to pick up troops. He called at the shipping office, hoping that the letter he had posted to his brother before leaving Hong Kong might have reached him to find, to his chagrin, that the letter was amongst a batch addressed to Graham and Catriona which was being held in the office, pending their return. On his identifying himself, the clerk told him that his brother had taken the lease of a furnished bungalow at Garden Reach and had left instructions that this was to be placed at the disposal of any member of his family who might arrive in Calcutta in his absence.

"He has given me two names, Commander," the clerk volunteered, leafing swiftly through the little pile of papers on his desk. "Yes, here they are . . . Mrs James Dorling and Mrs Thomas Hill. His—that is, your sisters, I presume, sir?"

Phillip nodded, tight-lipped. He cut short the clerk's offer to give him the keys of Graham's newly acquired residence and asked if there had been news of either of his sisters. "I was hoping that there might be a letter or letters, perhaps. They would be addressed to my brother, of course."

The clerk hesitated, eyeing him uncertainly. He was a young man, well mannered and anxious to please but clearly he doubted his authority to hand over mail to anyone to whom it was not addressed. "Where would such a letter or letters be from, sir?" he enquired cautiously.

"From the Upper Provinces—Lucknow probably. Or Cawnpore."

The clerk paled. "I trust not from Cawnpore, Commander. Have you not heard the news—the terrible news of what occurred there?"

Phillip shook his head. "I heard that it was under siege. There was a rumour in Singapore that terms for surrender had been asked for by General Wheeler and a wild tale of a massacre but neither had been confirmed when we sailed. We . . ."

The expression on the young clerk's face froze the words in

his throat. "For God's sake, man, surely it can't be true?"

"Unhappily the tale of the massacre is only too true, sir. Everyone here is still sickened by it, sickened and angry." In a few brief and bitter sentences, the boy described what had happened following the garrison's surrender and went on, "The survivors of the ghastly slaughter in the boats numbered about a hundred and twenty women and children, and the Nana confined them, with other poor fugitives from Fategarh, in a small house known as the Bibigarh in the centre of the native city. General Havelock was aware of this, sir, when he left Allahabad with his relief force and he made the most strenuous efforts to save them. He had a very small force, fewer than a thousand European troops, and they marched a hundred and twenty-six miles in ten days, fighting four successful actions against the Nana's army. The General re-captured Cawnpore on the sixteenth of July, sir, but that foul fiend, the Nana Sahib, had butchered our poor, defenceless countrywomen the day before, when he knew himself to be defeated. He fled the city, attempting to deceive his own people with a simulated suicide, but he is believed to be in alliance now with the rebels who are besieging Lucknow."

Phillip expelled his breath in a long-drawn sigh, feeling his stomach churn. It was a ghastly story, worse than anything he had ever imagined and he listened, only half taking in the horror of what was happening in India, as the clerk went on to recount other stories of uprisings in isolated stations, his young voice harsh with disillusionment.

"Is Lucknow still holding out?" Phillip asked, when the boy came to the end of his recital.

"Yes, sir. Despite the tragic loss they suffered when Sir Henry Lawrence was killed."

"Sir Henry Lawrence is *dead?*"

"Alas, sir, he is . . . he was killed at the beginning of the siege. News filters through, messages are carried by loyal native runners. We hear few details, just bare facts but it is believed that Sir Henry was killed when his room at the Residency was struck by a shell. General Havelock marched from Cawnpore on the twenty-eighth of last month to the relief of the Lucknow garrison. We heard that he had twice defeated the rebels and reached a town called Busseratgunj, thirty-six miles from Lucknow, but that heavy casualties and losses from cholera among his British troops might compel him to retreat. It is to be hoped that's not true." The clerk sighed. "Many people here feel that had the command of the relief force been confided to Colonel Neill—the officer who saved Benares and Allahabad, sir—Lucknow would have been relieved by now. But Colonel Neill has been left to command the force holding Cawnpore . . ." He talked on, extolling the merits of Colonel Neill and Phillip, recovering himself, interrupted him.

"Forgive me but . . . I have been a long time without news. One of my sisters, Mrs Dorling, was in Sitapur, I believe—that's an out-station, about forty miles north of Lucknow. Did you hear what happened there?"

"The native regiments mutinied in Sitapur, sir, as they did virtually everywhere else in Oudh. But"—the clerk frowned, in effort to remember—"I do recall hearing that a number of ladies from Sitapur managed to reach Lucknow. I very much hope that your sister was amongst them, I . . ." He hesitated, again leafing through the small pile of Graham's mail. "There's a note here, sir, addressed to Captain Hazard of the *Lady Wellesley*. I believe it came via Allahabad and is from Lucknow, smuggled out before the Residency was invested. In the circumstances, Captain Hazard surely would not object to my permitting you to read it, do you think, sir?"

"No, he would not." The boy had the note in his hand, still hesitating, and Phillip leaned forward and took it from him. The writing, he saw, was Harriet's and a wave of thankfulness swept over him when he opened it and read the heading and the date. On June 15th Harriet had been in the Residency at Lucknow, Harriet and . . . oh, heaven be thanked, her three children!

His throat ached as he read the rest of the note.

"We are permitted only a few lines," Harriet had written. *"My beloved Jemmy is dead, murdered by his own sepoys, but the children and I have come here safely and are lodged with other fugitives. There is no chance of our leaving until relief is sent. I have just been told that Lavinia and Tom are still in Cawnpore. Pray God they may be saved."*

"Is it—good news, Commander?" the clerk ventured.

For a moment, his thoughts with Lavinia, Phillip could not answer him. Then, controlling himself, he said flatly, "Yes, I thank you—my sister, Mrs Dorling, is in Lucknow." He returned the letter and, requesting pen and paper, left a note of his own for Graham. "I can be contacted aboard the *Shannon*," he told the clerk and was about to take his leave, after thanking the boy for his trouble, when a thought struck him. "Do you know whether any casualty lists have been published here?"

The clerk's eyes held pity. "A number, yes, sir. They're published each week. The Cawnpore casualty list isn't complete—I mean, all the lists are being added to and occasionally some names are deleted. Usually the officers and their wives who are known to be at each station are listed and the newspapers state that their present whereabouts is subject to confirmation, I . . . there are copies in our files, sir. It would not take me very long to extract any copies you wished to see and bring them to you."

"Thank you," Phillip managed. "Then the Cawnpore list, if you please."

He waited for twenty minutes, pacing restlessly up and down the office, watched curiously by its other occupants, and then the boy who had attended him returned and silently handed him copies of two Calcutta newspapers, folded open to reveal the list he had requested. He took them, his hands not quite steady and almost instantly the name he had been hoping not to see leapt out at him from the printed page. *"Hill, Lieutenant and Mrs T. F., H.M.'s 32nd Regiment . . ."* So Harriet's information had been correct, he thought dully. Tom and Lavinia were both dead, both . . . murdered.

He returned to the ship like a man living a nightmare, savage anger in his heart. His mother and father would have to be told, of course, but he postponed writing to inform them, unable to bring himself to commit what he had learned to paper. As the clerk had said, the lists of casualties had to be confirmed—it was possible that, at the last minute, Tom had been transferred, sent to join his regiment in Lucknow, perhaps or . . . He lay down on his cot without undressing and remained there, not sleeping but staring into space, his thoughts unbearable torment.

Next day, Captain Peel announced to his assembled ship's company that Lord Elgin had instructed him to place both *Shannon* and *Pearl* at the disposal of the Indian Government. "Arrangements are being made for the formation of a Naval Brigade to assist in quelling the mutiny, my lads," he told them. "The first four hundred men will leave here for Allahabad within a week, all being well, under my command. We shall be taking some of the ship's guns with us." The men, who had heard the story of the Cawnpore massacre, cheered him until they were hoarse.

Events moved rapidly after that. On 10th August, the troops were disembarked; on the 11th, the three hundred marines from the *Sanspareil* marched ashore to do duty as garrison troops in Fort William, and the *Pearl*—held up in the river—made her appearance to disembark the two hundred men of the 90th Light Infantry to whom she had given passage from Singapore. Two other transports arrived, bringing a wing of the 5th Fusiliers and two companies of the 59th Regiment, all of whom were dispatched up country by rail and road.

Phillip's hopes of a rapid journey to Allahabad by the same means were dashed when William Peel told him that it had been decided to send the Naval Brigade up by river, taking with them ten of the *Shannon*'s sixty-eight-pounder guns, with four hundred rounds of shot and shell for each gun, brass field-pieces, a twenty-four-pounder howitzer and eight rocket-tubes. On 13th, a large flat-transport, the *Gamma,* came alongside and the guns were hoisted out and loaded aboard her, together with medical and clothing supplies, tents, haversacks, water-bottles, and boots furnished by the military authorities. The men were issued with waterproof capes and cotton covers and sun-curtains to attach to their straw hats, and Minié or Enfield rifles, bayonets, and ammunition.

At 2 p.m. on Tuesday, 18th August, a ninety-horsepower steamer, the *Chunar,* was waiting in readiness for departure, with the straw-thatched flat in tow. Lord Elgin came on board the *Shannon* to address the men about to proceed on service and, an hour later, the first division of the Naval Brigade, three hundred and ninety strong, embarked in the steamer and the flat. As the *Chunar* got under way, those remaining aboard the

Shannon and the entire company of the *Pearl* lined the decks or ascended the rigging to exchange cheers, the *Pearl* saluting with seven guns.

Progress was, however, extremely slow. The *Chunar* developed a faulty feed-pipe and, on 20th August, unable to make any headway against the current for lack of steam, she was compelled to anchor off Barrackpore and Peel wrathfully sent the cutter, with Lieutenant Hay, to demand that she be replaced.

"Damned inefficiency!" Peel complained, to Phillip. "Devil take their so-called engineers! I'm going to put young Bone to supervise the engine room, if and when they manage to rake up another steamer for us. We're not having this again."

The *Chunar* was replaced by the *River Bird* the following day but her Commander contrived to foul the flat when endeavouring to take her in tow. After this had been dealt with, Peel had fresh reason for annoyance when, due to an error, a double ration of grog was issued to the seamen and Marines aboard the flat, and none to those who had transferred to the newly arrived *River Bird.* Led by a petty officer named Oates, a number of men came aft to demand aggrievedly that they be issued with their ration and the young Swedish officer, Lind, who had the deck, perforce refused their request, since no supplies had yet been received from the *Chunar.* The man replied insolently; Peel, who had been within earshot, promptly placed him under arrest and next day disrated him to able-seaman, with the forfeiture of his two Good Conduct badges.

"We may have a month of this," Peel said, when Oates and his escort had marched away. "The men have got to be made to work off their impatience—they're all so damned keen to come to grips with the mutineers and avenge Cawnpore that any delay upsets them. Well, we'll turn the inevitable delays to our advantage." He turned to Phillip, grinning boyishly. "I've been wondering what to do with you, Commander Hazard, but now, by heaven, I've got the answer! You shall take charge of training."

"Certainly, sir," Phillip agreed readily. "I take it you want your seamen transformed into soldiers?"

"Into *good* soldiers, Phillip. I want them to march and form square, exercise with the bayonet, learn to repel cavalry and to manhandle the guns, use the rifles effectively and, by God, drill like Marines! Above all, I want them to sweat, so that we'll have no more trouble from lads like Oates, due to inaction and boredom. They'll have to perform their routine duties, of course—hump stores, coal ship, and man the boats—this will be in addition. They shall have their grog all right but they'll earn every last drop of it . . . will you see to it that they do?"

"I will, sir," Phillip assured him. "Very gladly." He, too, was anxious to be distracted from the torment of his own thoughts and to regain fully his physical fitness, and he found release and a considerable measure of satisfaction in the results of the training programme he organised.

Each day, at first light, as steamer and flat steamed slowly up the broad and, at times tempestuous River Ganges, he exercised the small-arms men in rifle and infantry drill, dividing them into sections. The deck of the broad-beamed flat provided sufficient space for most of the drills, and he encouraged friendly rivalry between the various sections and the 50-strong Royal Marine contingent, whose two officers ran an unofficial "book" aided by the seamen's Divisional Officers, Edward Hay and Nowell Salmon.

During the heat of the day, lectures on military tactics occupied the men in batches, alternating with others covering such subjects as hygiene and first aid to the injured, given by the medical staff, and basic Hindustani and general talks on India and its people, contributed by one of the *River Bird*'s officers. At sunset, when both steamer and flat dropped anchor for the night, parties were landed to drill with field guns, practise infantry manoeuvres and make route marches and, before long, the *Shannon*'s "Jacks" became almost as competent in their military duties as they had previously been at sea.

They grumbled, as all British seamen will, but they worked hard and kept fit and, even when Phillip made attendence at certain lecture sessions voluntary, the numbers did not noticeably diminish. Breaches of discipline became fewer and finally almost ceased and William Peel's greatest anxiety was the number of men struck down by cholera, nine of whom died during the long, slow voyage up river. On reaching Dinapore on 10th September, a number of men had to be put ashore for hospital treatment and the *River Bird*—proving, in her turn, unserviceable—was replaced by the steamer *Mirzapore*. That evening, after transferring stores to their new ship, the entire Naval Brigade marched through the city headed by their band, to drill on one of the regimental parade grounds before an enthusiastic audience of British residents and troops, the bandsmen exchanging their Enfields for musical instruments for the first time since leaving Calcutta.

Phillip was pleased with the way the men acquitted themselves. They might still make mistakes in wheeling and other more complex manoeuvres, but their small-arms drill and their smart handling of the six-pounder brass guns evoked numerous compliments from the senior army officers who witnessed it. Disappointment was, however, in store for them—there was now no possibility that the Brigade would reach Allahabad in time to catch up with the troop reinforcements being pushed forward in a final attempt to relieve the hard-pressed Lucknow garrison. General Havelock, whose gallant little force had been reduced by cholera, dysentery, sunstroke, and rebel bullets to a mere eight hundred bayonets, had been compelled to retire to Cawnpore where, after defeating the pick of the Nana's army in a bravely fought battle at Bithur, they were now waiting for reinforcements to reach them.

"They've appointed General Sir James Outram to command this Division, which includes Cawnpore," a grey-haired Colonel stated with a shrug. "Recalled him posthaste from Persia, to supersede poor old Havelock, who's done as well as any Commander could, with the few regiments they gave him. But Outram has taken the Fifth and the Ninetieth from here and, if I know anything about him, he won't rob Henry Havelock of the glory if they succeed in relieving Lucknow. And Sir Colin Campbell's now Commander-in-Chief, which means there'll be no more dragging of feet in Calcutta. If we could just hear that Delhi's been recaptured, morale would soar sky-high. It's been a terrible business, though . . . and we've had our anxieties here, under a Commander who . . . well, I won't say any more, since he's been replaced. But firm action with the native regiments here would have given Havelock both the Fifth and the Ninetieth at the time he asked for them."

On Saturday, 12th September, the *Mirzapore* cast off with the flat in tow but, six miles above Dinapore, she was compelled to anchor, being unable to stem the current with her heavy tow. Phillip, accompanied by Lieutenant Nowell Salmon, returned to the city they had just left in the cutter to request the aid of a second steamer. The *Koel* was sent the following day, lashed alongside the flat to assist in towing and then, within two hours, the *Mirzapore* ran aground on a sandbank. She was got off, after some strenuous work, only to find that the *Koel*'s hawsers had parted and the flat was adrift. By 16th September, they had progressed no further than Durnapur and all three vessels were compelled by fading light to drop anchor.

Three more men died of cholera and fifty-one fell sick during the next two days; the *Koel,* her bunkers empty, returned to Dinapore to replenish them and Captain Peel ordered the flat to be lightened by transferring shot to the *Mirzapore,* but no sooner had this operation been completed than the steamer again took the ground. Finally when the *Koel* returned, she was refloated, but not before her worn hawsers had twice more parted and the extra shot, moved to her from the flat, had been loaded aboard the *Koel.*

On 22nd September, a wind of almost cyclone force struck the river from the westward and continued from 2:30 in the afternoon until dawn on the 23rd, again compelling the three vessels to anchor as it blew across the flat countryside on both banks, bringing a heavy rainstorm in its wake. The rain swelled the river to a muddy torrent, with every sort of flotsam hurtling down on the current, including native bodies in various stages of decomposition, which the *Shannon*'s seamen studied with growing excitement until informed by one of the steamer's officers that—far from being casualties from a British victory—they were the bodies of poor villagers, dead of natural causes, whose families were too poor to provide sufficient firewood for their funeral pyres.

On the 24th, with another man dead and 47 still sick with cholera or dysentery, the Brigade landed at Ghazipore, spending the next four days in barracks there and—on Peel's insistence—continuing with a full programme of training. On the evening of the 27th, the shore parties re-embarked in the *Koel* and the flat, leaving Lieutenant Wilson with the sick in the charge of an Indian Army surgeon and, after more frustrating delays caused by the inability of the two small steamers to make any headway against the current of the river, finally anchored off Benares City at three o'clock on the afternoon of 30th September.

Phillip had heard and read much about Benares and, at first sight, was as impressed by its size and extent and by the beauty of its graceful minarets and swelling domes as by the numerous flights of stone steps descending the river bank, which seemed always to be crowded with native pilgrims, come to bathe in the sacred waters of the river they called "Mother Ganges." On landing, however, he found it to be much less attractive than it had appeared from the deck of the flat. The magnificent mosques and temples were still imposing, but the approaches to them were filthy, the streets narrow and ill-kept, bordered on each side by mud-built native houses and teeming with people, with animals roaming at will, both in and outside the buildings. Although the fires of mutiny and rebellion had only recently been extinguished, the *Shannon's* landing party met with no hostility from the populace in general; a motley throng of beggars—many of them hideously deformed and crippled—followed them with plaintive cries, but the people seemed, for the most part, apathetic and indifferent to their presence, passing them by without a second glance. Only the hordes of monkeys in the vicinity of the Hindu places of worship displayed any animosity towards the new arrivals, their vicious assaults matched by that of the swarms of stinging flies brought out by the monsoon rain.

William Peel paid a courtesy call on the garrison Commander, while commissariat stores were loaded aboard the *Koel,* but he did not linger. With their destination now so close, he was impatient to reach it. Waiting only to receive the heartening news that Delhi had been re-captured and Outram and Havelock had succeeded in fighting their way into the Residency at Lucknow, he ordered his small fleet to cast off. The men, cheered by the news he had brought back with him, turned-to with a will to assist in coaling when they anchored off the town of Mirzapore the following evening, and there were few grumbles when they were called on during the night to pump out the *Koel,* which had shipped a quantity of water after dragging her anchor.

At 1:30 p.m. on Saturday, 3rd October, the advance party of the *Shannon* Brigade reached its destination in the *Koel,* anchoring off the Musjid Hospital at Allahabad. By five that evening, all shot and baggage had been landed with the assistance of coolies, and the detachment marched into a tented camp which was situated outside the massive Fort. The *Koel* was dispatched to pick up the invalids from Ghazipore and the ancient *Mirzapore* steamer towed the flat into the anchorage. Stores were landed and, with a detachment taking over garrison duties inside the fort, a start was made with the difficult task of getting the heavy guns ashore, of which Phillip was in overall charge. By the evening of 17th October, it was virtually completed, the party left at Ghazipore had rejoined and the second detachment of 120, under the First Lieutenant, James Vaughan—which had left Calcutta a month later than Captain Peel's—was reported to have reached Benares.

Phillip, who had been sleeping aboard the flat, marched his fatigue party up to the Fort and, almost for the first time since his arrival, was able to take stock of his surroundings. The Fort itself, situated in a fork made by the confluence of the Ganges and the Jumna Rivers, was, he knew, over two hundred years old. On the two river faces, its towering, loopholed walls and massive bastions of red sandstone presented the appearance of an impregnable stronghold of great antiquity, but the land face had been considerably modernised and the Main Gate, by which he and his party entered, was approached through a series of newly built brick prison cells and along a metalled roadway wide enough to admit a cavalry squadron riding eight or ten abreast. The barracks had accommodation for only six hundred men but about five hundred yards from the glacis, a permanent camp had been pitched, with messing marquees and huts, for the accommodation of troops passing through on their way up country, and the arsenal, occupying a series of flat-roofed storerooms within the Fort, was one of the largest in India.

The native city—as in Benares, composed largely of mud-built houses, temples, and open bazaars—nestled below the landward walls of the Fort, and the cantonments, previously containing the bungalows of civil and military families, lay two miles to the east. Few of the cantonment residences were now habitable; Colonel Neill's arrival had been too late to prevent the arsonists and looters indulging in a savage orgy of destruction, and the burnt-out buildings, in their abandoned gardens, still offered evidence of the violence which had characterised Allahabad's brief but bloody rebellion.

Captain Peel, when Phillip entered his office to report to him, was engaged in writing a letter to the Chief of Staff in Calcutta concerning the danger of fire to which the arsenal was exposed. He said testily, thrusting the letter to one side when he recognised his caller, "Imagine it, Phillip—those store-rooms contain most of the powder required for the approaching campaign and whole families of civilians, whose homes were presumably destroyed, have been permitted to take up residence in adjacent rooms! Many were actually camping in the storerooms until I threw them out and all the refugees housed in the Fort were nightly taking the air on the roofs, the men smoking their pipes!" He sighed in exasperation. "Now I've got sentries posted to check their identity at least, and I've told General Mansfield that I propose to remove the powder to detached buildings in cantonments or to powder boats on the river, where it will be considerably safer. And I've ordered the removal of the stocks of firewood the refugee families had painstakingly collected . . . If I can get *them* rehoused I shall feel much happier. Well . . ." His tone softened. "What have you to report? That our guns are safely unloaded?"

Phillip nodded. He made his report and then asked, "Is it true that you've been requested to send up a gunnery officer to Cawnpore, sir?"

Peel eyed him with raised brows. "News gets around, does it not?" he countered dryly. "It's true, I have received that request and I'm sending Edward Daniels. He's only a mid, I'm aware, but he had plenty of land gunnery practice in the Crimea—he'll do all they require and more. Why . . . had *you* any thought of volunteering?"

Phillip reddened. "Yes," he admitted. "I had thought of it."

"Damn it, I can't spare you, man!" Peel exploded. "I can't spare any of my lieutenants and, least of all, my senior training officer. The guns' crews have to learn how to handle bullock and elephant teams and all the officers, as well as some of the ratings, will have to become reasonably proficient at horseback riding. And we shan't have long to ensure that they are."

"You mean—" Phillip stared at him, his initial disappointment fading as comprehension dawned. "The Brigade will be going into action?"

William Peel smiled. He picked up a sheet of paper from among the pile on his desk. "Read this, my dear fellow—it's just come by telegraph from General Mansfield, Sir Colin Campbell's Chief of Staff."

The telegraphic message was addressed to Colonel Campbell, the commandant of the Fort and Phillip's pulse quickened as he read: *"The Inspector-General of Ordnance has ordered the equipment and forwarding of heavy guns to Cawnpore. See to this yourself and press forward the work. Beg Captain Peel to detach as many of the Naval Brigade as will be necessary to work this train under some efficient naval officers. One heavy battery with its ammunition, 200 rounds a gun, is to be completed first and sent off. Although there are no proper waggons for the transport of heavy ammunition at Allahabad, do what you can with ordinary carts of the country and press them forward. If no suitable carriage for naval sixty-eights, leave these in Fort and replace with Artillery twenty-fours. Beg Peel to employ his men in the arsenal to help in packing ammunition."*

"There is no suitable carriage for our sixty-eights," Peel said, when Phillip returned the message. "But the twenty-four-pounders are available. Even so, our most pressing problem will be transport. Help me solve that, Phillip, and get your Jacks to work on the gun teams. Elephants are the devil to control, they tell me, and bullocks can be awkward. As for the country carts . . ." He sighed. "At most we've got a couple of weeks and it may be only a few days, but we've *got* to be ready."

"Of course, sir. I'll do my best, I—"

"I know you will," Peel put in quickly. "And I know the anxiety you're enduring. The latest news from Lucknow is that, although Outram and Havelock fought their way into the Residency, the relief force suffered so many casualties—over five hundred, I understand—that they're trapped there with the original garrison. They cannot fight their way out and

Outram has said that he cannot risk an attempt to evacuate the women and children and the wounded with the force he now commands. But they are holding their own and have enlarged the Residency defensive perimeter. Their greatest anxiety is that their food is running low—dangerously low— so that they have had again to reduce their rations."

"Then there's need for haste?" Phillip suggested, frowning.

"Yes," Peel conceded. "The Commander-in-Chief is still in Calcutta but he's coming up to take command of the second relief force in person and should be here before the end of the month. We shall move on to Cawnpore to await his arrival as soon as our transport is arranged. The relief column will gather there and contact is to be made with the men Outram left to hold the Alam Bagh, who will be reinforced."

Phillip nodded. They discussed various details concerning guns and equipment and then William Peel said, "Jim Vaughan's party should be here by mid-day tomorrow, according to a signal from Allahabad. I propose to send him on to Cawnpore with four of the twenty-four-pounder guns and a hundred men, including Nowell Salmon's rifle company, as soon as I can—probably in a couple of days, if we can lay our hands on the necessary carriage. They've opened the railway as far as Lahonda but, as most of the engines were destroyed by the rebels, it's doubtful whether it will be of much help to us." He glanced at Phillip with a thoughtful frown. "Three of the mids can go in the first party . . . I feel that Kerr, Clinton, and Martin Daniel deserve the privilege, in recognition of the way all three of them have worked at their training, don't you? And a field-piece party—Clinton's, if you're agreeable."

Phillip nodded. Midshipman Lord Arthur Pelham Clinton, despite his rather effeminate good looks and diminutive stature, had sweated long and hard at his training for land warfare, and had drilled his six-pounder's guns' crew to a pitch of efficiency few of the other teams had reached.

"Right," Peel said, making a note on his desk pad. "The other twenty-four-pounders and two of the howitzers will go next, with Edward Hay's company and Gray's Marines as escort, and we'll follow with the rest of the field-guns and rockets—probably catch up with them on the way, with any luck, especially if the railway *is* functioning. Our total strength will be 516 officers and men when Vaughan joins although, of course, our effective strength will depend on the number of sick he has. We've got 57, but most of them are on the mend. We shall have to leave them, with about another two hundred, to garrison this place, until the Army can relieve them. Tom Young will command the second Cawnpore party—it's his due, as gunnery officer. And Phillip, I—"

"Sir?" Phillip acknowledged, his voice carefully expressionless.

"I can't give you a command officially, since you are here in a supernumerary capacity. You—"

"I understand, sir," Phillip assured him.

"No, old son, you don't." Peel laid a hand on his arm. "I want you to act as my second-in-command in the field because—supernumerary or not—you're the best man for the job. If I'm killed or disabled, you will assume command of the Brigade, unless and until some higher *naval* authority countermands my instructions—the military authorities aren't likely to. Is that understood?"

"It is, sir. And . . . thank you."

"It's your due, so don't thank me." Peel's firm mouth curved into a smile. "By the way, two other items of news you may not have heard. Sotheby and his *Pearl* Brigade are to garrison Buxar and should be at or near there now. And our mutual friend Henry Keppel is a Rear-Admiral and a K.C.B.. How's *that* for news?"

"I am simply delighted to hear it," Phillip answered, sincerely pleased. "And particularly delighted about his K.C.B.. Heaven knows, he deserved it!"

"But I imagine Her Majesty had to intervene in order to get it for him," Peel observed dryly. "Over the First Lord's dead body, no doubt." He arranged his papers in order, stifled a yawn, and rose. "Come and dine with me, Phillip. It'll give us a chance to get our transport requisitions sorted out."

Lieutenant James Vaughan's party of four officers and one hundred and twenty seamen—many of the latter volunteers, enlisted from merchant ships in Calcutta—arrived next day in the steamer *Benares* with a flat in tow, laden with tents and baggage, having accomplished the difficult journey up river in a month and suffered only a single case of cholera during the voyage. They were met and played into camp by the *Shannon*'s band, passing across the lowered drawbridge into the Fort between the ranks of a seamen's guard to receive a rousing welcome from the first detachment.

Three days later, Vaughan left on the one-hundred-and-twenty-mile journey along the Grand Trunk Road to Cawnpore in command of a party of one hundred seamen, his four heavy siege guns—each weighing 65 hundredweight—on Bengal Artillery carriages, drawn either by eleven yoke of oxen or two elephants. The gun ammunition was carried in bullock carts, the rocket-tubes mounted on horse-drawn hackeries and the rear of the lengthy procession was made up of baggage carts, with elephants and strings of camels laden with stores and camp equipment. Despite Phillip's misgivings and their hastily completed training, the bluejackets handled their strange transport animals reasonably well, aided by native drivers,

camelteers, and *mahouts*, and an interpreter—Captain
Maxwell, of the Bengal Artillery—now attached to the Naval
Brigade.

On 27th October, Lieutenant Thomas Young's party of 176
seamen and the Royal Marine detachment under Captain
Gray received orders to follow, taking with them the remaining four siege-guns, howitzers, field-pieces and rockets, and
the Brigade's reserve ammunition. Because of the importance
of this convoy, an escort of detachments from the 53rd and
64th Regiments was furnished by the Army and a company of
Royal Engineers, seventy strong, attached to it. Phillip left the
following evening, with Captain Peel and his two young
aides-de-camp, Naval Cadets Lascelles and Watson, the defence
of Allahabad Fort being entrusted to two hundred and forty
seamen—recovered invalids and the band included in their
number—under the command of Lieutenants Wilson,
Wratislaw, and Axel Lind.

It was a not unpleasant ride along the ten-foot-wide Trunk
Road, but everywhere evidence of rebellion could be seen in
gutted *dak* bungalows, burnt-out villages, and the grisly skeletons of long-dead mutineers still hanging from trees at the
road verge.

"Brigadier Neill's justice," the youthful Commander of a
patrol of Police sowars told them, his tone cynical, when they
halted at his camp-site. "There used to be a lot more . . . hang
'em first and prove their guilt afterwards, those were his orders
and his Blue Caps carried them out, until old Havelock put a
stop to it. But it's going on still in Cawnpore. Neill's dead, I
know, and he died fighting his way into the Lucknow
Residency, but drumhead courts martial and indiscriminate
hangings aren't really the best tactics if you're hoping to settle the country."

Captain Peel exchanged a wry glance with Phillip but said nothing.

At the village of Thurrea, after an overnight ride of twelve miles, their small party caught up with the siege-train and its escort. Scarcely had they dismounted at the camping ground than the convoy Commander, Colonel Powell of the Queen's 53rd, sought out Peel in a state of some agitation.

"I've just received a report that a force of rebels—made up of the mutinied Dinapore regiments, with some Irregular Cavalry and three guns—has crossed the Jumna and is preparing to launch an attack on Futtehpore," he announced breathlessly. "As no doubt you are aware, Captain Peel, we have only a small outpost garrison in a fort near the town—a company of the 93rd Highlanders and a battery of artillery and they're in danger of being wiped out or compelled to withdraw. Futtehpore is an important link in our line of communication. All our columns have to pass through the town on their way to Cawnpore and, in my considered opinion, we cannot afford to let it fall into the hands of the enemy. My orders are to escort your siege-train to Cawnpore without imperilling its safety but . . ." He hesitated, his faded blue eyes holding an eager gleam of anticipation as he studied William Peel's face. "The report is reliable—it's come from the outpost Commander, Captain Cornwall."

Peel gripped Phillip's arm. "Let's look at the map," he requested and then, as the convoy Commander clicked his tongue impatiently, "What do you propose to do, Colonel?"

"Strike camp at once and march to intercept them," Colonel Powell answered. "We can be in Futtehpore by midnight and join up with Cornwall's Highlanders before the Pandies realise what we're up to—they're still about 25 miles to the north-west. Somewhere near a village by the name of Bindki." He jabbed at the map Phillip spread out in front of them. "That means they've almost certainly come from Kalpi . . . and that's where the Nana's supposed to be, is it not? The bloody swine responsible for the butchery of our women and children in Cawnpore! For God's sake, Peel, this is an opportunity we've *got* to take . . ." He talked on, explaining his proposed plan of action and Phillip, studying the map over his Commander's shoulder, listened with growing excitement.

It was risky, he was aware; the column was strong enough for its purpose, which was to guard the slow-moving seige-train and the long line of lumbering bullock waggons along the well-patrolled Grand Trunk Road. But with no cavalry to reconnoitre the enemy position and a bare two hundred and fifty infantrymen to put into the field . . . He heard Powell say that, in addition to his infantry, he had some seventy Royal Engineers.

"I can use them in the line if necessary," the 53rd's Commanding Officer asserted. "With your seamen and Marines and at least a company of Highlanders, we could muster what? Five hundred bayonets, plus your field-guns. Leave the siege-train and ammunition and baggage waggons in the fort at Futtehpore and press on to Bindki at first light tomorrow and we'd have the element of surprise in our favour. By heaven, I believe we could do it! What's your opinion, Captain Peel? The alternative is to occupy the fort at Futtehpore and wait for them to attack us—which, in my view, would almost certainly cause them to shy off and leave the swine free to attack other convoys and outposts between here and Lucknow."

"How many are they, sir?" Peel asked.

The Colonel shrugged. "Between two and three thousand, according to the report. Two thousand are sepoys in uniform."

William Peel folded the map and passed it back to Philip,

his movements calm and deliberate. "My twenty-four-pounders travel deuced slowly," he warned. "But by all means let us make a forced march to Futtehpore, sir. We can make our final decision when we get there."

Camp was struck and the head of the column arrived at the Futtehpore camping ground just before midnight, to find Captain Cornwall and his Highlanders, with two 9-pounder guns of the Bengal Artillery, waiting for them. "Intelligence from spies confirmed the presence of the mutineers near Bindki," he said, and added, smiling, "Their cavalry are no longer with them—they've apparently gone off foraging on their own, leaving their infantry brothers from Dinapore to make camp at a place called Kudjwa, which is roughly twenty miles from here." He glanced expectantly at Colonel Powell. "We can get the siege-train into the fort while your fellows bivouac and break their fast, sir, and be ready to move off at first light. And . . ." He paused to make certain that his words would have the effect he was obviously hoping for, his gaze now directed at Peel. "I'm aware of the importance of this convoy, sir, but my spies tell me that they recognised the Nana of Bithur and one of his leading generals—a fellow named Teeka Singh—with the rebels, who number nearer four thousand than two. We shall need your naval rifle company, sir, and your nine-pounders."

Colonel Powell slapped his thigh and swore, loudly and vehemently. "Well, have you made up your mind, Captain Peel?" he demanded. "Are you with us?"

Peel nodded. "I'm with you, sir, as long as my big guns can be safely parked."

The march was along a narrow, rutted road through knee-high cornfields and across a wooded plain, interspersed with *jheels* which the recent monsoon rain had swollen to the size of miniature lakes. Only two halts were made, the men plodding doggedly along, many of them footsore and limping as the sun rose higher in the sky and the early morning chill turned to sultry heat, sapping at their strength and causing them to sweat profusely. They had covered sixteen miles when the third and final halt was called to consume haversack rations and the half-dozen mounted Police sowars, who had accompanied the column, were sent forward to reconnoitre.

Shortly after one o'clock the march was resumed and, at 1:30, after passing through the village of Bindki, Peel returned from a brief conference with Colonel Powell to announce that the rebel force had been sighted—as expected, near the village of Kudjwa—where they had made camp the previous night. Bugles shrilled and the Highlanders spread out to lead the advance in skirmishing order through fields of growing corn, supported by the detachment of Royal Engineers who, Phillip observed, had fixed bayonets on hearing the call to advance and pressed forward with great eagerness.

The 53rd and the Naval Brigade followed, still in column of march and the 64th's detachment, many of whom were recovered invalids, formed up in the rear to protect the baggage waggons and hospital *doolies.* Peel ordered four of the field-pieces brought up and, after an anxious inspection of the flagging gun-bullocks, gave directions for their positioning to Lieutenant Young and rejoined Phillip and Edward Hay, the rifle company's Commander, on the road.

"The rebels are occupying a line of hillocks to the left of the road," he told them briskly. "Their line is partly screened by a grove of trees and it continues to the rear of the village . . . something like this." With the toe of his boot, he traced the outline in the sand of the road. "Their guns are in the centre, two posted in front of the village itself and covering the approach to it and a third further back, mounted on a wooden bridge which spans a small stream—fordable by the look of it. The distance between the guns is approximately forty yards. Colonel Powell has ordered our four forward guns to engage theirs and give covering fire to the skirmishers, while he endeavours to turn their left flank with his light company, making a detour to the right of the road and using the village to cover his advance." Again his foot moved, describing an arrow in the sand. "He'll aim to take the bridge-mounted gun and the right-hand one from the rear—provided he can get his fellows across the stream—leaving the Highlanders to take the left-hand one, with the Marines in support, moving in from our left. The Bengal battery will engage the enemy line from the road. Is that clear?"

"It's clear, sir," Edward Hay confirmed, without enthusiasm. "But what about us? Do we just sit here?"

Peel put an affectionate arm round his shoulders. "Don't be idiotic, Ted my boy!" he admonished. "We go in to the right of the 53rd, taking Garvey's nine-pounder with us, and carry the left of the enemy's line whilst Powell's lads are dealing with the guns. Does that satisfy you?"

Hay beamed. "It does indeed, sir. And what about the Nana? *Is* he up there, too?"

"There's been no mention of his presence, alas. But—" Peel broke off with a smothered exclamation, as one of the enemy guns opened fire and a roundshot came bounding down the road ahead of them. The range was extreme and it rolled harmlessly out of sight, as the head of the column halted and the 53rd swiftly deployed, taking ground to the right of the road. Colonel Powell could be seen, mounted on a big bay horse, waving with his drawn sword to the men of his regiment to commence their detour. Scorning cover for himself, he trotted along the narrow, dusty track, directing the skirmishers, who were pushing forward on either side of him, the Highlanders half hidden amongst the sprouting corn, firing as they advanced with the practised skill of well-trained infantrymen. The Engineers, over-eager and untrained in skirmishing tactics, ran into a storm of grape from the two advanced enemy guns before Lieutenant Young got his nine-pounders into position, unlimbered, and opened a rapid and accurate fire which won a welcome respite for them.

To the left of the road, the two guns of the Bengal Artillery also opened and Phillip saw Thomas Grey moving up in the wake of the Highlanders with his redcoated Marines, the sun striking bright reflections from their steel-tipped Enfields as they advanced steadily through the trampled corn. Ahead of them and to their left, the fire of the British guns flushed out a number of rebels who had been concealed in the grove of trees in front of their entrenched position. Most were sepoys in uniform, who fled back to their comrades in the rear, pursued by a hail of Minié and Enfield bullets.

Peel said formally, "Be so good as to advance with your company in support of the Fifty-Third, Mr Hay."

Hay's "Aye, aye, sir!" was a trifle strained and, dropping formality, the *Shannon*'s Commander added, with a grin, "Let's see what sort of soldiers our Jacks are . . . keep well to the right, Ted, my boy, and use your cover for as long as you can. Then have at 'em with the bayonet!"

Hay's riflemen acquitted themselves well. Their weariness forgotten, they advanced through the trampled corn to charge the rebel line like veterans the instant they were clear of it, cheering wildly and those lining the embankment behind the village—again sepoys in white and scarlet—fired a last spasmodic volley and took to their heels. The single field-gun ordered to support them, commanded by a young acting-mate, Henry Garvey, lost two of its gun-bullocks and, finding that the rest would not advance, the gun's crew cut the traces and, with Peel and Phillip lending their shoulders, they manhandled the nine-pounder into position by the edge of the stream. From there, Garvey and his team fired shell after shell into the enemy-held hillocks, wreaking terrible execution amongst its yelling defenders.

But the line was a long one and, to the left, heavy toll was being taken of the advancing Highlanders and Engineers who, facing a steep slope, were unable to get to close quarters with the sepoy musketeers entrenched among the hillocks above them. Gradually they were being forced to fall back to the road to escape the deadly fire directed on their flank, the Marines—although better positioned—having to fall back with them. The two guns which had been the 53rd's objective had been taken, however, Phillip saw, as he and Peel and the two naval cadets forded the shallow stream to join Hay's company in their newly captured position. The third gun could just be seen through the drifting smoke, no longer firing, its gunners apparently about to withdraw with it, for horses had been brought up and already two were harnessed to an ammunition tumbril.

Colonel Powell had evidently realised their intention, for his stentorian bellow rose above the crackle of musketry. Phillip grasped Peel's arm, pointing through the smoke to where twenty yards ahead of his own men, the Colonel was galloping straight for the retreating gunners.

"He'll get himself killed!" Peel rasped. "And"—he had his glass to his eye—"devil take the Pandies! I believe they're moving out to attack our rear. Over there to the left, Phillip—d'you see them? They . . ." His voice trailed off as Cadet Lascelles' high-pitched treble announced that the Colonel had fallen. Peel dispatched the boy with an order to Lieutenant Young to move two of his guns to counter the rebels' new threat and scarcely had the cadet departed on his errand than one of the 53rd's officers—an ensign, with blood streaming down his face—came stumbling to a halt beside Peel.

"The Colonel's been killed, sir," he gasped. "Captain Mowbray requests you, as senior officer, to take command. Two of their guns are in our hands, sir, but they managed to make off with the third, I'm afraid."

"Right," Peel acknowledged. He sounded calm and confident as he said to Hay, "Hold on here, Mr Hay. I'll send another gun to your support as soon as I can. I'm going to launch a counter attack through the village and try to split their force. If it's successful, don't wait for orders—go in behind them and cut off their retreat. If it's not, fall back on our guns."

"Aye, aye, sir." Hay's voice was also calm.

Phillip accompanied Peel down to the bridge, the ensign—who gave his name as Truell—leading the way. The 53rd had brought in the body of their Colonel and laid it on one of the captured gun-limbers but now, exhausted by their charge, most of the men were squatting or lying in what shade they could find, in seeming indifference to the musket balls flying about their heads like a swarm of angry hornets. Captain Mowbray, wounded in the face by a charge of grape, greeted Peel's arrival with a grim assessment of the situation.

"They're too damned many for us, sir," he ended, his tone resigned. "And the men are worn out. I fancy our only course is to withdraw. Men can't fight in this climate after a 24 mile forced march in the heat of the day. The Highlanders are in a worse state than we are and, between us, we've suffered over sixty casualties. God knows how many those poor devils of Engineers have lost and—"

Peel cut him short. "We can turn it our way yet," he asserted. "Let's get those captured guns into action for a start and discourage their musketeers—Mr Watson, you know what to do. Bowse this gun 'round and send some grape into them . . ." He gave his orders with crisp decisiveness and the weary men, taking fresh heart, scrambled to their feet again, reaching for their rifles. *Doolies* were brought up and the wounded withdrawn; the two rebel guns, manned by scratch crews, opened up with devastating effect on their erstwhile owners. Phillip, having brought the second into action, left it under the able command of Midshipman Lightfoot—who appeared providentially with a message from Young—and set about collecting volunteers for the counter attack. There was no lack of them, despite the wounded Mowbray's gloomy assessment of their condition. Highlanders, Marines, and the 53rd formed up around him, and the baggage-guard of the 64th, fresher than the rest, came forward to a man, relinquishing responsibility for the baggage to footsore and slightly wounded men, while twenty of the Engineers, under a subaltern, grimly fixed bayonets again and took the right of the line.

Preceded by an accurate bombardment of the hillocks by Lieutenant Young's re-positioned field-guns, the attack was launched, led by Peel on the Colonel's big bay horse. Emerging from the village to pass round the embankment beyond, there was no slope to impede them and they drove their way right through the centre of the rebel line, cheering as they went. Hay's charge with his seamen completed the rout; the sepoys were soon in headlong flight, as position after position was taken at bayonet point. By half-past four, they had abandoned their hillocks and their camp-site, with its stores and ammunition, to the victorious British, leaving close on three hundred dead behind them.

Phillip, breathless and half-blinded by the streams of perspiration pouring down his face, came to a halt at last to find himself looking down at the body of a black-bearded Native Cavalry officer, whose pistol shot—fired at point-blank range—had miraculously skimmed over his head. He had no recollection of having killed the man but . . . He withdrew his sword from the medal-bedecked blue and silver jacket and saw that the blade was sticky with blood. Beside him, the 93rd's Commander, Captain Cornwall, dropped on one knee to examine the body and then looked up at him, a smile lighting his smoke-blackened face.

"Congratulations—you've just put a well-deserved end to one of the butchers of Cawnpore! This is Teeka Singh, the Nana's General of Cavalry . . . quite a prize, if I may say so."

"Are you sure?" Phillip questioned doubtfully.

"Yes, pretty sure." The Highland officer straightened up, brushing the dust from his bare knees. "For one thing, he's in the uniform of the Second Light Cavalry, the swine who mutinied at Cawnpore. For another, when our spies reported that he was here, I obtained a description of him from one of the Police sowars—short, inclined to corpulence, and with a black beard. He fits the description—it's Teeka Singh all right, Commander."

An eye for an eye, Phillip thought, with bitter satisfaction . . . a Pandy general, one of the Nana's men, had paid with his life for Lavinia's murder.

"Then I hope his soul will rot in hell," he said savagely and went to report to William Peel.

"We're going back to Bindki to make camp," Peel told him. "Pursuit, alas, is out of the question—the men are too done up and we've too many wounded. Hay's among them but it's only slight—a graze on the hand—and poor young Stirling's taken a musket ball in the leg. In all, I think we've nearly a hundred casualties, but I haven't got the surgeon's report yet." He expelled his breath in a weary sigh. "Dear God, I'm tired, Phillip! But our Jacks did pretty well, didn't they? They've had their baptism of fire as soldiers . . . I don't think they'll be found wanting when we get to Lucknow, do you?"

Phillip shook his head. "No, they won't, sir. And neither will you."

CHAPTER SIX

After spending a day at Futtehpore to rest the men, obtain fresh gun-bullocks and send the wounded back to Allahabad, William Peel's party resumed the march to Cawnpore with the siege-train, arriving there on 3rd November. The Lucknow Relief Force was under orders to push on to Buntera—10 miles from their objective, where Brigadier Hope Grant's Movable Column from Delhi was waiting to join forces with them for the final advance.

Two companies of the 93rd had already left; Lieutenant Vaughan's party followed and Peel was ordered to leave with the rest of the siege-train and its escort on the 8th.

Phillip was thankful at the prospect of putting Cawnpore behind him. During the time they spent in camp there, he had seen the heartrending relics of the siege and massacre, and had entered and wondered at the mud-walled entrenchment which the garrison had defended with such heroic fortitude for three long and terrible weeks. The crumbling walls, the shell-battered, roofless buildings, the pathetic holes scooped in the bare, foul-smelling earth which had provided the only shelter General Wheeler's people had had, seemed to him even more terrible than the sun-bleached skeletons which still, in places, littered the river bank. It was impossible to identify the skeletons but, as he had stood in the burnt-out hospital on the east side of the entrenchment, it had been peopled with ghosts and, at every turn, he had imagined that he saw Lavinia coming to meet him with a baby in her arms, weeping and crying to him for aid.

He had not intended to go to the Bibigarh, although the yellow-painted bungalow in the centre of the city, where the Nana's poor hostages had been butchered, had become a place of pilgrimage for every newly arrived member of the Lucknow Force. Finally, in the company of Edward Daniels, he had done so reluctantly and had regretted it ever since. Brigadier-General Neill had ordered that the house should be kept exactly as it had been when General Havelock's Force had recaptured the city, Daniels told him. The well in the court-yard, into which the bodies of the victims had been flung, had been filled in and a memorial Cross erected over it but, inside the house itself, Neill's orders had been carried out to the let-ter and—a stone's throw from its ghastly, blood-splattered walls—a gallows stood in stark reminder of the retribution which Neill had exacted, from guilty and innocent alike.

"They say that any native, who was even remotely sus-pected of having taken part in either of the massacres, was hanged," the midshipman added. "And they also say—I don't know if it's true, sir—that General Neill made each one of them clean up a measured patch of blood before they were executed. They were forced to go down on their hands and knees and cleanse the floor with their tongues. It sounds pretty revolt-ing, but apparently the mere touch of Christian blood defiles them and Neill wanted them to believe that he'd taken their immortal souls, as well as their lives, in revenge for what they'd done to our poor women and children. When General Havelock returned from Oudh in the middle of August, he put a stop to it. He's very religious, it seems, and doesn't believe

in what he calls meeting barbarism with barbarism. Not everyone agrees with him, I gather, but most people seem to think
that Neill went too far. I don't know what to think. After going
in there and seeing that room, I . . . I just don't know, sir."

He had chattered on but Phillip had scarcely heard him
as he had made his own, horror-stricken inspection of the
small, shadowed room in which the pathetic survivors of the
Suttee Chowra Ghat shambles had lived in fear for over two
weeks before meeting their hideous death. The blood had
dried—where it had not been cleansed and whitewashed
over—to a black stain, none the less evocative for its change
of colour and, from walls and verandah beams hung lengths
of cord by which, Daniels told him, the children had been suspended to witness their mothers' slaughter and await their
own. On the wall behind a door, a message had been scratched
with a knife or some other sharp instrument, and he had read
it, sickened.

*"Countrymen and women, remember 15 July, 1857. Your
wives and families are here in misery and at the disposal of
savages, who have ravished both old and young and then
killed us. Oh my child, my child! Countrymen, revenge it!"*

"They didn't write that, sir," Edward Daniels had assured
him. "Although it's probably true. But some of General
Havelock's soldiers are said to have carved the message with
their bayonets, after they'd been in here a few days after it
happened."

His assurance had been of some slight consolation but,
walking dazedly from the house of massacre, Phillip felt a savage anger well up inside him and it did not fade until long
after his return to camp, becoming then a nagging ache from
which, sleeping or waking, there was no relief. Most of the

men in the column—seamen, soldiers, and Marines—felt much as he did following their arrival in Cawnpore, and there was little grumbling, however arduously they might have to toil and however little rest was permitted them, as preparations for the advance on Lucknow were completed and they moved out to join Brigadier-General Hope Grant's camp at Buntera.

The Commander-in-Chief, Sir Colin Campbell, reached Allahabad on 1st November. Received at the Bridge of Boats by the *Shannon*'s cutter, with a guard of honour and a salute of seventeen guns, he had left at first light and entered Cawnpore on the evening of 3rd. The sight of his familiar small, slightly stooped figure in the immaculate blue frock coat put fresh heart into all of them and, in particular, into those who had served with him in the Crimea. Inevitably, he had aged but he had lost none of his energy; his temper was as explosive as ever, his eye as keen and searching, his voice, with its aggressively Scots accent, as rasping as Phillip remembered it from that day at Balaclava when—his "thin red line" of 93rd Highlanders all that stood between the Russians and the Harbour—he had warned them that they must die where they stood, if need be, and had then admonished them for their eagerness.

Another Crimean veteran, Major-General Windham—one of the heroes of the British attack on the Redan at Sebastopol in 1855—had been chosen by Sir Colin to assume the unenviable responsibility of the Cawnpore command during his absence. Despite the ever-present threat posed by the Gwalior contingent—five thousand well-trained sepoys, with twenty-four guns, only forty miles away, across the Jumna at Kalpi—and the Nana's levies, also amounting to about five thousand, only five hundred British and five hundred and fifty Madras troops could be spared from the Lucknow Relief Force for

Cawnpore's defence, and William Peel had returned from his first meeting with the Commander-in-Chief looking strained and anxious.

"Sir Colin has asked me to leave an officer of lieutenant's rank and two guns' crews here," he told Phillip. "Fifty of our best gunners, he specified, to assist in General Windham's defence. You've seen the entrenchment General Neill constructed at the Baxi Ghat, to cover the Bridge of Boats across the river, haven't you?"

"Yes, I have, sir." Phillip waited, frowning. If Sir Colin Campbell's request was complied with—as obviously it would have to be—the strength of the Naval Brigade would be barely two hundred, including Marines and rifle companies.

"The entrenchment's solid enough," Peel went on thoughtfully. "And well supplied with guns and ammunition. Whatever happens, Windham should be able to hold it with a thousand men—even if the Gwalior contingent and the Nana attack him simultaneously. But Sir Colin is anxious, so I've had to agree . . . although it's going to leave us pretty short. Ted Hay's the obvious choice to command the guns' crews, with young Garvey as his second-in-command and the two cadets . . . and you'd better select the men least able to march, Phillip, and detail them to stay here."

"None of them will like it," Phillip said reluctantly.

"For God's sake, I know they won't!" Peel sighed. "But I can't refuse a direct request from the Commander-in-Chief, can I? As he pointed out to us this morning, he's taking a hell of a gamble by going to Lucknow at all, before securing his base here. He's on the horns of a dilemma. If he attempts to meet and defeat the Gwalior rebels and the Nana, they can hold him up indefinitely. Since they're on the other side of the Jumna and all the boats are in their hands, they can choose their own time and place to do battle. If the Chief waits, Lucknow could well fall—they've been under siege for over four months, poor souls—and if he goes to their relief, he knows that the Nana will almost certainly attack Cawnpore. His only chance and the one he's gambling on, is that he can push on to Lucknow, evacuate the garrison, and return here before the Nana and his allies have had time to launch their attack."

"He'll be cutting it fine, will he not?" Phillip demurred.

"Yes, he will," Peel agreed. "But what else can he do? Even with the addition of Hope Grant's column from Delhi, he only has . . . what? About five thousand men of all arms available to him. In the circumstances, the minimum number he can leave here is a thousand, the absolute minimum. With the rest, he must defeat an estimated sixty thousand Pandies at Lucknow."

Phillip eyed him sombrely. "Then it *is* a gamble?"

Peel laughed shortly. "Sir Colin said himself, at the end of our conference, that this is the greatest gamble he's ever taken in his life . . . and he said it a trifle cynically, reminding us that he's always had a reputation for being overcautious! But I think he's right to take the gamble—Lucknow *cannot* be allowed to fall, whatever the cost. If Outram is forced to surrender, he'll be served as poor old Wheeler was served—and my God, Phillip, another Cawnpore would be more than any of us could bear!"

Phillip shuddered, thinking of the yellow-painted bungalow in the heart of the city and of Harriet and her children. There was not a man in the Relief Force, he knew, who would not gladly give his life to prevent another Cawnpore. War was one thing, the brutal slaughter of defenceless women and children quite another . . .

"As I said," the *Shannon*'s Commander went on, "the entrenchment Windham has to defend is a strong one—poor old Wheeler's doesn't compare with it. Sir Colin has instructed him to 'show the best front possible'—his words—but not to move out to the attack unless he's compelled to do so by the threat of heavy bombardment."

"Then as long as General Windham can hold the entrenchment and keep the bridge across the river intact, all should be well?" Phillip suggested.

Peel nodded. "Yes, it should—after all, the late General Neill held the same entrenchment with only three hundred men, when Havelock's Force was in Oudh. I gather that Windham intends to post one of our twenty-four-pounders on the bridge itself, under a strong guard, to prevent any attempt by the enemy to blow it up. In any event, we move out tomorrow, ahead of the Chief and his staff, and join up with Hope Grant's column and our advance guard at Buntera. We've to be there by the tenth, which will mean two marches of seventeen miles. The Chief hopes to push on to the Alam Bagh and relieve the holding force there on the twelfth. The Alam Bagh garrison has been reinforced and supplied, and their wounded evacuated, so they will join us in the attack on Lucknow, being replaced by Hope Grant's sick and footsore men." William Peel smiled suddenly, his blue eyes gleaming. "When you come to think about it, Phillip," he said, with a swift change of tone, "*we* took a hell of a gamble at Kudjwa, didn't we? According to Sir Colin we did"—his smile widened—"but it came off. Given a modicum of luck and the guts and determination our fellows displayed at Kudjwa, so will this one, God willing! This force doesn't lack guts and Hope Grant's column has carried all before it since leaving Delhi—having taken part in the recapture and then saved Agra, which was no mean achievement. We could hardly ask for better comrades in arms, could we? Not to mention the 93rd and poor Colonel Powell's 53rd, both splendid fighting regiments." He rose, still smiling. "First light tomorrow, Phillip—make sure that we leave on time, if you please, with all officers mounted. I'll join you in a little while but first I'll have to find Ted Hay and break the bad news to him that he's to stay here. Edward Daniels can come with us in his place—he's earned it, he's done a fine job here."

The siege-train moved out the following morning, the men in great heart despite the long hours spent loading stores the previous day, and Buntera was reached on the evening of 10th November. On the 11th, Sir Colin Campbell reviewed the combined Relief Force which, during the afternoon, was drawn up in quarter-distance columns in the centre of a flat, sandy plain surrounded by trees.

Pickets were posted and the Commander-in-Chief, mounted on a small white hack, rode out with his staff to inspect them. With him—although few of the assembled troops were aware of his identity or of the perils he had faced in order to reach them—was a civilian clerk named Henry Kavanagh. A tall, red-bearded Irishman of the Lucknow garrison, he had made his way through the rebel lines during the hours of darkness, in native guise and accompanied by a trusted Hindu *cossid,* in order to offer his services as guide to the Relief Force.

Phillip, when the parade was dismissed, wrote a description of it and of their journey to his father. He had, as yet, received no mail from England and, reluctant to write more than was strictly necessary of Cawnpore, simply mentioned that he had passed through the city on the way to Lucknow.

"We march, on average, twelve miles a day," he wrote. *"But coming here we did seventeen—as much as our gun-bullocks can*

stand in a day. We have with us six 24-pounder guns—two had to be left with General Windham in Cawnpore—and two 8-inch howitzers, with bullock-draft, and our rocket-tubes, which are mounted on country carts, known as hackeries. Our siege-train, when complete with ammunition waggons, stores, tents, and camp followers, is nearly three miles in length, so you can understand why all officers, including mids, have to be mounted. Our baggage animals include camels, elephants, and, of course, oxen and horses and, apart from the gunners and Marines, our blue-jackets serve as rifle companies to defend the train. They are armed with Enfield and Minié rifles and drill with the soldiers, under their own divisional officers.

"There are certain differences, however. The troops frequently set out on a march before daylight and without breaking their fast—which they do at the first or second halt—but Captain Peel has issued orders that our men are always to eat before they leave camp. He also insists on our paying very strict attention to camp hygiene and shaving daily and, although the soldiers are permitted to grow beards, we are not. It is a chore sometimes but we are really none the worse for it and our men, in blue frocks, with white duck trousers and polished black boots, always present a smart appearance. As protection from the sun, they wear cotton sun-curtains over their straw hats, extending down the back of the neck, and the officers' are similar, but worn over caps or pith helmets.

"William Peel is the best of Commanders, taut enough but considerate and immensely popular with all ranks, and discipline in his brigade—like morale—has never been higher. At today's parade, held prior to the advance on Lucknow, Sir Colin Campbell inspected us and, we were told, made most complimentary remarks concerning us, which was gratifying.

"It was a very impressive and colourful parade, with our Lucknow column joined to that from Delhi, and divided into three

nominal brigades of Infantry and one each of Cavalry and Artillery with attached Engineers . . . in all, I believe, numbering 3,400 men. We were most interested in the troops from Delhi. Their guns looked blackened and service-worn, but the horses were in good condition and the men very tanned and seemingly in perfect fighting trim.

"The 9th Lancers—their Commanding Officer is the Brigadier, Hope Grant—looked workmanlike and ready for anything in their blue uniforms, with white turbans twisted 'round their forage caps, flagless lances, and lean but hardy looking horses, and their bearing is most soldierly. By contrast, the Sikh cavalry—which includes Hodson's Horse—are wild-looking fellows, clad in loose, fawn-coloured robes, with long boots, blue or red turbans, and armed with carbines and sabers. (They call them 'tulwars' I believe.) Their British officers dress as they do, even to the turbans and look extremely picturesque, especially those serving in Hodson's Horse, who wear brilliant scarlet turbans and ride splendid horses, in appearance as wild as themselves. The only ones who can match them are the Punjab infantry, fine, tall men in sand-coloured uniforms, all of them bearded and wearing enormous turbans, which add to their height.

"The poor Queen's regiments—the 8th and the 75th—which apparently suffered very heavy casualties in the assault on Delhi, looked worn and wasted. Their uniforms, which were originally white, are now a dull slate-colour and during Sir Colin's inspection, they stood silent and wearied, lacking the spirit even to cheer him, although he paid them compliments and praised them highly for their achievements.

"The 93rd Highlanders made up for this a little later, though. They were on the extreme left of the line and, out of a thousand of them, more than half were wearing medals for the Crimea so, of course, the Chief is well known to them and they revere him

greatly. They made a grand sight in Sutherland tartan and plumed feather bonnets—the latter, they tell us, afford ample protection from swords as well as sun and, in addition, serve them as pillows at night. Certainly they look well, although, being intended to serve in China, on the Canton River, when they left England they were issued with brown holland blouses, with scarlet facings, instead of their normal scarlet tunics, this in no wise detracted from their appearance.

"At all events, when Sir Colin came abreast of them, they received him with such tumultuous cheering that I swear it must have been heard in Lucknow, ten miles away! He addressed them at some length, telling them that when he had taken leave of them, after the Crimea, he had never thought to see them again. 'But,' he said, 'another Commander has decreed it otherwise. There is danger and difficulty before us. The eyes of Europe and of the whole of Christendom are upon us, and we must relieve our countrymen, women, and children, now shut up in the Residency of Lucknow. You are my own lads, 93rd—I rely on you to do the work!'

"That brought more cheering, for he delivered his address in the broadest Scots, and the men shouted back that he could depend on them—they would bring the women and children out or die in the attempt. I was moved close to tears when I heard of it, thinking of Harriet and her three little ones and praying, with all my heart, that we may succeed in bringing them safely out."

Phillip paused, the pen in his hand. He had not intended to make more than passing mention of either of his sisters; his father and mother would have heard the terrible news of the Cawnpore garrison's massacre and read of it in the London papers weeks before his letter could arrive. Anything he might write concerning Lavinia and her husband would serve only to open old wounds; he could offer them no comfort, since he did not know when or how either had died and—until Sir Colin

Campbell's Relief Force gained the Lucknow Residency—Harriet's fate was a matter for prayer and speculation. The four-month siege must inevitably have taken heavy toll of the women and children—from sickness and semi-starvation, as well as from enemy shot and shell, so that . . . He sighed and took a fresh page, to finish his description of the parade with a list of the other units and detachments which had taken part.

"The 93rd are the only regiment of ours at full strength," he wrote. *"For the rest, our Infantry Brigade is made up of detachments—a wing of the 53rd, two companies of the 82nd and of the 23rd Fusiliers. They will be augmented by detachments from the Alam Bagh garrison, which will bring our total strength up to almost five thousand with, I think, about fifty guns. We—that is to say, the Naval Brigade and the Royal, Bengal, and Madras Artillery—are under the command of Brigadier-General Crawford, four batteries being horsed and ours the only siege-guns."*

There was nothing more he could write . . . Phillip put his pen down. The mail was going out that evening, he knew; after that, there would be little time for letter-writing with the fate of the Lucknow garrison in the balance. He added a few personal messages and was about to seal his letter when the tent flap parted and, looking up, he saw Edward Daniels's tall, thin figure framed in the aperture.

"I hope I'm not disturbing you, sir," the midshipman said uncertainly. "If you're busy with your mail, I can come back, I . . ." He sounded as if he would have preferred to postpone his visit but Phillip, gesturing to his letter, invited him to come in.

"No, I've finished. Sit down, Mr Daniels. A drink . . . I've only got whisky, I'm afraid."

"That's all right, sir. To tell you the truth, I've developed quite a taste for whisky since my attachment to the Army. They drink a lot more than we do and without Captain Peel to tell me my mess bill's too high, I . . . well, as I said, I've developed quite a taste for whisky. And champagne, sir. The Army officers regard champagne as a necessity in this climate . . . some of them even have it at breakfast. Or they did in Cawnpore. And I . . . that is, sir—"

His voice, Phillip realised, was slurred and his over-thin young face unusually flushed. "Mr Daniels," he demanded curtly, "are you sober?"

The boy shook his head. "No, sir, not very. I . . . well, I've been dining with some of the Delhi column . . . the Cavalry. They seem to think we're . . . well, a bit out of the ordinary because we're sailors and I . . . I've got rather a thick head now. But I needed some Dutch courage to come to you, sir."

"Dutch courage to come to *me*, Eddie?" Phillip challenged wryly. "In God's name, why? Here, sit down, there's a good fellow, and I'll get you some coffee."

Midshipman Daniels sat down. "I don't need coffee, sir, thanks all the same. It's just that I—I've something to give you but I'm not sure if I should or whether you'd want it because . . . well, you see, sir, it *proves* something you might rather not know for certain and . . ." He was floundering helplessly and Phillip eyed him in some astonishment. Normally Edward Daniels was the most composed, as well as the most efficient of the *Shannon*'s "young gentlemen"; Captain Peel had chosen him to go to Cawnpore as artillery officer because of his reliability, yet here he was now what the bluejackets called "half seas over" and fumbling for words, like some newly joined cadet, as if . . .

"Pull yourself together, Mr Daniels," he said, an edge to

his voice. "I suggest you go to your tent and sleep it off—for heaven's sake, lad, you don't want the Captain to see you in this state, do you?"

"God forbid, sir!" Daniels answered feelingly. "But"—he was fumbling in his pockets and finally succeeded in bringing to light a small, leather-bound book. Holding it as if its very touch were painful to him, he blurted out unhappily, "It's this, sir. I got it from Captain Mowbray Thomson—he was one of the only four survivors of the Cawnpore garrison and now he's acting as Garrison Engineer in General Windham's entrenchment. That was how I met him, you see, sir, and we . . . that is, we talked quite a bit about the siege and the massacre. I told him that your sister and brother-in-law were in the garrison—General Wheeler's, I mean—and, of course, he asked their names. I remembered you'd told me that your sister's name was Lavinia and that her husband was one of the Queen's 32nd officers and—"

"*I* told you?" Phillip questioned, feeling the colour drain from his cheeks. "I don't recall that I—"

"You let it out, sir," Edward Daniels explained apologetically. "When we were in that house where—the one they call the Bibigarh—and I remembered. Captain Thomson remembered too, of course, and he—he gave me this to give you. An officer of Havelock's Force found it in the Bibigarh and entrusted it to him for safe keeping, it . . . it's a Bible, sir." He held out the leather-bound book, opened at the flyleaf and Phillip saw, as he took it, that both binding and flyleaf were ominously stained. Written on the flyleaf was an inscription and he felt a lump rise in his throat as he recognised the neat, masculine hand and read: *"For my darling Lavinia . . . with fondest love from Tom."*

"I do hope, sir . . ." Daniels's anxious and still slightly

slurred voice broke into his thoughts and Phillip roused himself, forestalling the boy's question.

"You were right to give me this," he said, forcing himself to speak without emotion. "I'm grateful, my dear lad, I . . ." A vision of the room in which Lavinia's Bible had been found swam before his eyes, in all its remembered horror. He had prayed, often and fervently, that she had died in the entrenchment or even in the attack on the boats and might thus have been spared the final appalling torture of confinement in that darkly shadowed room and death, at the hands of brutal, merciless butchers, at the end of it. But now . . . He looked at the little leather-bound book and could not suppress a shudder as he thrust it into the breast pocket of his frock coat. Dear God, how could he say that he would treasure the hideous, blood-smeared relic? How could he . . . He met Daniels's unhappy gaze and managed to smile at him reassuringly. "I shall always keep it. I'm only sorry it caused you so much heart-searching and . . . distress."

Young Daniels looked relieved. "I wasn't sure if you'd want it, sir. But Captain Thomson said you would. He also said, sir, that Lieutenant Hill was a very gallant officer." He rose, obviously thankful that his self-imposed task had been completed and added, before taking his leave, "He was one of those who formed a guard of honour for poor old General Wheeler, Thomson said. The terms of the surrender granted them the honours of war, so the guard formed up outside the entrenchment when the General was leaving to go down to the *ghat*. They presented arms to him and then marched ahead of him to the boats and most of them were killed, trying to push the boats out into the channel. Thomson thinks that your—your brother-in-law was among them. I . . . that is goodnight, Commander Hazard."

"Goodnight, Mr Daniels," Phillip responded automatically. "And . . . thank you again."

Left alone he sat for a long time, his head resting on his hands. He must seal his letter, he knew—the Chaplain was collecting mail for dispatch and would be here soon, asking for his, and he had not yet written to Graham. That could wait, of course—in all probability, Graham and Catriona had not yet returned to Calcutta—and in any case, mail to Calcutta was getting through fairly regularly and quickly now, thanks to the re-establishment of the *dak* and the recently opened rail link from Lahonda to Allahabad. But the letter to his father must go and . . . He opened it, to read through what he had written. It was a cheerful letter, he decided, and was better so. He picked up his pen again and added a postscript.

"*One thing may amuse you, Father*," he wrote. "*The natives apparently have a wholesome fear of our Jacks. They believe them to be 'little men, four feet high and four feet in the beam, always laughing and dragging their guns about.' Some wag—I suspect one of our younger lieutenants—spread the story that we are cannibals, who salt down the bodies of the slain for future use and, for this purpose, each man carries a clasp-knife at his side! Despite its patent absurdity, this tale has gained credence even among our native camp followers who, it seems, will believe anything.*"

They also believed that the kilted 93rd were the ghosts of the women massacred at Cawnpore, Phillip recalled, and a knife twisted in his heart. But the cannibal story would undoubtedly give the old Admiral a quiet chuckle, so he signed his name and sealed the letter. It was ready when the Naval Brigade's Chaplain, the Reverend Edward Bowman, came to collect it.

At daybreak the following morning, the advance began. After marching for some three miles, the advance-guard came under attack by a body of rebel infantry with two guns, positioned near the old fort of Jellalabad on the right. Captain Bouchier's Field Battery, from the Delhi Column, swiftly and efficiently silenced the enemy's guns, while a squadron of Hodson's Horse, under the command of Lieutenant Hugh Gough, made a detour and under cover of some fields of cane, came up unseen on their left flank. Although there were an estimated two thousand sepoy and *zamindari* troops opposed to them, the squadron made a spirited charge through swampy ground and, taking them completely by surprise, succeeded in routing them and capturing both guns.

Camp was pitched that evening in the rear of the Alam Bagh, a large walled palace four miles from Lucknow, which had been held by three hundred men of Havelock's first Relief Force, under the command of Major McIntyre of the 78th Highlanders, since 25th September. McIntyre had maintained contact with the Residency by means of a semaphore, mounted on the roof and, whilst waiting for the arrival of Sir Colin Campbell, his garrison had been supplied and substantially reinforced from Cawnpore and by Hope Grant's Delhi Column, which had evacuated his sick and wounded. Now his gallant garrison, formed into a batallion of detachments from the regiments besieged in the Residency and commanded by Major Barnston of the 78th, marched out to join the Relief Force, their places being taken by the three hundred-strong 75th Regiment* and fifty Sikhs.

Baggage, tents, and reserve supplies were moved into the Alam Bagh and each man of the Relief Force was issued with three days' haversack rations as, by semaphore, Sir Colin

---

* The 75th had suffered very severe casualties in the siege of Delhi and was reduced to three hundred officers and men.

Campbell signalled to Sir James Outram in the Residency that it was his intention to continue the advance at first light on the 14th. William Peel, returning from a brief unit Commanders' conference next day, explained the plan of action that had been decided upon to his assembled officers, a map of the area spread out before him.

"We are to advance due east from the Alam Bagh, gentlemen," he told them. "Across flat country, much of which is under cultivation, to the Dilkusha, which is a double-storied palace standing on a plateau near the river—here, to the northeast." His finger jabbed at the map, as he went into details concerning the terrain. "When the Dilkusha is occupied, the advance will continue northwards for half a mile, to the Martinière, which is a vast pile of buildings with a central tower and four turrets. This, in turn, will be occupied and Sir Colin intends to use it as his base for the next part of the operation with which we shall be directly concerned—the capture of a very formidable obstacle indeed, the Sikanderbagh Palace. This, I am told, is a very extensive building of strong masonry set in a large garden and encircled by a twenty-foot-high wall— loopholed, for musketry, of course, and with bastions at each angle. To reach it, the canal must be crossed—here—we must follow the river bank for about a mile, and then swing sharply to the left—or west—to join a road which runs to the rear of the Sikanderbagh." He paused, inviting questions, and Lieutenant Vaughan asked about expected opposition.

"Sir Colin expects little from the Dilkusha and the Martinière." Peel grinned. "The worst you'll have to contend with will be getting our guns across the fields and streams, whilst the advance guard and the Horse Artillery clear the way ahead to the Martinière. There's a bridge over the canal but some villages will have to be cleared—here and here—before it can be used. Two of our twenty-four-pounder guns are to take up position to cover the leading infantry brigade as it passes the Martinière and heads towards the canal . . . here. We shall have to use our best endeavours to get them there by noon, which is the time Sir Colin estimates that the Martinière will be in our hands. He intends to make a strong reconnaissance towards the Char Bagh Bridge—here—in the hope of deluding the Pandies into the belief that he'll follow General Havelock's route to the Residency but he'll call on the horsed guns for that, because the terrain is difficult."

Again he went into details and Phillip listened with rapt attention, peering over his shoulder at the map.

"As to opposition," Peel went on, "that is expected to be heavy at the Sikanderbagh. It is said to be held by about two thousand trained sepoy troops and there's a village, also occupied by Pandies, close to it, so the advance may be held up there. However, once it's been taken, Sir Colin intends to use the shortest route to the Residency—the one Havelock took—westwards, to aim at joining up with Outram at the Moti Mahal . . . here. He'll make a sally and set up gun batteries to cover our advance. Between us and the Moti Mahal is a flat plain . . . here. It's approximately twelve hundred yards wide, gentlemen, crossed by a good road. About three hundred yards along it is a village, with garden enclosures round it, which is expected to be held and a mosque, called the Shah Nujeef, beyond and about a hundred and fifty yards east of the Moti Mahal, which we know to be very strongly held. Well . . ." He paused. "We need not to go into that part of our route in detail now, because Sir Colin doesn't expect today's advance to take us further than the Martinière."

A number of questions were asked and answered, with admirable lucidity, by Peel; commands were allocated and the order of march settled. As First Lieutenant, Jim Vaughan was officially designated second-in-command and Phillip, to his own surprise, was appointed to act as naval liaison officer to the Commander-in-Chief . . . the same role that he had played, three years before, at Balaclava, when Sir Colin Campbell had commanded the Highland Brigade.

At dawn on 14th November, the column began to form and at nine o'clock the advance began across a wide, flat plain, well cultivated with corn and sugar-cane and dotted with clumps of trees. Screened by cavalry, the advance guard moved forward steadily for three miles and encountered the first opposition at the wall of the Dilkusha, which was lined by musketeers. They were quickly driven back by the guns of the Horse Artillery; a gap in the wall was found and cavalry and guns galloped through, the enemy retreating before them. The Dilkusha Palace was occupied with scarcely a shot fired but, on reaching the crest of the plateau, the cavalry advance guard came under a heavy fire of artillery and musketry and was compelled to halt until Captain Remmington's horsed battery, a Royal Artillery howitzer, and Captain Bouchier's eighteen-pounder Field Battery could unlimber and reply to the enemy guns.

Under cover of their fire, the main body of the British infantry continued the advance, driving the rebels from the Martinière at the point of the bayonet, and the cavalry—led in a stirling charge by Lieutenant Watson's Punjab Horse— chased them right up to the canal bank. By noon, as Sir Colin Campbell had estimated, both the Dilkusha and the Martinière were in British hands and Phillip—who thus far had been a mere spectator—was sent to guide the Naval Brigade's two 24-pounders into position between the wall of the Martinière and the canal. Scarcely had they reached the wooded compound, however, than guns and gunners came under a very heavy fire of roundshot and musketry and Phillip, after making a swift reconnaissance, rode back to advise Peel to change their position. This was done rapidly and the enemy driven off before they could inflict any casualties and, when Captain Bouchier's eighteen-pounder battery came up in support, all opposition ceased. With night coming on, the men were ordered to bivouac, the gunners sleeping beside their guns.

Unhappily, the accidental explosion of one of the howitzers caused the death of a petty officer named Cassidy and wounded two others and Peel—learning that the same explosion had also killed one of the Highlanders—was beside himself with distress.

Next day, while stores and reserve ammunition were brought up and small holding forces took over the two newly captured palaces, Sir Colin Campbell's feint attack on the Char Bagh Bridge was launched, the artillery being massed on the left front, with orders to keep up a continuous bombardment of the city throughout the night. The Naval Brigade's rockets were used with great effect and the howitzers shelled the Begum's Palace and the rebels' defences along the canal bank whilst, in the rear, the 93rd beat off a number of heavy infantry attacks on the baggage and ammunition waggons, making their slow way from the Alam Bagh to the Dilkusha Palace.

Sir Colin Campbell was at his most abrasive, angered by the delay in sending up the ammunition, without which he could not advance, and Phillip—in common with the rest of his staff—spent the day galloping from post to post with orders and bringing back reports which, if they did not please the Commander-in-Chief, resulted in the man who delivered them receiving the rough side of the C-in-C's tongue. By evening, however, all was in readiness for an advance on the Sikander-bagh; it was ordered for eight o'clock the following morning and Campbell made amends to his staff with apologies and compliments.

CHAPTER SEVEN

Little sleep was possible that night; disturbed by the ceaseless roar of cannon fire, Phillip tossed and turned restlessly, and Sir Colin Campbell paced, only partially dressed, on the steps of the Martinière as he anxiously awaited the arrival of the last convoy of camels, laden with small-arms ammunition, which he had ordered up from the rear. By eight o'clock, the advance guard of Hodson's Horse, Blunt's troop of Bengal Horse Artillery, and a company of the 53rd, was in motion. Brigadier Hope Grant's main body—the 93rd, the rest of the 53rd and the 4th Punjab Infantry—followed, with the Lancers, the 23rd, and two companies of the 82nd, under Brigadier Russell, in support.

Finally the long line of guns, with limbers and ammunition waggons, joined the column, with the Engineer Park and Brigadier Greathead's 8th Regiment, the 2nd Punjab Infantry, and the Battalion of Detachments forming up in the rear. The canal was found to be virtually dry—the rebels, believing that the British advance would be made by the Char Bagh Bridge, had dammed it at that point—and even the great twenty-four-pounder siege guns of the Naval Brigade were able to cross without much difficulty, to William Peel's elation. Following the river bank through narrow, tortuous lanes between thick plantations and enclosed gardens, little opposition was met with but, when the advance guard made the sharp, left-hand turn on to a narrow, sandy track leading to the Sikanderbagh, a galling fire of musketry greeted them.

This came, Phillip saw, appalled by its volume, from a village on the left and from the Sikanderbagh itself, to the right. The great 150-yard-square enclosure was bristling with musketeers and from its bastions and loopholed walls, from the sandbagged windows and flat, parapeted roof of its extensive interior came a triple-tiered fire, which mowed down the advancing cavalry and sent the infantry scattering for cover. The cavalry, unable to retreat for the column to their rear, had no choice but to go on and they made for the village, only to find themselves trapped, with Blunt's troop, in a narrow lane with high banks hemming them in on either side.

Sir Colin Campbell showed his mettle then. Spurring into the thick of the tumult, careless of his own safety, he ordered the cavalry to disperse into side lanes to clear the way and then shouted to Blunt to mount the bank with his battery and bring it into action. With the 53rd lining an enclosure to the right, to give what covering fire they could, the gallant Blunt put his guns in motion, swung the horses' heads round and, with whip and spur and shout, his gunners drove their teams up the bank and forward, into an open space beneath the walls of the Sikanderbagh. They unlimbered and opened fire, to be joined by Captain Travers's eighteen-pounder battery, his guns dragged bodily up the bank by infantry volunteers. Sitting his small white horse behind the foremost gun, Sir Colin himself directed their fire, unmoved by the musket balls whining over his head and—as he always was under attack—the personification of coolness and courtesy. The two batteries were compelled to fire in three different directions—right-handed, to keep down the musketry fire from the Sikanderbagh, left-handed to check a deadly fusillade from the village, and then to their front, in an attempt to reply to a cannonade which the enemy opened, at long range from their principal fortress, the Kaiser Bagh.

As the Highlanders and the main body of the 53rd advanced under Hope Grant's command to clear and capture the village and the enclosure to the left, Phillip—waiting perforce amongst the Commander-in-Chief's entourage—received the order he had hoped for. "Be so good, Commander Hazard," Sir Colin said, over his shoulder, "as to request Captain Peel to bring us up some artillery support, if you please. A field battery and the rocket-tubes will suffice, I think, for he'll not get his siege-guns up here. We have to blow a breach in the wall of the Sikanderbagh and that"—he took a watch from his pocket—"and that right soon, kindly tell him."

Predictably, Peel was already on his way, anticipating the order, and Phillip jerked his panting horse to a halt beside him to be greeted with cheers from the eager seamen as he delivered the Commander-in-Chief's message.

It took a further half hour's bombardment by the combined batteries before a small breach was made in the massive wall some twenty yards to the right of the main gate, on the river side of the enclosure. Seen through a cloud of smoke and dust, it looked scarcely large enough to admit one man and the *Shannon* seamen concentrated all their efforts in a desperate attempt to enlarge it. Casualties were beginning to mount; the guns became heated, so that a lengthy pause had to be made between salvoes to enable the barrels to cool and, as the gunners waited, roundshot from the distant Kaiser Bagh came hurtling into their midst, while sharpshooters on the walls of the Sikanderbagh took steady toll of them.

Sir Colin Campbell was struck in the thigh by a spent

musket ball but he made light of his wound, shaking his head firmly to pleas from his A.D.C.s and his Chief of Staff, General Mansfield, that he submit to having it dressed. Twice, scorning the enemy's attempts to shoot him down, he trotted across to where the men of Hope Grant's infantry brigade lay—as he had ordered them to—in the shelter of a low mud wall, to bid them curb their impatience. Hearing the crash of falling masonry, as more of the wall came down, the Highlanders besought him to give them the order to go in and take the palace by storm, but he shook his head.

"Lie down, 93rd!" he rasped at them hoarsely. "Lie down! Every man of you is worth his weight in gold to England today . . . and the breach is not yet of a size to admit you."

The tall, black-bearded Sikhs of the 4th Punjab Infantry, grasping their bayoneted rifles, began to edge forward, as eager as their Highland comrades to come to grips with the foe, but still Sir Colin sat his horse, giving no sign, as shells screamed overhead and musket balls raised the dust from the ground about him. A veteran sergeant of the 53rd, whose company was occupying a shallow trench to the right of the line, called out to him urgently.

"Sir Colin, let the infantry storm! We'll make short work of the murdering villains, Your Excellency, if you'll just give the word!"

The old Commander-in-Chief recognised him. "D'ye think the breach is wide enough, Dobbin?" he shouted back.

"Aye, sir—let the two Thirds at it and you'll see!" Sergeant "Dobbin" Lee assured him.

The Sikhs could be restrained no longer. Without waiting for orders, they surged forward, a section of their turbanned Sappers with them, carrying crowbars with which to enlarge the breach, and led by a young British officer and a huge

Subedar-Major, both with drawn swords. A terrible fire of musketry met and mowed them down; for a moment, brave though they were, they hesitated and, above the roar of the guns, Sir Colin shouted to the 93rd's Colonel.

"Bring on the tartan, Colonel Ewart!" he commanded. "Let my own lads at them!" He lifted his pith helmet from his head and held it high and the Highlanders sprang to their feet, determined to be first at the breach, even now. Led by their pipers and cheering wildly, they tore after the Sikhs, and some of the 53rd went with them, vying for the honour. Some hurled themselves in through the narrow, littered opening, others made for the towering wall to tear at its line of iron-barred windows and force a way in thus, while the main body of Highlanders blew in the lock of the gate and burst it open. A great shout went up—more an expression of concerted fury than a cheer—as they fought their way into the enclosure and were lost to sight in the smoke of the guns.

"They'll take that place or die in the attempt, every man-jack of them!" William Peel said, his normally calm voice sounding oddly shaken. "Just listen to the appalling din, Phillip! Dear God, there'll be no quarter given or asked inside there now . . . the Highlanders will remember Cawnpore!"

He mopped at his sweat-streaked face as, in the sudden lull which had fallen outside the enclosure, the guns ceased fire. *Doolies* were being brought up, led by their Chaplain, and the gunners roused themselves and turned to attend to wounded shipmates who, until then, had been compelled to lie where they had fallen, their cries unheard in the fury of the battle.

Returning to his post with the Commander-in-Chief's staff, Phillip waited, with growing anxiety, for news of the fight still going on inside the walls of the Sikanderbagh. It came, just before noon, when the 93rd's Commanding Officer, Colonel Ewart, emerged at a shambling run and, after looking dazedly about him, saw Sir Colin Campbell and came hurrying towards him. He was bare-headed, his uniform stained with blood, and slung across his shoulder was a roll of scarlet cloth which, as he approached, he shook out to reveal the regimental Colour of the 71st Native Infantry.

"We are in possession of the Sikanderbagh, sir!" he gasped. "I have killed the last two of the enemy with my own hand and here is their Colour!"

The staff, with one accord, started to cheer him but Sir Colin Campbell, his explosive temper frayed by the strain of waiting, silenced them with a raised hand.

"Be damned to your Colours, sir! It's not your place to be taking Colours," he told poor Ewart wrathfully. "Go back to the regiment you command and bring them out. There's more fighting to be done before this day is over and your wounded must be attended to."

Crestfallen, the Highlanders' tall Commander saluted and retraced his steps to the shambles of the Sikanderbagh where—as William Peel had predicted—his men had taken terrible vengeance for the dead of Cawnpore.

"There'll be another apology from the Chief tonight," one of the A.D.C.s observed to Phillip, his tone wryly amused. "When he finds out that Colonel Ewart's brother, with his family, was murdered at Cawnpore. But Sir Colin's always the same in action. Butter wouldn't melt in his mouth when the shots are flying and he's in the thick of it . . . but when he has to wait, whilst other men are facing the danger, there's no pleasing him and he becomes as sour as an old crab apple. I've learnt to keep out of his way on such occasions. All the same," he added, with feeling, "I'd follow the old man anywhere—he's a damned fine soldier and, when he campaigns, he leaves nothing to chance. Look—the field hospital's coming up! *That's* what I mean, Commander Hazard . . . the Chief ordered it up an hour ago, with the water carts and the reserve ammunition."

The field hospital was set up under the outer wall of the Sikanderbagh and, within a short while, a long procession of laden *doolies* emerged from the interior and the surgeons and orderlies unpacked their instruments and dressings and started work among the wounded. The column reformed, *bhisties* with their goatskin carriers answered calls for water from the parched and weary men, as ammunition limbers were replenished and the infantry refilled their cartridge pouches and munched dry rations from their haversacks, waiting for the muster roll to be called.

It was well on into the afternoon when bugles sounded the advance, and leaving some two thousand rebel sepoys dead behind them, the column turned again in the direction of the Residency. Now they were following almost the same route as Outram and Havelock had followed—but had reached more directly, via the Char Bagh Bridge—their objectives the one-time Mess House of the Queen's 32nd, the Khurshed Manzil, and the Moti Mahal Palace, in which Havelock's gallant rearguard had been trapped, with their wounded and their heavy guns, in September. Here, Campbell had arranged by semaphore, Outram and some of his defenders were to make a sally to meet him when he signalled that both buildings were again in British hands.

But before they could hope to join forces, there was another formidable obstacle to be overcome. The road led across a wide plain, open and seemingly undefended for the first few hundred yards, but the advance guard had scarcely started to cross it when a murderous fire of grape and musketry assailed them from a fortified village on their left. The column halted, just out of range, while this was cleared by Colonel Gordon, with two companies of the 93rd, and then the advance was resumed towards the Shah Nujeef—a domed mosque, surrounded by the inevitable walled garden—which lay a hundred yards ahead and to the right of the road. Henry Kavanagh, the volunteer sent by Outram to guide the Relief Force to the Residency, had warned that—apart from the Kaiser Bagh—the Shah Nujeef was the rebels' mightiest stronghold, specially reinforced and fortified to bar the road to the Residency and Sir Colin Campbell's preliminary reconnaissance had confirmed Kavanagh's warning.

Recalling Captain Peel's earlier description of their route, Phillip took out his Dollond and subjected what he could see of the Shah Nujeef to a careful scrutiny. Jungle grew right up to its walls which, as always, were loopholed; there were walls and huts, affording cover for sharpshooters, lining the narrow defile of the approach and, he saw, the entrance gate had been covered by a regular work in masonry, with what appeared to be a gun emplacement to the rear. The flat top of the building, below its mushroom-shaped dome, had been crowned by a breast-high parapet, now lined with scarlet uniformed sepoy musketeers.

The afternoon was already well advanced but the Shah Nujeef would have to be taken by dusk, Sir Colin announced grimly, consulting his watch. He rode forward to make a personal reconnaissance, under a fire so heavy that two of his aides were wounded and five or six had their horses shot within the space of five minutes. After an unhurried inspection with his gilt-and-ivory field-glass, he lowered it and motioned Phillip to his side.

"Inform Captain Peel, if you please, Commander, that I

require his siege-guns and mortars with all possible speed. We've no scaling ladders, alas, so he'll have to breach those walls." With one of his rare smiles, he added, "You had better remain with him—he will need every officer and man he's got, unless I'm much mistaken."

Phillip swung his horse 'round and went at a gallop to deliver his message. The guns were brought up with what seemed to him agonising slowness, the long train of bullocks straining at their wooden yokes, reluctant to face the hail of fire into which they were being goaded. One team, drawing the howitzer commanded by Midshipman Martin Daniel, lost two yokes of the poor beasts but the seamen of Lieutenant Salmon's rifle company slung their Miniés and manhandled the great squat gun into position. Men, horses, and bullocks went down in the ghastly hail of fire and Sir Colin Campbell, in an attempt to reduce it, sent a company of infantry to burn some of the huts which were giving the sharpshooters cover. Remmington's troop of Horse Artillery went with them.

William Peel was everywhere, bearing a seemingly charmed life as he dashed from gun to gun, exhorting his men to further effort, laughing and making boyish jokes with them, urging them on.

"Stay on hand, Phillip," he warned, his smile briefly fading. "If they get me, you and Jim Vaughan will have to take over." Then, his voice rising above the yells of the sepoys and the incessant crackle of their musketry, "Come on, lads—get that gun into action! One more heave will do it!"

At last the guns were in position, a scant twenty yards from their target, the battery's left resting on the newly captured village, from which smoke and flames rose sullenly skywards. Young Martin Daniel was the first to report his gun ready.

"Fire the howitzer, Mr Daniel!" Peel yelled.

The boy's high-pitched "Aye, aye, sir!" ended in a cry of horror from one of his crew as a roundshot took the right side of his head away and, bounding on, killed two of the yoked bullocks thirty feet behind him. Lieutenant Young sent Lightfoot to take the dead midshipman's place and the howitzer opened with the rest.

For three hours, the *Shannon*'s siege battery pounded the towering walls, firing salvo after salvo at virtually point-blank range, stripping them of mortar but unable to breach them. From the Kaiser Bagh and the Mess House and from an enemy battery across the river, roundshot hurtled amongst the sweating gunners as, from the mosque itself, the rebels kept up an unremitting hail of grape and musket balls, screaming their hatred from the parapet. Rockets hissed high into the sky, to descend in a shower of incandescent flame into the enclosure, shells burst above the parapet and smashed against the bulbous dome but still, it seemed, there was no diminution in the number of the mosque's defenders, whilst the *Shannon*'s casualties steadily increased.

Phillip laid one of the twenty-four-pounders for over an hour, losing two men of his crew when an uncannily accurate shot from the Mess House battery blew up an ammunition tumbril behind them. One of Arthur Clinton's crew had his left leg carried away above the knee and, long after the battle ended, Phillip could hear his voice in memory, mouthing oaths and crying out dazedly, "Here goes a shilling a day, a shilling a day! Go at the bastards, boys—go at them!" until death mercifully silenced him.

Little Clinton, himself wounded in the arm, left his gun only long enough to have the bleeding staunched and then returned to it, yelling frenziedly to his gun-captain to keep on firing. Lightfoot had an Engineer named Bone and two of Gray's Marines making up his howitzer crew; Thomas Young and Edward Daniels were, Phillip saw, like himself, working guns, coatless and bare-headed. Pausing for the long minutes necessary to cool his own twenty-four-pounder, he wiped the sweat from his blackened face and saw, through the swirling smoke, that Sir Colin Campbell was still sitting his horse like a statue barely thirty yards off. He had evidently sent for infantry support for, as he watched, he saw the old General rise in his saddle and wave on Major Barnston's battalion of detachments, who were advancing in skirmishing order towards the fringe of jungle and the walled enclosures to the right of the mosque. A burst of grape thinned their leading rank and the stout Barnston fell forward on his face. Two of the skirmishers ran to pick him up and the rest hesitated, some flinging themselves down on their faces, as their leader had done, either wounded or seeking cover. Sir Colin roared an order and another officer of Greathead's brigade spurred his horse forward to lead them to their objective. Gallantly they attempted to scale the wall, but, without ladders, it was impossible and they were compelled to retreat, firing as they did so.

Minutes later, Captain Middleton's battery of Royal Horse Artillery galloped up to lend further support to the *Shannon*'s hard-pressed gunners. Waving their caps and cheering, they passed the seamen's battery on the right, to unlimber and pour round after round of grape on to the parapets of the mosque and its enclosure.

"We're doing no damned good!" William Peel gasped bitterly, halting by Phillip's side. "We've scarcely made an impression on those infernal walls and the light'll be gone in half an hour." He slid from his horse, holding out his hand gratefully for the pannikin of water Nowell Salmon offered him. Wiping his smoke-grimed lips inelegantly with the back of a clenched first, he swore under his breath. "There's one particular black swine, who's a deadly marksman, perched up on the wall over there and I swear he's hit more of our poor Jacks than all the rest put together. A fellow in a green turban—look you can just see his head, behind that tree growing up the wall." He pointed and Salmon said excitedly, "Yes, I see him, sir."

"He's been up there for at least an hour," Peel said aggrievedly. "The devil take his black hide! We've all taken a pot at him and we can't knock him down."

"I believe I could, sir," Salmon offered. He checked his Enfield carefully. "I'm not a bad shot, after all the practice Commander Hazard has made us put in and if I were to shin up that tree, sir, I think I'd have a clear view of him. May I try?"

"I'll see you get a Victoria Cross if you succeed, Nowell," Peel promised recklessly. "But for God's sake, have a care! He's as liable to hit you as you are to knock him down. Take a man with you to hold your rifle until you get into position in the tree."

"Aye, aye, sir!" The young lieutenant thrust his rifle into the hand of the man nearest him and they ran forward together, dodging bullets as they made for the tree.

Peel met Phillip's gaze and shrugged resignedly.

"I shouldn't have let him go . . . damn it, he'll get himself killed! And I can't afford to lose officers, least of all officers of his calibre. But we've lost so many good men today, I . . . oh the devil! This is worse than the Crimea, Phillip, isn't it?" He did not wait for Phillip's reply. Wearily, shoulders bowed, he walked over to his horse. "Another broadside, gentlemen, if you please!" he requested, his voice husky with the strain of shouting above the thunder of the guns. "Give the swine another broadside! And, Phillip—"

"Sir?" Phillip waited, guessing what his Commander was about to say.

"I shall have to tell Sir Colin it's no use," Peel said regretfully. "I don't want to admit defeat but we can't smash those walls with roundshot in the time that's left to us. The only answer will be to wait till after dark and then try to explode a couple of charges under them."

Phillip felt his pain, aware of how much the admission would gall him when he had to make it to the Commander-in-Chief. "Shall I tell Sir Colin for you?" he offered. "I'm supposed to be naval liaison officer. If you can find anyone to replace me on this gun, I'll go and—"

"No." William Peel shook his head. "Reporting failure is my responsibility. The worst of it is, I don't see how the column *can* pull out now. Damn it, the entire road is blocked by the baggage train coming up behind and that has to be got under some sort of cover before nightfall, in case they attack from the rear. We . . ." He was interrupted by a shout from one of Nowell Salmon's rifle company.

"Captain Peel, sir!" The man was grinning his delight. "Mr Salmon did it, sir—he shot down that bastard in the green turban! Took one in the leg while he was doing it but he's not badly hurt. Harrison's helping him back now, sir, and he sent me to get a *doolie.*"

"Good lad!" Peel exulted. His mood of depression left him. "By heaven, if I live long enough, I'll see the boy gets his Cross! All right, Phillip—I'll take you up on your offer after all. Give the C-in-C the bad news for me. Tell him I'll prepare charges and call for volunteers to lay them, if he wishes, and in the meantime I'll try to take the rocket-carts in a bit closer. If we could clear the enclosure to our front, we might be able to get the charges in place before dark."

Phillip found Sir Colin Campbell already aware that the attack had been a failure. He said gruffly, "Captain Peel did everything possible, and with zeal and gallantry. But I—" he broke off, as a company of the 93rd came marching along the road towards him, the setting sun glinting on their long bayonets. They halted and the officer in command crossed to his side.

"The 93rd are in close column and ready, sir," he stated. "Five companies, sir."

"Thank you, Colonel Hay," Sir Colin acknowledged. "I had not intended to call on your regiment again today but it is five o'clock and the Shah Nujeef must be carried." Motioning Phillip to wait, he rode over to the column of Highlanders and addressed them, his voice firm and clear. "Remember, men, the lives of women and children are at stake in the Residency and they must be saved. It is not *will* you take that mosque, my lads—you *must* take it! And I will lead you at it myself."

There was a chorus of protest. "We can lead ourselves, Sir Colin," a voice from the ranks assured him. "And we'll take it, never fear."

Uncannily as if they had sensed the presence of the Highlanders, the rebels in the Shah Nujeef enclosure set up a tremendous hubbub. Bugles sounded the "Advance" to be followed, moments later, by the "Double" and suddenly all firing ceased. Sir Colin looked round in frowning puzzlement and then Brigadier Hope Grant, who had been supervising the collection of his wounded, came cantering over, a sergeant of the 93rd running beside him, clinging to his stirrup.

"Sir Colin!" Hope Grant's tone was urgent. "This man"—he gestured to the sergeant—"Paton, sir, of the 93rd, has found a

breach in the rear wall. It seems the naval guns have succeeded after all—some of their roundshot must have rico-
cheted and brought it down. I'd like your permission to take
fifty men to inspect it."

Permission was readily given. The Brigadier, with Colonel
Allgood of his Staff, dismounted and, with fifty Highlanders
and a party of Sikh sappers, both officers set off to investigate
under the guidance of the sharp-eyed Sergeant Paton.
Darkness fell and tension grew among the little knot of Staff
officers gathered about the Commander-in-Chief. The firing
had not been renewed and, in the oddly unnatural silence,
they spoke in whispers, as if fearful that raised voices might
bring about its resumption.

Then, shattering the silence, came the welcome skirl of
the 93rd's pipers, coming from inside the great mosque which
had defied them for so long, the tune they played to signify
their hard-earned victory one that brought a beaming smile to
Sir Colin Campbell's lined and weary face.

"'The Campbells are coming!'" he exclaimed. "Aye, they've
done that fine today, God bless their gallant hearts!"

Colonel Allgood galloped back, his forage cap held high
above his head. "The enemy have gone, sir," he stated triumphantly. "We entered through the breach in time to see the
last of them fleeing into the darkness!"

"Convey the good news to Captain Peel, if you please," Sir
Colin said, turning to Phillip. "With my thanks for his noble
exertions, tell him that he may withdraw his guns."

As the moon rose, the old Chief and his Highlanders
entered the Shah Nujeef enclosure to bivouac for the night,
the men sleeping fully accoutred, their arms piled, each rifle
loaded and capped. Pickets were posted, sentries paced beside
the guns, and the rearguard spread out, alert for any attack

which might be launched against the long procession of carts and tumbrils, camp followers and beasts of burden.

When all the necessary precautions had been taken, the dead were buried, William Peel and his ship's company standing bare-headed as Chaplain Bowman read the service, hearing in the distance the pipes of the 93rd playing "The Flowers of the Forest" as they, too, lamented their dead.

Next day—Tuesday, 17th November—the Naval Brigade was early astir. Anxious to reduce the number of casualties, which already exceeded four hundred, Sir Colin ordered a preliminary bombardment of the Mess House of the 32nd before bidding his infantry advance.

Leaving his First Lieutenant, Jim Vaughan, to move the siege-guns and mortars into position, Peel took Phillip with him to visit the wounded. They found both Nowell Salmon and young Arthur Clinton in good spirits but the field hospital in so exposed and dangerous a site that Peel was horrified. During the night a rumour had been spread that the Sikander-bagh contained large reserves of powder and, fearing that this might explode, the senior surgeon, Dr Dickson, had moved the wounded in their *doolies* into open ground.

"The reserves of powder are in the Shah Nujeef," Peel told him grimly. "Tons of it! No doubt that was why the Pandies evacuated the place so suddenly last night—we were firing rockets into the enclosure. They probably feared we'd blow it and them to smithereens . . . as, indeed, we should have done, if we'd known the stuff was there. But"—he sighed—"you can't stay here, Doctor. I'll speak to General Mansfield and see if he'll arrange for you to get your patients under cover."

Thanks to his intervention, the hospital was removed, a few hours later, to a captured village which, although under occasional fire from an enemy battery across the river, at least afforded shade and shelter for the wounded.

The bombardment of the Mess House lasted for almost three and a half hours. It was stubbornly defended but eventually the fire from its loopholed walls slackened and Sir Colin Campbell gave the order to storm. The column advanced, led by a company of the Queen's 90th, with the Battalion of Detachments in support, and soon two figures in British uniform could be discerned on the roof, planting their Colour on its summit.

Now less than a thousand yards separated the Relief Force from the Residency defenders. The previous day, two gun batteries from the Residency had been set up in the courtyard of the Chuttur Manzil Palace and an intervening wall partially breached by the explosion of a mine to afford a clear field of fire on the Hirun Khana and the Kaiser Bagh. Seeing the British flag flying from the Mess House roof, Sir James Outram ordered his two batteries to open fire and the storming party of twelve hundred men, drawn from each of the Lucknow regiments, set out to capture and occupy some of the intervening courts and buildings. This they did in heartening style, cheering as they charged, and the rebels fled before their vengeful bayonets, as Campbell's troops pressed forward with equal determination from the Mess House to the Moti Mahal. Here the enemy made their last stand, putting up an obstinate resistance but, sensing victory, the men of the Relief Force went surging through gaps blown in the walls, to drive the sepoys from enclosure and palace at bayonet-point and, once again, to plant their Colour triumphantly on its roof.

Between the courts and buildings occupied by the Residency defenders and the newly captured Moti Mahal lay a scant four hundred and fifty yards of shell-torn ground but, although the distance was trifling, the passage was a dangerous one. Every foot of the way was under continuous fire from guns and muskets in the Kaiser Bagh and from a tall, sandbagged tower, built as an observatory, to the right of the Mess House, which was strongly defended. An officer of Havelock's Force, Lieutenant Moorsom of H.M.'s 52nd, however, successfully ran the gauntlet from a building known as the Engine House, whilst Henry Kavanagh, unable to restrain himself, dashed over in the opposite direction, to be received with cheers by the comrades he had thought never to see again. Ten minutes later, General Sir James Outram and Brigadier-General Havelock, with their respective Staffs, made the perilous crossing to greet their Commander-in-Chief on the road outside the Moti Mahal.

The prolonged outburst of cheering, which signified that the 140-day siege of the Residency was over, reached the men of the *Shannon* Brigade as they continued to work their guns. Their target now was the massive bulk of the Kaiser Bagh Palace—occupied in force by several thousand picked sepoy troops and the key to the rebels' position in the city—a vast maze of buildings, courtyards, and gardens, crowned by gilded domes and cupolas, and defended by batteries of eighteen- and twenty-four-pounder guns. To have taken it by storm would have cost thousands of lives and Sir Colin Campbell, intent only on evacuating the garrison of the Residency without further loss, had decided to bypass it.

"Our task," William Peel told his officers, later that evening, "is to make the Pandies believe that an assault will be made on the Kaiser Bagh. To convince them, we must bombard the infernal place night and day, while first the sick and wounded and the women and children, and then the garrison, are withdrawn from the Residency. They will be taken by road to the Sikanderbagh—most of them, including the women, on foot—and from there, where *doolies* will meet them, to the Dilkusha and the Martinière, and finally to the Alam Bagh and Cawnpore. All these buildings are held by our troops and, to protect our left flank, Brigadier Russell's brigade has occupied a line of enclosures and houses between here and the Dilkusha. The evacuation will begin the day after tomorrow— the nineteenth. It is hoped that the garrison can be withdrawn by the twenty-third. Between then and now, gentlemen, we have to keep our guns firing . . . even if they melt! It'll be watch and watch for your guns' crews, and the small-arms men, when they're not on picket, will erect screens out of canvas or any material that comes to hand, and dig a shallow trench, to enable the women and children to pass our position without fear of being hit by enemy musketry."

He went into careful detail and his officers nodded, asking no questions.

"No leave is being granted to enter the Residency," Peel added. His hand rested for a moment on Phillip's arm. "I'm sorry but I need you all. You must sleep by your guns as and when you can, gentlemen, because this, if it's to deceive the Pandies, must assume the character of a regular breaching and bombardment. We've got to keep them in the Kaiser Bagh and the only way we shall do so is if we afford them no relief from our fire. And—needless, I feel sure, to tell you—two of our 24-pounders are to remain, with Colonel Ewart and four companies of his Highlanders, as rearguard. Nearer the time, I'll call for volunteer crews to man them." He grinned at them affectionately. "God bless you all, my boys—I know you'll do what has been asked of you in the true *Shannon* spirit."

They were wearier than they had ever been but they

responded with new-found energy. At times, Phillip wondered whether any of them would ever know peaceful sleep again, for the roar of the guns was continuously in their ears; they wakened to it, from catnaps snatched in the trench they had prepared for the evacuation; they ate beside the belching monsters, their food tasting of gunsmoke and burnt powder, their mouths parched and dry. But it had to be done and they endured it with what cheerfulness they could muster, conscious that the success or failure of the garrison's withdrawal depended largely on their efforts.

Phillip, anxious for news of Harriet, hid his anxiety. Enquiries for her, difficult to pursue in his present circumstances had so far yielded no concrete result but he clung obstinately to the hope that his sister and her children were alive and waited with ever-growing impatience for the evacuation to begin. Preparations were well advanced; the guns of the Artillery brigade were moved to strategic positions along the canal and the road to Dilkusha, and young Arthur Clinton, reporting again for duty during the afternoon, was sent with his nine-pounder and a scratch crew to cover the road between the Moti Mahal and the Sikanderbagh. That evening, the most severely wounded men of the Residency garrison were carried safely along the hurriedly prepared route and, although Brigadier Russell's thinly spread brigade had to beat off two attacks near the canal bridge at dusk, the attackers vanished with the coming of darkness and the *doolies* crossed over the canal unmolested.

The following afternoon, it was announced that the women and children, with the rest of the sick, were leaving the Residency entrenchment. They took a considerable time to pass through the intervening palaces and walled enclosures, and the light was fading when the head of a long, slow-moving

procession of carriages, bullock carts, and litters reached the
sap below Phillip's gun position. Here all had to dismount from
their conveyances in order to walk in single file along the
scarp, past an area of open ground which was under fire from
the Kaiser Bagh, and then up a slight slope on the far side,
protected from enemy musketry only by the makeshift wood
and canvas screens Peel had devised. Many of the women and
most of the older children were already on foot, Phillip saw,
and he turned his glass on them, only to lower it a few
moments later when he realised that, in the dim light, it was
impossible to make out individual faces among the crowd.

"Commander Hazard . . ." Peel's voice came from behind
and he spun round, startled, not having heard his approach
for the thunderous clamour of the guns, whose fire—by order
of the Commander-in-Chief—must continue, despite the
women's presence.

"Sir?" he acknowledged, a hand to his ear as Peel drew
level with him.

"Take a party of twelve small-arms men, if you please,"
the *Shannon*'s Captain requested formally. "And give those
poor souls what assistance you can. I'll relieve you here." He
added, smiling, "I hope you find her, Phillip—and the children
too. Good luck!"

Phillip thanked him and, with his twelve seamen, descended to the sap. Quite a number of the women had already
entered it, some walking slowly and feeling their way, others
—anxious for an end to their ordeal—picking up their skirts
and running as fast as they could, obedient to the advice of
their escort to keep their heads low. He crossed to a mud-
spattered carriage, drawn by two emaciated horses and, opening its door, offered his hand to assist the occupants to alight.
They did so apprehensively, staring about them as if unable

to believe their eyes and Phillip studied them covertly.

They looked wan and ill, as though for a long time they had been deprived not only of food but also of sunlight and fresh air and he found himself wondering whether he would recognise his sister, even if she were among them. It had been almost seven years since he had seen her; she would have changed, in any event, with the years. The Harriet he remembered had been tall and slim, with long fair hair and the bluest of eyes, a beautiful girl just on the verge of womanhood, vivacious and . . . one of the women grasped his arm.

"Oh, sir . . ." She was thin and dark, clad in a torn cotton dress, and she sounded frightened. "Do we really have to run across that trench?"

"I'm afraid you must," Phillip told her. "But don't worry, it . . ." He saw her legs then and could not suppress a shudder, for they were grossly swollen and covered with open sores. "I'll get one of my sailors to carry you across," he amended lamely. "Don't worry, it won't take long."

He yielded his burden to a stalwart young seaman and returned to shepherd a little group of children into the trench, surprised and faintly shocked by their gravity and silence. They asked no questions, gave no greeting, obeyed his instructions instantly and did not flinch when a shower of grapeshot struck the edge of the parapet, spattering them with dust and stones, and he watched them go, sick with pity. Then another woman claimed his attention, a grey-haired, smiling woman, upon whose arm a pale and sickly girl was leaning. She refused his help, assuring him that she could manage and then asked, still smiling, if he was really a naval officer.

"We heard that a naval party had come to our rescue but until I saw you, I did not really believe it. What ship do you belong to?"

"Her Majesty's ship *Shannon,* ma'am," Phillip answered.

"God bless you!" the grey-haired woman said quietly and he saw that there were tears in her eyes, although the smile remained. As he walked beside her to the trench, he asked about Harriet but she shook her head. "I'm sorry, I don't know for certain. Mrs Dorling, you say, from Sitapur? I remember the ladies from Sitapur arriving, just before the siege began but I . . . I'm not sure. So many of us have died, you see—the Chaplain, the Reverend Harris, told me only a little while ago that he had conducted five hundred funerals. His wife might know—she's in that carriage just behind us. I'm so sorry I cannot help you."

Phillip missed the Chaplain's wife in the confusion, as darkness fell and a hail of musket balls struck the carriage from which she and half a dozen others had just descended, killing its syce and causing the horses to bolt. By the time order had been restored and the straggling line of women resumed the crossing, Mrs Harris and her companions had vanished and he was kept too busy to search for her. There were many who had to be carried now, pathetic, puny children and women too weak and ill to walk, and he and the seamen of his party lost count of the number of times they trudged the length of the sap and stumbled up the slope beyond, to hand their burdens to some soldiers of the escort on the other side.

The moon rose and the enemy fire, although random and inaccurate, increased in volume, and several times the procession had to be halted until it slackened sufficiently to permit them to proceed. It was when he had almost given up hope that he saw a little boy of about five or six, dressed in a grubby white sailor suit, coming towards him. The boy was by himself, marching along with grave purposefulness, a tiny rifle roughly fashioned of wood held to his shoulder with military precision. In the moonlight, his face was so like Harriet's, as he remembered it from childhood, that Phillip guessed instantly who he was.

Dropping to his knees beside the small, erect figure, he asked, his voice not steady, "Tell me, youngster—is your name Phillip Dorling?"

The boy stared at him, his thin, unwashed little face puckered in surprise. "Yes, sir, it is," he confirmed. Then, puzzled, he looked at Phillip's uniform. "You're a sailor, sir, aren't you? Not an Army officer?"

Resisting the impulse to hug him, Phillip nodded, bracing himself to ask the question. "Is your mother with you? Your mother and your sister Augusta?"

"My mother? Oh, yes, sir—she's just behind. Over there." He pointed. "Augusta's asleep, I think—she's not very well and Mamma is carrying her. Shall I take you to them, sir?"

"If you please," Phillip said, his throat tight.

Harriet came to meet him, weary, stumbling with the weight of the child in her arms, but with a glad cry of recognition. He could find no words to say, could only repeat her name, as relief flooded over him. She was thin, as all of them were after the long siege, and the lovely fair hair he remembered was cropped short and flecked with silver but . . . She was alive and he had found her. He took the sleeping child from her and, with his free arm about her shoulders, led her across the sap.

EPILOGUE

The women and children reached the Sikanderbagh to find Sir Colin Campbell himself waiting to receive and welcome them and a meal set out on cloth-covered trestle tables. The dead from the battle for its possession had been counted and hurriedly buried but still the taint of death hung over the great, one-hundred-fifty-yard-square enclosure, with its battered walls and shot-pitted buildings and Harriet shuddered as she entered it with the rest.

But Sir Colin's welcome was warm and the food, to those who had existed for almost five months on a near-starvation diet, unbelievably lavish, the sight of fresh meat, white bread and butter, fruit, and great urns of tea almost more than they could bear. Exhausted after her long walk through the shell-torn darkness, Harriet contented herself with cups of tea and a ham sandwich, but little Augusta, waking at last, could scarcely contain her delight at the sight of so much food, pointing to it excitedly.

"Mamma, there is a loaf of bread on the table! I'm certain of it—I can see it with my own eyes!"

Phillip, his mouth crammed, asked suddenly, "Mamma who was that gentleman who spoke to me? The one in sailor's uniform, who carried Augusta through the sap?"

"That," Harriet told him, tears of happiness misting her

eyes, "was your Uncle Phillip, darling . . . the one you are named after. I never expected to see *him* here."

At eleven o'clock, the march was resumed, with *doolies* or carts for almost all of them, and they reached the Dilkusha at a little after 2 a.m. There were tents pitched into which they all crowded, to sleep the sleep of the exhausted, after partaking of tea and bread and butter provided for them by the officers of the 9th Lancers. Next morning, they were issued with rations by the commissariat and—indescribable joy, to women who had heard nothing from the outside world for so long—letters from home, which had been held in Cawnpore pending the relief, were distributed.

Harriet sat reading her mail for most of the day; there were letters from her parents, from Lucy and Graham, one from Phillip, posted in China and, tragically, a scrawled little note from Lavinia, addressed to her in Sitapur, which had somehow reached her with the rest. She wept over it and then resolutely folded and placed it in the bosom of her dress. Life, she told herself sadly, had to go on and, for the children's sake, she must not yield to grief, for they were still in danger. The gunfire never ceased and on Saturday 21st the Lancers and the Artillery had to beat off a rebel attack on their camp. But gradually the garrison was being withdrawn from the Residency. Each day they came in, the gaunt, war-worn men of the Queen's 32nd, the Highlanders of the 78th in tattered tartan, the gallant sepoys of the 13th Native Infantry, who had defended the Bailey Guard Gate throughout the siege, and the Sikhs of Hardinge's Cavalry, on foot but still bearing themselves proudly, a handful of faithful household servants behind them.

Harriet found many friends in camp and from them, she learnt the incredible story of how the withdrawal had been made under the very noses of the rebel host. Guns in the Residency had been spiked and lights left burning; the defenders had filed out, leaving to Brigadier Inglis the sad honour of closing the gate of the Residency and, marching in tense silence, the last of the old garrison had passed along the route the women and children had followed, the outlying pickets falling in behind them, still without a shouted word or a bugle call. Covered by the guns of the *Shannon* Brigade and of the Horse Artillery, the rearguard of the 93rd had bivouacked five hundred yards from the Kaiser Bagh in which, still pounded by the *Shannon*'s twenty-four-pounder broadsides, the rebels waited for the attack that never came. Then, as cheers from the sailors signalled another breach in its massive walls, the Highlanders had heaped logs on their bivouac fires and silently slipped away to serve as rearguard to the slowly moving guns as they, too, received the order to withdraw.

On the 24th the women and children were told that they were to move to the Alam Bagh and they heard, with intense sadness, that General Havelock—so recently promoted to a knighthood and the rank of Major-General—had died from an attack of dysentery in a tent in the Dilkusha. His body was borne to the Alam Bagh by a party of the soldiers he had led to nine valiant victories and there interred, the pipers of his favourite regiment, the 78th, playing him to his last long resting place.

Harriet was worn out when she and the children lay down at last in their tent at the Alam Bagh. The journey was only one of four miles but, starting at 11 a.m., they had been all day on the road, crowded with a dozen others into an open bullock cart. With so great a mass of waggons, carts, camels, bullocks, and elephants all loaded with baggage, the sick and wounded, and the women, clutching their children, in litters or on carts, confusion was inevitable and, every ten minutes, the long procession came to a standstill. Sir Colin, fuming at the chaotic lack of organisation and the delays, sent his Staff officers galloping this way and that and, after a while, some sort of order was restored, but the dust was suffocating, the heat almost unbearable. Tents had not been pitched when the head of the column reached the camp-site and, when finally this was rectified, the women and the wounded were found to have suffered a number of deaths.

Harriet wakened next morning to realise that, for the first time in five months, no cannon were firing. Anxious for Phillip, she sat up, straining her ears. The children continued to sleep but . . . She recalled a young midshipman, who had given his name as Lightfoot, who had sought her out during the march to tell her that her brother was with the two naval guns covering the retreat.

"Commander Hazard's compliments, ma'am," the boy had said. "And I'm to tell you that he will be with you as soon as his duties permit."

Weary and spent, the children fractious, she had scarcely taken it in but now she remembered and began to feel anxiety. General Outram, she had been told, was to remain in the Alam Bagh with artillery and four thousand troops, to prevent pursuit from Lucknow when the column took the road, and to hold the rebels in check, until the Commander-in-Chief returned with reinforcements to recapture the city they had now been compelled to abandon. Would Phillip, she wondered unhappily, be left behind with his guns? It seemed on the cards but no one was able to tell her and the naval guns had not yet left the Dilkusha.

All day she fretted, learning without enthusiasm that the column was under orders to leave for Cawnpore, guarded by the three thousand remaining troops, on the 27th. Most of the old garrison and the regiments of Havelock's Force were to go but, probe and question as she might, Harriet could glean no news of whether or not the Naval Brigade would accompany them.

On the evening of the 26th, as she was picking up her scanty possessions, she heard a glad cry from little Phillip and, running to the tent flap, saw that he was pointing excitedly to a long line of yoked bullocks pulling the great, unwieldy siege-guns. Overcome with relief, Harriet dropped her tired head into her hands and wept.

She was still weeping when Phillip found her.

"It's all right," he told her gently and took her into his arms. "We'll get you back safely—nothing is more certain." Harriet clung to him, smiling through her tears.

The worst was over, she told herself thankfully. From now on, every step she and the children took would be a step nearer to freedom. And Phillip would be with them, to help them on their way.

BOOKS CONSULTED

CONTEMPORARY

The Mutinies in Oudh and the Siege of the Lucknow Residency: Martin Gubbins (Richard Bentley, 1858).

A Lady's Diary of the Siege of Lucknow: Mrs G. Harris (John Murray, 1858).

Lucknow and Oudh in the Mutiny: Lt.-Gen. James Innes (A. D. Innes, 1895).

The Siege of Lucknow: The Hon. Julia Inglis (Osgood, MacIlvaine, 1892).

A Middy's Recollections: Victor Montagu (Black, 1898).

Memories of the Mutiny: Col. F. C. Maude & J. W. Sherer (Remington, 1894).

Journal of the Siege of Lucknow: Maria Germon (privately printed 1870: Edited by Michael Edwardes Constable).

The Relief of Lucknow: William Forbes-Mitchell (1893; Edited by Michael Edwardes for The Folio Society, 1962).

Memoirs of Sir Henry Havelock: Marshman 1867 (Longman's, 1891).

The Shannon's Brigade in India: Edmund Hope Verney (Saunders, Otley & Co., 1862).

Recollections of a Winter's Campaign on India: Captain Oliver Jones, R.N. (Saunders, Otley & Co., 1859).

Letters from Lord Canning to Vernon Smith Esq. (private papers, kindly lent by Jane Vansittart, author of *From Minnie with Love*).

The Illustrated London News, 1857–8–9.

Papers of Dr N. Cheevers, Medical Secretariat, Calcutta (private collection of letters, cuttings from Indian newspapers, printed Orders in Council, telegraph messages 1857–9, obtained from Mr H. J. Varnham, Blackheath).

HISTORICAL REFERENCES

The Naval Brigades in the Indian Mutiny: Edited by Commander W. B. Rowbotham, R.N. (Navy Records Society, 1948).

The Second China War: Edited by Captain D. Bonner, R.N., and E. W. R. Lumby (Navy Records Society, 1954).

History of the Indian Mutiny: T. R. Holmes (Macmillan, 1898).

History of the Indian Mutiny: Charles Ball (London Pub. Co., 1858).

History of the Indian Mutiny: 3 vols. G. W. Forrest, C.I.E. (Blackwood, 1904).

The Tale of the Great Mutiny: W. H. Fitchett (Smith, Elder, 1904).

The Sound of Fury: Richard Collier (Collins, 1963).

Eighteen Fifty-Seven: S. N. Sen (Govt. of India, 1957).

My thanks for aid in obtaining reference books to York City Public Library and Mr Victor Sutcliffe of Stroud, Glos., and research undertaken by Mr Peter Gaston.

GLOSSARY OF INDIAN TERMS

Ayan: nurse or maid servant
Baba: child
Bearer: personal, usually head, servant
Bhisti: water bearer
Boorka: all-enveloping cotton garment worn by purdah women when mixing with the outside world
Brahmin: high-caste Hindu
Chapkan: knee-length tunic
Charpoy: string bed
Chitti: a chit, a written order
Chuprassi: a uniformed door-keeper
Daffadar: sergeant, cavalry
Dhoti: a loincloth worn by men in India
Din: faith
Doolie: stretcher or covered litter for conveyance of wounded
Eurasian: half-caste, usually children born of British fathers and Indian mothers
Ekka: small, single-horse-drawn cart, often curtained for conveyance of purdah women
Fakir: itinerant holy man
Feringhi: foreigner (term of disrespect)
Ghat: river bank, landing place, quay
Godown: storeroom, warehouse

Golandaz: gunner, native

Havildar/Havildar-Major: sergeant/sergeant major, infantry

Jemadar: native officer, all arms

Ji/Ji-han: yes

Lal-kote: British soldier

Log: people (baba-log: children)

Mahout: the keeper and driver of an elephant

Mem: wife, woman

Moulvi: teacher of religion, Moslem

Nahin: no

Nana: lit. grandfather, popular title bestowed on the Mahratta chief

Oudh: kingdom of, recently annexed by Hon. East India Company

Paltan: regiment

Pandy: name for mutineers, taken from the first to revolt, Sepoy Mangal Pandy, 34th Native Infantry

Peishwa: official title of ruler of the Mahratta

Pugree: turban

Raj: rule

Rajwana: troops and retainers of native chiefs

Rissala: cavalry

Rissaldar: native officer, cavalry

Ryot: peasant landowner, cultivator

Sepoy: infantry soldier

Sowar: cavalry trooper

Subedar: native officer, infantry (equivalent of Captain)

Sweeper: low-caste servant

Talukdar: minor chief

Tulwar: sword or sabre

Vakeel: agent

Zamindar: landowner

Zenana: harem

More Action, More Adventure, More Angst . . .

This is no time to stand down! McBooks Press, the leader in nautical fiction, invites you to embark on more sea adventures and take part in gripping naval action with Douglas Reeman, Dudley Pope, and a host of other nautical writers. Sail to Trafalgar, Grenada, Copenhagen—to famous battles and unknown skirmishes alike. All the titles below are available at bookstores. For a free catalog, or to order direct, call toll-free 1-888-BOOKS-11 (1-888-266-5711). Or visit the McBooks website, www.mcbooks.com, for special offers and to read excerpts from McBooks titles.

ALEXANDER KENT
The Bolitho Novels

___ 1 Midshipman Bolitho
0-935526-41-2 • 240 pp., $13.95

___ 2 Stand Into Danger
0-935526-42-0 • 288 pp., $13.95

___ 3 In Gallant Company
0-935526-43-9 • 320 pp., $14.95

___ 4 Sloop of War
0-935526-48-X • 352 pp., $14.95

___ 5 To Glory We Steer
0-935526-49-8 • 352 pp., $14.95

___ 6 Command a King's Ship
0-935526-50-1 • 352 pp., $14.95

___ 7 Passage to Mutiny
0-935526-58-7 • 352 pp., $15.95

___ 8 With All Despatch
0-935526-61-7 • 320 pp., $14.95

___ 9 Form Line of Battle!
0-935526-59-5 • 352 pp., $14.95

___ 10 Enemy in Sight!
0-935526-60-9 • 368 pp., $14.95

___ 11 The Flag Captain
0-935526-66-8 • 384 pp., $15.95

___ 12 Signal – Close Action!
0-935526-67-6 • 368 pp., $15.95

___ 13 The Inshore Squadron
0-935526-68-4 • 288 pp., $13.95

___ 14 A Tradition of Victory
0-935526-70-6 • 304 pp., $14.95

___ 15 Success to the Brave
0-935526-71-4 • 288 pp., $13.95

___ 16 Colours Aloft!
0-935526-72-2 • 304 pp., $14.95

___ 17 Honour This Day
0-935526-73-0 • 320 pp., $15.95

___ 18 The Only Victor
0-935526-74-9 • 384 pp., $15.95

___ 19 Beyond the Reef
0-935526-82-X • 352 pp., $14.95

___ 20 The Darkening Sea
0-935526-83-8 • 352 pp., $15.95

___ 21 For My Country's Freedom
0-935526-84-6 • 304 pp., $15.95

___ 22 Cross of St George
0-935526-92-7 • 320 pp., $16.95

___ 23 Sword of Honour
0-935526-93-5 • 320 pp., $15.95

___ 24 Second to None
0-935526-94-3 • 352 pp., $16.95

___ 25 Relentless Pursuit
1-59013-026-X • 368 pp., $16.95

___ 26 Man of War
1-59013-091-X • 320 pp., $16.95

___ 26 Man of War
1-59013-066-9 • 320 pp., $24.95 HC

DOUGLAS REEMAN
Modern Naval Fiction Library

___ Twelve Seconds to Live
1-59013-044-8 • 368 pp., $15.95

___ Battlecruiser
1-59013-043-X • 320 pp., $15.95

___ The White Guns
1-59013-083-9 • 368 pp., $15.95

___ A Prayer for the Ship
1-59013-097-9 • 288 pp., $15.95

___ 5 Hazard in Circassia
1-59013-062-6 • 256 pp., $13.95

___ 6 Victory at Sebastopol
1-59013-061-8 • 224 pp., $13.95

___ 7 Guns to the Far East
1-59013-063-4 • 240 pp., $13.95

DEWEY LAMBDIN
Alan Lewie Naval Adventures

___ 2 The French Admiral
1-59013-021-9 • 448 pp., $17.95

___ 8 Jester's Fortune
1-59013-034-0 • 432 pp., $17.95

DAVID DONACHIE
The Privateersman Mysteries

___ 1 The Devil's Own Luck
1-59013-004-9 • 302 pp., $15.95
1-59013-003-0 • 320 pp., $23.95 HC

___ 2 The Dying Trade
1-59013-006-5 • 384 pp., $16.95
1-59013-005-7 • 400 pp., $24.95 HC

___ 3 A Hanging Matter
1-59013-016-2 • 416 pp., $16.95

___ 4 An Element of Chance
1-59013-017-0 • 448 pp., $17.95

___ 5 The Scent of Betrayal
1-59013-031-6 • 448 pp., $17.95

___ 6 A Game of Bones
1-59013-032-4 • 352 pp., $15.95

The Nelson & Emma Trilogy

___ 1 On a Making Tide
1-59013-041-3 • 416 pp., $17.95

___ 2 Tested by Fate
1-59013-042-1 • 416 pp., $17.95

___ 3 Breaking the Line
1-59013-090-1 • 368 pp., $16.95

JAN NEEDLE
Sea Officer William Bentley Novels

___ 1 A Fine Boy for Killing
0-935526-86-2 • 320 pp., $15.95

___ 2 The Wicked Trade
0-935526-95-1 • 384 pp., $16.95

___ 3 The Spithead Nymph
1-59013-077-4 • 288 pp., $14.95

C. NORTHCOTE PARKINSON
The Richard Delancey Novels

___ 1 The Guernseyman
1-59013-001-4 • 208 pp., $13.95

___ 2 Devil to Pay
1-59013-002-2 • 288 pp., $14.95

___ 3 The Fireship
1-59013-015-4 • 208 pp., $13.95

___ 4 Touch and Go
1-59013-025-1 • 224 pp., $13.95

___ 5 So Near So Far
1-59013-037-5 • 224 pp., $13.95

___ 6 Dead Reckoning
1-59013-038-3 • 224 pp., $15.95

Classics of Nautical Fiction

CAPTAIN FREDERICK MARRYAT
___ Frank Mildmay OR
The Naval Officer
0-935526-39-0 • 352 pp., $14.95

___ The King's Own
0-935526-56-0 • 384 pp., $15.95

___ Mr Midshipman Easy
0-935526-40-4 • 352 pp., $14.95

___ Newton Forster OR
The Merchant Service
0-935526-44-7 • 352 pp., $13.95

___ Snarleyyow OR The Dog Fiend
0-935526-64-1 • 384 pp., $16.95

___ The Phantom Ship
0-935526-85-4 • 320 pp., $14.95

___ The Privateersman
0-935526-69-2 • 288 pp., $15.95

NICHOLAS NICASTRO
The John Paul Jones Trilogy

___ 1 The Eighteenth Captain
0-935526-54-4 • 312 pp., $16.95

___ 2 Between Two Fires
1-59013-033-2 • 384 pp., $16.95

WILLIAM CLARK RUSSELL
___ The Yarn of Old Harbour Town
0-935526-65-X • 256 pp., $14.95

___ The Wreck of the Grosvenor
0-935526-52-8 • 320 pp., $13.95

RAFAEL SABATINI
___ Captain Blood
>*0-935526-45-5 • 288 pp., $15.95*

MICHAEL SCOTT
___ Tom Cringle's Log
>*0-935526-51-X • 512 pp., $14.95*

A.D. HOWDEN SMITH
___ Porto Bello Gold
>*0-935526-57-9 • 288 pp., $13.95*

Military Fiction Classics

R.F. DELDERFIELD
___ Seven Men of Gascony
>*0-935526-97-8 • 368 pp., $16.95*
___ Too Few for Drums
>*0-935526-96-X • 256 pp., $14.95*